PRINCES

ANITA RENAGHAN

Cover Design by Denise Collie www.deedesign.com

Cover Illustration by Eve Johnston

©2013 by Anita Renaghan

Kitchen Entertainment

ISBN-13: 978-0-9838700-3-6

DEDICATION

This book is dedicated to my little girl, who has opened up
a whole new world of adventure in my life.

Chapter 1
No One's Son

When Myra George summoned the queen's doctor only to find out that he was dead, she locked herself in the king's suite to deliver the queen's baby herself. It was an extraordinary task in unusual times. This doctor had already been a replacement for the queen's long time doctor whom had taken a fall while horseback riding and had died only months earlier. A little voice was telling Myra that, in this hour, the queen needed protection. Myra knew that most importantly the king's new baby needed protection. It was no secret to Myra, who knew everything that was whispered within the castle walls, that Counselor Glenn hoped to be next in line as ruler, and Myra thought he would probably do anything to remove an heir to the throne.

The queen screamed, shuddering a typically graceful Myra George into dropping the empty water basin onto the floor. Myra's plump arms scooped it up. "There, there, Queen Samantha. You relax until the next contraction comes. We're almost there."

Myra didn't have children of her own, but she was from a large family and had assisted in all of her sisters' child births so, while she was not a doctor, she knew the procedure well.

The queen screamed a second time and Myra drew near, pulled up the queen's skirting, and prepared for the birth of the next royal child. The queen pulled her frail shoulders forward and tried to curl over her plump stomach. Myra saw her small, dimpled jaw harden as the queen grit her teeth, but then a smile curled up on Samantha's lips.

"How did you talk me into doing this without my aids?" Queen Samantha asked.

"Pish posh," Myra responded with a smile on her large, strong face, "Your aids are not having this child, my queen, you are. They would just suck the fresh air out of the room and get in my way. But we will have to deal with King Birch when he returns from hunting. I suppose there is no getting around him." Myra allowed her eyes to meet Queen Samantha's, and they shared a moment. They were very unlike one another: Queen Samantha was fair, petite, royalty; and Myra was strong, bold, practical, and loyal to the core. Myra had been serving King Birch's family for two decades, and had been nanny to Princess Zaria for six years. The queen respected Myra for her wisdom and confidence, and Myra had respected Queen Samantha for her assuredness that she would bring an heir to the throne. Their moment ended when the queen pulled her eyes tightly closed in a rush of pain.

"I can see the head," Myra said excitedly. "One more push, m'lady."

Pale and out of breath, Queen Samantha did as she was told. A roar erupted from the frail figure of the queen, and then silence. It was all over quickly, and Myra allowed silent tears to escape down her cheeks.

The newborn was a tiny speck of a baby having been born a full four weeks early, and it was the miracle of the soft cry that brought tears to Queen Samantha's eyes. The queen had been frail in the months of her pregnancy, and Myra could see now that the delivery was taking its toll. There was an unusual amount of blood, and it didn't seem to be slowing. In the queen's happiest moment, the life was running out of her. Myra could see now that after carrying her child for nine months, the queen would only spend minutes with her baby.

Myra held the baby up before her, the tiny back of the rump facing the queen. She smiled boldly at Queen Samantha before gritting her teeth. Myra George could see from this angle what the queen could not. It was impossible for Myra to tell the dying queen that after years of trying and hoping, and eight months of enduring a difficult pregnancy, she had failed to produce an heir to the throne of Fontanasia. As Myra gently cleaned the tiny figure, she considered her options. Queen Samantha had promised her husband it would be a boy, a future for the Royal Hall family, and just the miracle to put an end to all of the rumors that there had been bickering for control within the King's Council. Seeing the blood continue to collect under the queen, and knowing that this was the one time that Queen Samantha would look upon her newborn daughter, Myra did the only thing she could find within herself at the moment. She lied.

"It's a boy," Myra cleared her throat. "Just let me wrap him properly." There were pink and blue robes laid out in the trunk next to the bed. Myra hesitated, but ultimately reached past the pink and took the blue robes to swaddle the baby girl.

The queen slumped back on her pillows, and the fading sun that shone through the window lit up her deep black eyes. "I knew it," she told Myra as she wiped her tears away. "I knew that I would have a son. Birch will be so pleased to have a son and heir to the throne."

Myra pursed her lips into a slight smile and cleared her throat. "The king will be happy to know that he has a healthy baby in any right."

Queen Samantha tried to leverage her arms on the bed so she could sit up to get a look at her son, but she was too delicate and would have to wait for Myra to finish cleaning and wrapping him before she could hold him for the first time.

There was a loud knock on the locked door and Myra's face turned beet red in anger. Two hours earlier she had locked herself and the queen alone in the king's suite and told the servants that they were not to be disturbed. It was not a typical thing to do, but none of her subordinates questioned her because she had always been Attendant to the royal family, and her tall and broad frame was little compared to her direct and imposing demeanor. The George family had served the Hall family for seven generations, before Fontanasia had been founded, and there was no more attention to care and trust anywhere in the land.

Myra finished wrapping the baby in the blue cotton and silk and handed the tiny girl over to the queen who held her newborn ever so gently in her weakening arms. Just then the rapping on the door was followed by a pounding, and Myra's thick shoulders raised as she barged toward the noise.

"I said no interruptions!" she barked as the bolt was thrown back and she easily pulled the heavy oak door inward. They were the same height and saw eye to eye, and King Birch gave Myra a stern look. She winced and stepped aside. Myra had sent word into the forest that Queen Samantha was in labor. She could see that the king had come straight from the hunt, but Myra couldn't understand how King Birch had appeared so quickly. He should have been at least a day away, not hours.

As King Birch entered the chambers, the growing crowd in the hall began to murmur a barely audible whisper, and the king turned on his heel and bellowed.

"Silence!" In an instant, all was quiet. "I have a son whom I would like to see, and then you shall have your turn." His voice had cracked like a whip, and Myra's heart jumped in panic. How could he think it was a boy? He'd not even been in the room for three seconds. She looked to the queen and saw the blue bundle at the queen's chest. It must have been the blue color of the baby's wrap that had made King Birch assume it was a boy. Myra should have corrected him then and there, but she softly closed her eyes as the king slammed and bolted the door. Although he was by her in a matter of seconds, Myra noticed the dark circles beneath King Birch's eyes and the minute quiver on his strong lip.

King Birch removed his thick leather wrap and let it fall to the floor as he washed his hands in the side basin. He unclasped his buckle and placed his sword and dagger aside before sitting his muscular frame on the corner of the bed, and the queen summoned enough strength to reach her hand out and rest it on her husband's cheek tenderly. She smiled, but all the king could see was how truly pale and weak his wife looked. His deep brow furrowed and cracked as he held back an ocean of tears.

Myra George returned to the bed tending to the queen, cleaning and covering her as best she could while staying out of the gentle moment being shared by the royal couple. They gazed at their new child.

"A son, Birch. I knew it would be a son. You have your heir." Queen Samantha should have been glowing, but her face had turned blue.

"You have done well, my love," King Birch told her as he helped support the tiny bundle against her chest. "What shall we call him?" the king asked softly.

"Avalon," the queen whispered.

"Avalon," the king repeated. "Named for the brightest star in our skies."

"Yes, Avalon, my guiding light." The queen tipped her head forward to peak at the perfectly tiny face exposed in the swaddled blankets. "Hello, Avalon. I love you, my baby boy." Then the queen's neck went limp, her black and pearl watered eyes having lost the soul that had given them life these thirty years.

King Birch sat still holding their son to his wife's lifeless chest. When Myra noticed the queen's slumped position, she rushed over and tried to find a pulse. She held Queen Samantha's dimpled jaw and stared into the lifeless, black void, calling out to her. She brought the smelling salts forward, but before opening the jar, Myra noticed how still King Birch sat with his newborn baby pressed tightly between his right hand and the queen's breast. He took Queen Samantha's neck with his left hand and gently tipped her head back onto the pillow.

"She's gone," he whispered. It was only then that Myra saw King Birch had been silently crying over his newborn child and the wife he had lost. He had been painfully torn in half.

The king's suite was magnificent. One wall of the room was ornately carved gray rock etched into the side of the mountain that Fontanasia was built upon. Building the castle into the mountain was part of what gave Fontanasia a heavenly look as it climbed high into the mountain's often floating fog. The curtains billowed and the stone ceiling was raised on an arc with little hand carved cherubs in the center. There were beautiful antique tables and lounge chairs placed neatly around the room, and the light passed through the circular colored glass windows opposite the rock leaving a meditative glow along the walls. That glow faded now with the sunset as all attention had remained on the grand four-post bed draped over with patterned silk.

"It isn't a boy," Myra again confessed to King Birch guiltily, not knowing if he had heard her whisper the first time she had dared to speak. "I mean to say, you have another daughter, sir."

The king now seemed to awaken from his trance. "What?" he growled. Myra's look toward the door cautioned him, and King Birch lowered his voice but remained visibly angry, the bulk of muscles in his body turning to stone. "What are you talking about?"

"I'm sorry, sir. I meant to tell you sooner, but..." Myra's voice trailed off as she cowered and again looked to the door. The king tenderly pulled his newborn from his wife's chest and placed it at the foot of the bed. He then swept over and made sure the chamber was locked.

"Show me," he commanded.

Myra dared not make eye contact with the king. She quickly laid the bundle next to the queen's body and unwrapped the powder blue blankets. King Birch looked at the sweet face and tuft of sandy blond hair on his newborn child, and then gazed down. Myra was not lying; it was a girl. He glared back at his most trusted servant who still didn't look at him but re-bundled the baby. He thought that the expression on her face was one of apprehension but wasn't sure because in all the year's he'd know her, he'd never seen her intimidated. Then King Birch's heart jolted as he realized Myra hadn't lied outwardly to him. She had never said it was a boy. But the blue blankets had spoken for themselves.

"The queen, sir," Myra begged as she felt the urge to explain herself, "she was bleeding out and there was nothing to be done. I've seen it before." Myra looked at the queen's limp figure and then to the baby. "And, well, it was her wish, sir."

King Birch was frozen in place, his eyebrows dancing as he thought through the moment.

"I panicked, sire," her voice quivered. "It's just that I sent for her doctor and learned that he had died, or had been killed. And after that attempt on your life last month…"

"There was no attempt on my life!" King Birch bellowed. "It was an accident while hunting, that is all." His tone closed the door on the topic and Myra bit her lip.

Myra had heard from her brother, who was on the royal guard, that the king had run a man through with his sword on their last hunting trip. King Birch claimed that the man had stumbled into the blade as he approached to get a closer view of the etching on the grip, but Myra had never heard of such a thing. There had been hunting accidents that involved the bow and arrow at long range, but never accidents with the sword. She could only assume King Birch didn't want anyone to know that someone had come so close to threatening his life. There was trouble in Fontanasia, but Myra George knew King Birch well enough not to point it out twice in one night.

Myra pursed her lips and then continued. "In either case, I didn't know what else to do but deliver the baby myself." Myra rambled on. "She wanted a boy so badly, I didn't see the harm. It was her dying wish after all."

Myra was regaining her typically unshakeable composure as her rant ran out of steam. She paused to make eye contact with her old friend, the king. "And I didn't know you were going to come in and announce it to everyone before I could change the robes to the pink." Not one to push blame on others, she stopped herself. "I am at your mercy, sir." She sighed heavily as she half bowed. She'd have tipped all the way to the ground in sadness and regret but for the baby still tucked in her arms.

King Birch coughed and Myra could see that he was swallowing hard and trying to suppress his grief and disbelief. She gave him a moment, and then stepped forward, handing him his young daughter. Seeing King Birch so weak caused Myra's voice to shake. "Your princess, my king. Avalon Hall."

The king let Myra place his daughter in his arms. Such a large man, the baby covered barely one tenth of the king's chest. He sat with her for a few long moments, taking in her smell and her striking black eyes. He remembered his daughter Zaria constantly sleeping as a baby, and was surprised to see Avalon so alert.

There was a brisk knock at the door followed by muffled voices. "King Birch!" He recognized the voice of Counselor Robert. Myra moved to unlock the chamber door, but the king shook his head and cleared his voice.

"One moment," he bellowed causing the baby to jump. And then softer, "Sorry, my princess." King Birch's eyes never left his daughter as he crept toward a chair and sat. Myra remained frozen. She hadn't been nervous around King Birch since they had first met as children. Back then, she was still unsure how to address royalty, and he was still unsure how to accept a bow. Now, she was anxious for the lie she had facilitated and the predicament the king was in because of it. She had never been good at silence, but she waited the long minutes as the king drew in the sight of his baby. The king's face continued to undulate between sadness and joy, never resting for more than a few seconds between the heights of both emotions.

"But I dreamt you would be a boy," he quietly scolded the blue bundle in his arms. "I dreamt it."

The color ran out of Myra's face.

There was another knock at the door and a muffled, "Sir?"

King Birch clenched his jaw and closed his eyes, his body tense but for his hands which held his daughter with reverence. The staff had to check on him, he knew. He was their king and doors were not locked to them very often. But if he'd ever needed a moment to himself, this was it. He rose and slowly handed the baby to Myra. Then he moved to the door, his grief turning to anger, and his patience well tested. He flung open the oak monstrosity and grimaced with his lips pressed closed over his teeth.

"I am fine, you can see." King Birch swept his hand in front of his body. "I need some time with my family."

If anyone was prepared to speak, they lost their courage quickly. Myra could see the king's men begin to bow as he shut them out with the slam of the door.

"Birch," she called him as she had when they were children and did so now seldomly when they were alone. "You have a daughter, not a son. This is a girl; there is no getting around it."

"I dreamt it was a boy, last night," he stated.

Slumber for most descendants of the Hall family was a black void, but for some, when they did dream, it was a rare night vision of something that would happen the next day. When Birch was twelve years old, he'd had his first dream the night before his birthday, and the next day when he saw his birthday gifts, he already knew what was inside each package. When he was thirty-nine, he'd had a dream that he was at a dance and spilled his drink on the most beautiful woman in the room. The next evening he did accidentally spill his drink, and in turn met his future queen. And dreaming is how King Birch had learned of his wife's passing before it had happened. When he awoke this morning, twenty miles from home on a hunting trip, he knew already that he would have a son. He closed his eyes and remembered his vision vividly: the blue robes perched on his wife's chest, the light smile she mustered to have given birth to an heir to the throne, the way her head fell forward into death as she admired her son. As the memory from the night before played over and over, King Birch realized he had assumed it was a boy in his dream because of the blue robes. Nothing had to be said, the evidence was there. He had also known that Queen Samantha would die, and as he rode straight away like the devil back to the castle, he had already begun to grieve the imminent loss of his wife. For there was nothing he could do about it. When he dreamt, his dreams always came true.

King Birch could not fault Myra for wanting the queen to be happy in her last moments. He was actually content that Samantha was allowed to die with her wish fulfilled and some joy in her heart.

Myra watched as the king took the baby to the window. The sun was setting and the sky was painted a bright red. It took a tidal wave of emotion to make either cry, but Myra could again see a tear on King Birch's cheek as she wiped her own away with her apron. Long moments passed before King Birch broke the silence.

"She has to be a boy." His huge hands engulfed the newborn.

"You can't keep that kind of secret," Myra softly protested.

"I can and I will. And you will, too," King Birch commanded.

"And who else?" Myra begged. "Princess Zaria? Prince Hawker? Counselor Glenn?"

"Don't be ridiculous, Myra. Counselor Glenn has been my acquaintance as long as you have, but many years have passed since we saw eye to eye. He is half the reason I am in this predicament." Myra didn't ask what the other half was as her face blushed candidly.

"So," she stated slyly, "you have heard the way he talks about you and the crown."

"I have no time to debate politics with you now, Myra. Please, I am asking you for your help, and for your silence."

There was no need for him to ask, her alliance was always his. She simply nodded.

"Zaria will know. She is only six, but she is Avalon's sister and they will be close. Avalon will need Zaria. She will need both of you."

"And Prince Hawker?" Myra asked hesitantly of the king's half-brother. "The queen didn't like him and didn't trust him."

"He is my brother."

"Half brother," Myra muttered. "And his mother was a witch who never liked you."

"That is true, but Hawker is my brother and has always stood by me."

Myra half-stifled a loud huff.

"You've never liked Hawker."

"He lit my skirt on fire when I was ten, and you didn't see the evil look of pleasure on his face!"

"He was a boy. He probably liked you and meant to get your attention."

"Well that he did, and I will never turn my back on him again."

Myra could see King Birch deliberating and thought it best not to press her luck. She stood quietly waiting.

"No," King Birch finally whispered. "Hawker is my brother, but I will not tell him. I am afraid this is too big of a secret to ask anyone to keep." King Birch looked to Myra, and she returned to him a look of supreme confidence before holding her fingers up to her lips and turning an invisible key. Then King Birch looked into his daughter's black eyes that matched her mother's. He touched his nose to hers. "Samantha should be your proper name, after your mother."

The air inside the room was crushing, its heavy intonation rippling the future. When the king looked away, Myra's sharp jaw set as she clenched her teeth, knowing that although she did not agree with King Birch's decision to announce his daughter as a son, she would help her friend, her king, at any task, and would take his secret to the grave.

King Birch didn't notice Myra bow to take her leave and slip out the side entrance to Zaria's room. All of his attention was on his baby girl as he talked tenderly to her. "I am going to teach you everything that I can. I will protect you, my daughter, until the end of my days." For a long time, Birch stared out at the darkening sky as it began to fade to gray and night emerged, and he weighed his choices one last time.

He could still change the blue robes for pink and let everyone know that Avalon was in fact a girl. Those close to the queen knew that Samantha's one wish was to produce an heir, and her friends would fully understand that the lie upon her deathbed now allowed Queen Samantha to rest in peace. If King Birch decided to do this, Avalon would be raised a princess like her sister Zaria, and life for his girls would go on naturally.

This should not have been a difficult decision, but he had announced that he'd had a son, and King Birch was certain that the moment he emerged from the room with a daughter, Counselor Glenn would have him brought up on charges of treason for trying to dupe the whole of Fontanasia with an heir to the throne. King Birch didn't think that anyone else in council would challenge him, but he could no longer be certain of the depth of Counselor Glenn's reach and what power he might wield if able to trap the king in a lie.

King Birch did not like believing this of the man who had been his dearest friend when they were young men. His own naïve faith in those around him had brought him to this uncertain moment. He had announced that the baby was a boy because he'd seen it in his dream, but he couldn't tell the whole truth about his dreams because no one but Birch, Hawker, and Myra knew about the Hall's dreams of the future. It was a family secret that Birch was not willing to give up. As conflicted as he was at this second, he knew that he had already committed himself.

"Your mother has passed. I don't know why that had to happen, but it did." King Birch's eyebrows pressed together in a stilted line as he whispered to his sleeping daughter. "I had a dream last night that she would die, just as I had a dream that you would come. Just as I was sure you would be a boy by the blue robes your mother held you in." Everything he had seen so clearly less than a day earlier was obscured behind a cloud of uncertainty now. King Birch spoke without distinct direction, and Avalon was not bothered by her father's tender tone. The king was working things out loud for his own conscience.

"There are deceptions at play here, Avalon, lies that are spreading their slow poison. I need a foothold." King Birch looked straight at her when he said this, trying to explain to a child who did not yet know the meaning of the words. "Your life has scarcely begun, yet your fate is already changing, Avalon." Before this day, King Birch had not cried in three decades. Losing his wife and now looking into his daughter's face had caused him to expose his heart several times in mere hours.

"I will lie to you, my daughter, but only once, and that lie comes now." He cleared his throat. "You, S. Avalon Hall; you are my son."

"It's time," Myra George announced as she returned through the side door from Zaria's room carrying a bundle of blankets. As nanny to the king's six year-old, Zaria, she had checked on her young charge and instructed the nanny that she should remain close for the evening. Then she ran an errand no one was to know about.

Myra was an old friend to the king, but the four decades bond they held before tonight had paled in comparison to the tie that was now building by the minute.

"I am not sorry that I lied for Queen Samantha's sake, God rest her soul…" Myra trailed off. "I want you to know that I understand why you have to do this, but I do not agree. Avalon will be confused when she is old enough to know that she is not a boy." The entire time she spoke, Myra was quickly moving about the room. On sight, her tall, bulky frame kept her from appearing very polished, but her every movement held a purpose and in turn she looked graceful in her work. She placed her bundle of blankets on the bed and removed a silk robe from the queen's trunk.

King Birch's eye caught the bundle. It had moved.

"I suppose, if she takes after you, she will grow to understand that her people need her. They need her to be a boy now, as they will need her to grow into a king." Myra continued her chore as she rattled on.

The bundle on the bed made a sound, and King Birch swore he'd heard the bird like call of an unattended baby. The king didn't understand where the sound could have come from because Avalon was still pressed to his chest. Myra unwrapped the bundle of blankets she had placed on the bed, and a plump baby boy appeared in front of the king. Myra promptly rewrapped this other baby's naked figure in the queen's silk shawl.

"They'll need proof, your majesty. You know that," Myra stated as if that explained everything.

"She'll have to understand, Birch. Dare I say, she may not. She may come to hate both of us in time." Myra's cheeks were rosy and she sighed deeply as she reached down to the bottom of her white apron and pulled it up over her face, wiping the sweat that King Birch hadn't noticed until now.

Myra watched the soft miniature hands curled above miniscule feet, as Avalon lay bundled in her father's warm arms.

The baby's pointed chin matched her father's, but her huge, smoky black eyes were all her mother.

"Have you changed your mind?" Myra asked, all action, but not yet fully committed herself.

King Birch held his breath as he looked over to the limp body of his queen. Myra had managed to lay clean sheets over the queen and positioned her flat on the bed, her hands folded as though she was resting. Birch grit his teeth. He let the tears to the surface again hoping this release could possibly heal the heartache. It didn't. Queen Samantha lay dead in their bed where she had delivered their new baby. The king wanted to rest with the queen, to spill his emotions out over her. He had been strong all of these years never asking much of her, but he needed her guidance now.

He knew that the citizens of Fontanasia had already heard the news as the chatter of a growing crowd outside built into the start of a celebration. The council would be waiting for the king on the parapet above the five fingers. They would be waiting for the proof that a son and rightful heir to the throne had been born. King Birch noticed the bundle that Myra now held.

"My great nephew, sire. Just please be quick about it before my niece expects him back for feeding." King Birch allowed the shock to guide him toward Myra. He handed his daughter to Myra's waiting arms. Myra placed Avalon on the bed and replaced the tiny newborn girl with the silk bundled boy. She swiftly changed Avalon's wrappings to plain, white cotton in case anyone saw her while the king had the boy. Myra finished the swaddling and in another moment was holding Prince Avalon, looking into the baby's smoky pitch black eyes, her innate womanly rocking taking over as she settled the tiny figure back to sleep. It was difficult for Myra to believe that this tiny girl was in line to become the next King of Fontanasia.

And King Birch noticed how at ease Myra was with the baby, as though her entire destiny was to care for children, or maybe this one child.

Three stories below the king's suite, the King's Council and personal guard awaited the arrival of King Birch for their first look upon the new heir to the throne. Prince Hawker Hall looked down at the crowds of townspeople gathered below. It was not one massive crowd as it was when the castle was first built, but rather four large crowds separated by thick, brick walls that ran from the castle to just inside of the city walls. When he first took the throne, King Birch had the walls constructed at the advice of his lead guard, Walthan. There was a small walkway on each wall, enough for men to stand back to back and defend the city if they were ever attacked. From the hills at the foot of the town, the castle looked like the back of a hand running down from the wrist into giant fingers that latched onto the side of the mountain. Hawker found himself annoyed with the fingers, as they were called. He didn't understand why his brother had ordered the project completed since Fontanasia was a world on its own, never having even seen one stray stranger in its two hundred years, much less an invading army. He watched now as the arched gates between the fingers were raised, allowing the citizens to travel easier between the burrows without having to walk all the way down the hill and around the wall.

Within each burrow, small pyres were being lit as the sky grew dark. The people streamed up toward the castle and began their celebration, the word of the new prince having made its way to the outer wall as the king's men waited two hours for him to emerge with the newborn babe. The rotund Counselor Glenn sidled close to the towering Prince Hawker and smiled.

"It looks like you have lost your place in line, *Prince* Hall," Glenn leered at Hawker.

Hawker's nose twitched like a rabbit's and he laughed, but he did not take the bait. Hawker knew that his position under the crown had always been invalid because his parents had never married. He was shrewd and unaffected in public, keeping his rants far behind closed doors.

Counselor Glenn pressed on. "The Council is ready to rule Fontanasia, to be the true voice of the people." Glenn's eyes came only to Hawker's shoulders, and he looked up but couldn't force eye contact with Hawker who kept looking over the counselor's head at the others gathering on the parapet. "It would all go much smoother if you would be our voice, if you could convince those counselors still devoted to your brother that it is time for a change."

"It is time for a change," Hawker said. His eyes rolled to the sky but just as quickly were back down to the sea of people gathering below. Always calm and diplomatic, he'd eased his jaw almost the very moment he'd begun clenching his teeth. "You must be desperate talking this way. I had heard rumors that you were becoming pompous enough to speak out, and you couldn't get more brazen." Hawker leaned forward and held his hands out noting that Counselor Glenn was talking treason on the King's own parapet.

"I will not be your voice," Hawker answered calmly, a smile curling up at his lips. "Perhaps you have not heard, but my nephew is next in line to be king now. You might have better luck with him. It will be at least a year before he learns to speak though, so you will have to be patient in your plotting."

Just then the gaggle of voices on the parapet fell silent as Prince Hawker's brother, King Birch, moved into view. Hawker turned his back but looked down at Glenn. "*King* Birch will never concede, and I am sure my brother won't let you anywhere near the boy, so maybe it is time to lay your plans to rest." Hawker brandished his cape and moved away from an insulted Counselor Glenn to get a closer look at his nephew.

King Birch swept onto the terrace above the crowd, his presence instantly shifting the positions of those waiting. He was holding Myra's nephew bundled tightly in the queen's ivory robes, and his brother, Prince Hawker, stepped to his side at once before the King's Council surrounded them. As a precaution, Walthan and Brick, the king's first guard, moved in closer behind King Birch and Prince Hawker. Counselor Glenn eyed the small white bundle with an unhidden skepticism.

King Birch instinctively held tighter to the baby knowing Counselor Glenn must have been seething with rage that his step up to the throne had been postponed by an heir. King Birch looked back over the years of their friendship turned rivalry and wished he had trusted his closest advisors and turned Counselor

Glenn out several years earlier. He didn't want to believe then that Glenn would have acted on any personal ambition, and now, holding this baby, he felt helpless to stop what had begun. To turn Counselor Glenn out now would show weakness. King Birch needed a year or two with a rightful heir to quiet any whisper of change, and to earn back the trust of any counselor who had been willing to listen to Glenn's urging for the council to take control.

Birch concentrated on the baby in his arms. He stepped to the front of the parapet, and the scene in the burrows filled King Birch with hope as the crowd sounded up cheers of congratulations and applause. Samantha's passing devastated him, but the people of Fontanasia had not heard yet that she had died, only that a son was born. It was getting dark now, but the flaming pyres lit the crowd below. The moon over Fontanasia was full and bright, its gleaming points of light glistening like the sun on water.

"Congratulations, King Birch," Counselor Glenn greeted, his crow's nose pecking at the air. Those who knew him well did not think for a moment that he was sincere.

"Thank you," King Birch heaved before turning to Hawker. "Brother, meet your nephew, S. Avalon Hall." King Birch tipped the sleeping baby's head up on his arm so Hawker could see the face. It was round and pudgy and white as the moon.

"Congratulations, Birch," Hawker responded informally. Being brothers, Hawker rarely referred to his brother as King. "A strong boy. He looks like a fighter to me."

Counselor Glenn's eyes squinted and his lips became two thin sticks.

"Help me, brother," King Birch said to Hawker, although his gaze was aimed toward Counselor Glenn.

Hawker moved closer to his brother, his wafer thin frame, though much taller, looked feeble next to Birch's bulk. He helped the king fully unwrap the queen's robe, and everyone on the porch could plainly see that the king was holding a boy.

At that moment, Counselor Nelson stepped to the front of the parapet and took a deep breath in. "It's a boy!" he rejoiced, followed officially by, "Prince S. Avalon Hall is born!"

The crowd went wild as King Birch cradled the naked boy over his head in his sturdy hands. The baby, chilly and startled by the crowd, began to cry.

"You are truly blessed," Counselor Glenn conceded before offering a slight bow as the king wrapped Myra's nephew back in the robes. An attendant held out her hands to take the heir, but the king held tight.

"I will take him to our chambers," the king announced as the attendant melted back.

"S. Avalon?" Hawker asked. Everyone on the parapet remained silent, and King Birch's lips pressed tight. He instinctively pulled the baby closer before remembering it was not really his baby in his arms.

"The 'S' is for Samantha," he said softly to Hawker. Then to his council and the guards on the parapet, "Let the people have their night, for tomorrow they shall learn that their queen died giving birth to our son." King Birch swept past without another word as the mouths dropped on his inner circle's shocked faces.

Chapter 2
First Council

ᴰawn spread quickly over the green valleys of Fontanasia. Prince Avalon deftly sprang forward and hit her attacker with her sword causing him to heave forward into a heap on the ground. Three other men lay on the ground around her clutching their sides, and she whipped the air with her broadsword preparing to counter her final opponent. Her smoky, pitch black eyes carved their own line down his figure, and she knew that he was an opponent with which to be reckoned. Metal clanged as they danced around each other; jumping, spinning and stabbing. The others had fallen easier than this, and Avalon pulled in a deep breath of the crisp morning air hoping that her attacker would make a mistake. She had been using a sword for ten years now and had learned that the counter attack was her key to survival.

She sprung back out of the way of three strikes and then lunged forward herself. Her attacker slapped her back with the blunt edge of his sword as he spun out of her reach. Avalon's face turned red, but she did not falter. He lunged at her, she retreated and then side stepped as he pounced forward into her trap. He overstepped, and as she spun to meet him, Avalon's blade held still at her attacker's neck. She did not draw blood though, and after a moment, her attacker made a silent gesture of defeat when he put two fingers on the side of her blade and pushed it away from his skin. Avalon allowed her muscles to relax making a quick step back but keeping the ever-present composure of the Prince and heir to the throne of Fontanasia. She handed her dull practice heavy sword to the keeper and retrieved her steel broadsword, placing it back on her hip as the other defeated men stood and dusted themselves off.

"You are ready, Prince Avalon," her attacker told her as the four men bowed simultaneously. A flower of happiness unfolded inside her chest. She smiled as the men collected their swords and practice packs, moving off toward the castle.

"The festival is still a month off, Gamon. I expect to see you here tomorrow morning so that I can continue."

"It is my honor, Prince Avalon," the king's guard bowed. "I would like to be the first to wish you a happy birthday, and suggest that you might want to skip tomorrow's practice."

Avalon beamed. "As you wish, Gamon."

"As you wish, my Prince."

Gamon was very tall, and his long muscles tied around his frame making him a quick swordsman. Avalon had chosen him as her trainer for his skill and his height. For a boy, she was tall for her age, but Myra told her that girls typically sprouted earlier than boys, and Avalon knew that the boys would soon grow taller than her. She wanted as much experience as possible fighting with those who had a longer reach. She would need Gamon's skills to continue to be a capable fighter.

Gamon bowed again, waiting for the prince to move on ahead, but Avalon tipped her head toward the path signaling to Gamon to leave without her. Used to his Prince's insatiable appetite for practice, he simply nodded and moved off, jogging to catch his men.

With two of the guards looking sharp, although they were long bored with the early morning ritual, Avalon remained in the grass doing footwork drills for the larger part of an hour. She loved to train and felt at home with a sword in her hand, channeling the fierce spark of competition that she had inherited from her father. She was not pretending here, just lunging, retreating, attacking, and enjoying herself. Training was the one place where she felt equal to the men around her because she wasn't overthinking their actions or wondering if they knew her secret. She was simply allowing her body to do what it knew.

She stayed as long as she dared, but it was her birthday, and there were rituals that she would not be able to outrun. She looked up the expanse of Fontanasia, built high into the side of the mountain. From the low grass, the castle looked like the back of a hand rested on the steep rock above, fingers ready to curl up and pull the whole of Fontanasia from the mountain. The guards brought her horse forward and together they rode along the center wall. They were in the largest of the fingers as the road changed from dirt to brick and steepened up to the castle. Each day that she trained with Gamon, she took this same path home, but being in the street made her self-conscious. Food merchants were out preparing their carts and shops for the day, and a group of small boys walked ceremoniously behind Avalon and her guards. The people tipped their heads and bowed low, but they would always look up at her again after she passed by. She knew that they looked because she was the prince, but she worried that they looked because they knew she was a girl.

She lost sight of the castle in several areas where the shops were tall enough to block out the mountain, but she knew that as long as she was following the center wall up to the castle, she would find the entrance. Avalon had not visited the other burrows since she was little. Ever since she had started hiding the fact that she was a girl, she didn't feel safe. She wouldn't allow the possibility of being exposed to anyone finding out. So she only remembered this one path, this one finger that led her up to the safety of home.

They made their way to the angled entrance, and Avalon left the guards where the horses could no longer find footing. Her muscular legs took the walkway with even strides as the two fingers came to a close. She crossed into the castle and climbed three circular staircases to her sister's room. She hesitated outside the carved, wooden door to the king's suite. For as long as she could remember, her birthday had always begun in Zaria's room. Myra George had kept Avalon to a ridiculous yearly tradition, but this year was different because this year Avalon was fourteen. Instead of entering the royal suite, Avalon moved back out onto the parapet and took a deep breath, soaking in her country's glory.

Fontanasia was nicknamed Heaven's Bed by its inhabitants. A green, rolling land bordered on the east by sea, and protected on the west and north where the castle was hugged by a wide, white, rocky mountain, thick mist appeared like feathers a hundred feet above the castle each morning of spring. The city had grown over the decades to house over ten thousand tenants, and six separate burrows each held their own shops of bakeries and clothing stores, and professional businesses of smiths and carpenters, and homes for all of the families within. The great curving castle was built inside heavy, chalk colored, brick city walls with a secondary wall built two miles away guarding from mountain to sea. The heavy barriers were sturdy and meant to protect the inhabitants in case of attack, but in the over two hundred years of its existence, Fontanasia knew neither enemies nor any other people at all. They were contented alone in their reality, with only the fading tales of their forefathers' journeys to paint any picture of a past life spent outside these city walls.

Avalon pulled in a deep breath and watched the sun's heat dissipate the last of the mist. She was fourteen today, and in the eyes of all of Fontanasia, she was old enough to take the throne. Avalon knew that it would be many years before she would be king, but she felt the weight of the day upon her. There was one task ahead of her that she'd been avoiding, but it was time to face it. She walked the short distance back to the king's suite and into her sister's room. Princess Zaria never looked back at Avalon as she watched herself in the mirror. She curtsied and smiled to herself before sliding her hands over the cloth on her skirt, turning this way and that, her eyes staying trained on her image. Avalon wondered how her sister could care so much about materials, dresses, and her hair. It had to be an empty life.

Avalon cleared her throat as she crossed the room to gain her sister's attention.

"I'm here for my torture," Avalon stated, resigned.

Zaria had been eagerly awaiting Avalon's arrival and tousled her little sister's walnut colored hair.

"That is disgusting, Avalon," Zaria complained of the sweat that she now wiped back on Avalon's sleeve.

"You shouldn't pet me like a dog, then, should you?" Avalon retorted, already dreading what was to come. She moved into the washroom and locked the door behind her as there was a slight knock on the outer door.

"Good morning, Zaria. Sorry I am late," Myra George announced in her sing-songy voice. Myra touched her curly silver hair and closed the door and locked the bolt so no one else could enter.

"You haven't missed anything. Avalon came back late, on purpose," Zaria signaled to the closed door next to her.

"I had to train, Zaria," Avalon's voice hounded back from behind the closed door.

"She just doesn't want to dress this morning," Avalon's twenty year-old sister sassed while patiently standing at her closet, three magnificent dresses on hand.

Myra shot a stern look at Zaria for referring to Avalon as a girl. Of course Zaria knew that Avalon was really her sister, but Myra had made Zaria always refer to Avalon as 'he' to keep the promise that she had made King Birch fourteen years earlier. She shook her head realizing in wonder that their charade had somehow lasted all this time.

"Pish posh," Myra told them both. She double knocked and then jerked open the washroom door to expose a muscular Avalon dressed in boy's undergarments. "Happy Birthday, my Prince. Come now, it's time to get dressed."

In the kingdom of Fontanasia, where boys wore pants and girls wore dresses, it would be as awkward for a teenage girl to feel comfortable in slacks as it would for her to bow instead of curtsey. But Avalon felt as natural as any boy to wear pants and to bow, because she had been raised as a boy and simply knew no other way.

"This isn't right. I'm a boy," Avalon answered in the deeper voice she used as a prince.

"You are a boy," Myra agreed, "but you're a girl, and your mother would never forgive me if I didn't remind you of that."

"But my mother wanted a boy."

Myra reached down and cradled Avalon's pointed chin in her warm hand and looked into the mirror of Avalon's smoky, black eyes. "Your mother wanted a healthy, happy child, and she would love you for who you are." Myra gulped down her sentiment and hugged Avalon, pulling her out in front of the mirror in Zaria's dressing room. "Besides, you are a girl and may eventually have feelings such as a girl does. And someday you will bloom just as Zaria did, and you will want to wear a dress, if you have the chance…" Myra tapered off.

As soon as she was old enough to know the difference, Myra had made Avalon wear a dress behind closed doors. There was not much negotiating room with Myra George, but as the years passed, Avalon had protested more and more until declaring that she would never wear a dress again. They ended up compromising that only once a year Myra would make Avalon put on a dress in honor of Queen Samantha. Still, Myra held on to several dresses in each size once Zaria grew out of them, believing one day Avalon would come to change her mind. Knowing she was beat, Avalon prepared to endure her yearly torture, but she still didn't believe that there would ever be a day in which she would want to wear such impractical clothing.

Zaria bounced lightly, excited as she readied the gown that she had chosen to dress her sister in. She bustled around Avalon who was trying not to look at herself in the mirror. Even more than the yearly ritual itself, Avalon hated dressing in Zaria's old clothes. The waist fit, but her arms and legs were larger than Zaria's because of the physical tasks she undertook in training, and Avalon felt trapped in the too small top. She tried not to move in fear of tearing the delicate silk and lace. Zaria was also taller than Avalon at any age, so the bottom of the dress sagged on the floor and the disproportion between the small top and long bottom were almost comical.

Avalon's shoulders slumped over in the mirror. She was a very self-confident boy, but as a girl, she was awkward and indifferent. It was more than that though. She hated looking at herself this way because although it was the truth, seeing herself as a girl in a dress felt like the real lie. She didn't like losing the assuredness that she enjoyed as Prince Avalon.

"Are we done here?"

"Oh," Myra squeaked, honestly touched. "You really do get more and more beautiful each year."

Beautiful was not the word a prince was used to hearing, and Avalon rolled her head with her eyes. Compliments of beauty were more equated with Zaria who was tall and lean and had at twenty years-old become the statuesque woman that their mother had been. Avalon was shorter and always dressed in layers to look stouter like King Birch, which came in handy while pretending to be a boy.

"Stand up straight, dear, let me see you," Myra insisted. Avalon made a face at Myra. Not out of disrespect, but because she knew that her keeper was right and that her body would transform someday. As it was, she looked in the mirror every morning to make sure nothing had changed yet. Avalon pulled her shoulders back and looked at her reflection, relieved as the fabric of the dress hung off of her chest.

"Myra is right, Avalon. You are ravishing," Zaria flourished. "Let me do your hair." Zaria stepped forward to play with the short sandy brown strands of Avalon's hair but was too slow for her agile sister who ducked and leapt away from the mirror but then fell over the train of her dress and tore the shoulder seam wide open.

"What hair?" Avalon countered in her normal, deep, everyday voice, not at all concerned with the hole she had just torn.

Zaria didn't allow her little sister to change her voice into the deeper male tone when they were alone, and she waited for Avalon to repeat her question.

"What hair?" Avalon repeated in the natural voice of a young girl. It felt strange to talk without effort.

"Really, sister." Zaria's bird-like tone matched her small, chiseled face. "You should let me dress you in a wig." Even though most men kept their hair shaggy, Avalon's was cropped neatly to emphasize that she was a boy. "I could dress you up and have you to one of my gatherings. It would do you some good to get out."

Myra had sat quietly taking in every moment of Avalon the princess, but she cleared her throat to deter Zaria's invitation.

"Just a suggestion," Zaria conceded. "No one would notice her anyway." Zaria was in the mirror again admiring her own reflection. She was full of the confidence King Birch had instilled in her, *and sometimes a little pompous,* Avalon thought.

"Don't worry, Myra, I wouldn't go. Although, it would be fun to watch her suitors trip over themselves," Avalon teased her sister. At twenty years-old, Zaria was the marrying age, and the princess enjoyed the attention of several admirers.

"Are you worried that someone might make himself a fool for you?" Zaria countered with a smile.

Avalon turned to Myra trying to will out the pink that was flushing her cheeks. "Can I change back now?"

Myra admired her young charge. "Just a moment longer. It is your fourteenth birthday, and your mother would wish for you to celebrate your coming of age dressed properly."

"May I call her Samantha?" Zaria joked.

Avalon's throat caught, but she wouldn't let herself ruin the moment with guilty thoughts of her mother's death. She winced and mockingly curtsied to Myra and then to Zaria before attempting to dance about the room in the torn dress, but all of the layers slowed Avalon down. She realized that as difficult as it was to always pretend to be a boy, and the added pressure of becoming the next king of Fontanasia, Zaria must have had a much more difficult life with her dresses and made up party conversation. Zaria's job was to find a husband and marry and have children, nothing about which Avalon could find importance. Her sister wasn't even really permitted to have an opinion in public, only to appease others with a smile.

Avalon got to play at sword fighting, and spent hours reading and learning everything she could. The only inconvenience she found was that she had to return to her suite to use the bathroom for privacy because they couldn't chance her being revealed.

King Birch had himself revolutionized the elaborate washroom and water system using the mountain springs and gravity. It benefited all in the castle, but was designed to keep his daughter's true gender safe, and the ruse had worked.

Zaria disappeared into her immense closet and returned with a small colorful box.

"Happy birthday, *sister*," she announced, catching Avalon as she mock swirled in front of the mirror.

"Don't taunt," Myra chided as she looked around the room. She was paranoid someone might have heard, although they were locked in and there was clearly no one else present. She clucked her tongue and looked to the locked door as she shushed Zaria who was holding the package out to Avalon.

Avalon opened the gift and held it up to Zaria with a look of incomprehension. It was a silver hair comb that adorned several black jewel stones. It was stunning, but nothing Avalon would ever wear in her tightly cropped hair.

"Speechless?" Zaria sassed. "I expect you to wear it to your first council today. My feelings will be hurt if you don't." Zaria was teasing her younger sister again, and Avalon began to peel off her morning attire.

"Over my dead body," Avalon countered.

Myra held her breath, and Zaria softly took the comb from Avalon's hands.

"It was mother's," Zaria gently whispered. The mood in the room turned cold as she placed the comb in Avalon's hair. It didn't hold for long in the short strands though, and Zaria pressed it into Avalon's palm again.

"Thank you," was all Avalon could manage. She didn't have anything of her mother's, aside from her first initial. King Birch was practical but paranoid. He hadn't allowed any of Queen Samantha's jewelry or trinkets to be passed down to Avalon. Avalon swallowed hard, but before she could get caught up in the moment, there was a loud knock at the door.

"Why is the door locked? I am here for the birthday..." there was a pause, "the birthday boy!" King Birch shouted.

"Just one minute, Sire!" Myra jumped faster than Avalon had ever witnessed of her nanny, and the frantic woman unpacked some fresh clothes for Avalon and began to straighten them as fast as she could. Avalon needed little prodding and she was out of the dress in five seconds and pulling her pants on. King Birch didn't know about Myra's ritual, and he would be furious if he found out.

"Am I to be kept waiting?" King Birch bellowed. Myra let out a fearful squeaking sound and gasped, her normal controlled façade crushed to bits. Another minute passed, and Avalon unlocked the door and pushed herself past the king and out of the room buying time for Zaria and Myra to clean up the mess. Avalon did not enjoy Myra's yearly ritual, but she enjoyed her father's temper less.

"Father, I didn't expect to see you until this afternoon's council," Avalon admitted as she led him away from Zaria's door.

The reigning king of Fontanasia towered over his daughter. Though insulated by his massive frame, he wore heavy furs well into the spring as he was often chilled to the bone. Avalon ducked into her father's bear hug. He wasn't often overly affectionate, but when he meant to show his love, he held on tight and squeezed the breath out of her.

"You're crushing me, sir," Avalon voice was muffled in the heavy furs. King Birch slowly let go but kept his huge hands on Avalon's shoulders. She smiled up at him but looked down uncomfortably when she saw the start of a tear on his eyes.

"Son," King Birch said softly. "Son, you are fourteen years-old, and in the eyes of the people, you are a man now." King Birch paused, and Avalon, having been wearing a dress a moment earlier, tried not to laugh out loud.

Mistakenly sensing Avalon's aloofness, King Birch tensed. "There are things you should know, Avalon. Things have been done," he stuttered, "decisions have been made…" the King trailed off, his eyes looking everywhere but into Avalon's. He took a deep breath as he tried to find the right expression, and his face melted into a sensitivity that Avalon had never seen. She would like to have turned to begin their walk to council, but he still held her shoulders tight as the air between them became the most serious she could remember.

"Life, your life, might have been different."

Avalon now knew what her father was trying to say, and she immediately withdrew.

"I don't want my life to be different," Avalon blurted. She was sure that her father was trying to lead into a conversation that he had never had with her, a conversation fourteen years overdue. He had always greeted her with an expression due a strong boy, but the growing vulnerability on his face told her that he was, for the first time, trying to tell her that she was a girl.

Avalon's stomach tightened in an effort to control the unsettling weightlessness it was beginning to feel. She had wondered if this day would ever come, and she had played this scene through and through in her head. When she turned thirteen, she presumed her father would never broach the topic because by then she would have had to know the secret. And now, surprised that the moment was upon her, she realized that she didn't want to hear her father say the words. She was a girl, but more, she was Prince Avalon of Fontanasia, and she didn't want anything to taint that. Myra and Zaria might remind her of her gender on occasion, but that was unofficial in some way. She didn't need her father to see her as a girl. She needed him to see the boy he had raised and was proud of, but now with each word, it was as though he was erasing the life she had built.

"But your life could be different," he tried again.

"But I like my life as it is." Avalon had never been short with her father, but she felt her chest rising and did not want him to see her panic.

King Birch clasped the back of Avalon's neck with one of his huge hands and gently lifted her chin so that she would be forced to look into his eyes. She let her fear turn her head away from him, and the King allowed her neck to pull away from his engorged hand. The time she usually spent with her father was much easier, and she had never disobeyed him. He continually looked at her with confidence, and she always felt that he truly believed she could accomplish anything. But for the first time in her life she had pulled away from him. King Birch only looked at her in dismay, his brows furrowed and his eyes wary and burdened. Avalon realized that she was shaking.

"Avalon?" a voice called, searching from the outer chamber. "Avalon!" they heard again as Prince Hawker entered the royal suite and Avalon, grateful for the disturbance, left her father to run and hug her uncle.

"Happy Birthday, my Prince," Hawker sang. His nose twitched like a rabbit's causing the happiness on his face to look out of place.

"Thank you, Uncle."

"You are getting taller each day," her uncle told her, although he towered over her.

"Ahh, Hawker," King Birch appraised his brother. "Your day has come too. Now that Avalon is of age to take the throne, you shall cease being his advisor and have the freedom to focus on your own interests again."

"I shall always be here for Avalon, as his advisor and uncle," Hawker proclaimed.

"Well said, my brother. See you tonight?" King Birch asked, but he didn't wait for an answer. They watched King Birch leave, his large steps causing him to walk side to side like a toddler, yet his muscles allowing him the grace of a ballet dancer. He was fifty years old, and had now been king for twenty-seven years. Avalon felt bad for the way their conversation had been left, and her Uncle Hawker could see the disappointment on her face.

"That is how it is between fathers and sons, Avalon. Boys become men and then move on, and father's become either angry or despondent for it," Hawker advised Avalon when he noticed her lingering on her father's retreat. Hawker was taller than most, and he seemed to lean over to one side like a slender tree as though he had only one muscle in his body which ran from his toes to his forehead. His soft skin was always pale white, even in the height of the sun in summertime, and he looked like a ghost next to Avalon's fair but freckled skin.

"Not father and I. We have always been close," Avalon proclaimed.

"It looks as though you are not as close now, young man. You are a teenager and making your own way. It is only natural that you and Birch wouldn't agree on everything."

"But we always agree," Avalon said longingly as she eyed her feet.

"The son wants to please, and the father wants the son to be better than he ever was. That causes tension. It's not a winning combination," Hawker advised. "It is an age old tale."

"That's not it." Avalon's throat tightened and she swallowed hard. She wanted to tell her uncle that this was not the way with her and her father, and that the tension was because she was a daughter and not a son.

"Then what is?" Hawker asked Avalon as he swayed over her.

She couldn't tell him the truth though. "I don't know."

"You see?" he took Avalon's elbow. "I am right."

Avalon decided she should turn the conversation. "Is that the way it was between you and Grandpa?"

There was a flash of disgust as his face pulled in on itself, his nose twitched, and then in a instant Hawker smiled as his face softened. It happened so fast that Avalon wasn't sure what she had just seen on her uncle's face. "No, it was not tense between me and my father. He didn't regard me very well." Hawker's smile only extended to his lips, but his tone remained even. "Your father was already of age to take the throne by the time I was born, you know. So my father had already had a son for many years, and he spent most of his time with Birch making sure he knew how to rule Fontanasia when the time came."

Hawker's black robe trailed as he took a few short steps around Avalon with a faraway look on his face. "Much like Birch is with you now, Avalon. He is preparing you; he has been for years. So you see, my father didn't have the time of day for a second son."

"Oh." Avalon felt sheepish for a moment until Hawker snapped out of his reverie.

Avalon could easily imagine her father as a child learning to become king, as most of her time spent with him was the spent learning to do the same. Although, her father did also spend a fair share of his time with Zaria as well.

"Well, my young Prince," Hawker reflected, "this is how it is in royal families with the eldest son learning the family business, so to speak." Hawker put his arm on Avalon's shoulder. "You will learn to live through it as so many before you have, and that will be that."

Avalon looked out the window of her room at the rolling lands of Fontanasia. Green and beautiful, nestled between lake and mountain, she noticed that there were no roads in or out like the castles she had read about as a child in fairy tales. But knowing her history, she knew that it was because there was no one to come or go, just the people of Fontanasia living within their own existence, with no neighboring towns or villages. The people were all free to go wherever they desired with no beaten path required, but there were no foreigners in and out of this city, and no road had ever taken shape.

Avalon's thoughts turned to her first official council meeting. She had been in the room over the years listening to her father's council talk about the food stores or little squabbles that arose, but it never piqued her interest. She would rather be out climbing or practicing at swordplay. Her father and her Uncle Hawker had also taken her there on separate occasions over the years to teach her about the protocol involved and about each councilman and their views on the future of Fontanasia. Avalon listened intently to both, silently noting their very different opinions.

Myra George had told Avalon about her birth, and about Counselor Glenn and the reasons King Birch had decided to raise her as a boy. Myra said that having an heir to the throne had stifled most of Glenn's standing. Her father never confirmed this when he took her to the council room, but he did admit that Counselor Glenn had maintained some control of the council's trust. He watched Counselor Glenn, but never forced him off of the council, explaining to her that he knew Glenn so well, there was no real danger anymore. So he kept his former friend and now enemy close. As for the other five councilmen, the king valued them and took them at their word.

Hawker on the other hand had sat in the king's high, ornate, metal chair and regaled Avalon with the differing personalities, bonds, and arguments that the councilmen had over the years. The council members would say things in front of the king's brother that they would not in front of the king, so Hawker had a very different view of each member of the council. He had told Avalon that she should disband the council should she become king. He told her that it had been foolish of their forefathers to give them a voice in the first place, and that Counselor Glenn was not as subdued as Birch thought. Avalon had never told her father what Hawker had said, but it was always there in the back of her mind, and she held on to her own childhood memory as reason to not trust Counselor Glenn. She told herself that today she needed to pay attention to every word the council uttered as though her life hung in the balance because she would be part of the council, and even the tedious matters were hers now.

There was a quick knock at her door before the knob turned and Avalon stretched her limbs as her father pushed in. Avalon paused, worried that he would revisit their last conversation, but instead of the wrinkled concern on his face that he had left her with, she saw a smile.

"Are you ready to attend your first council, son?" King Birch asked.

Avalon was relieved by the word 'son'. It held more meaning to her than her father could have imagined.

"You are of age, Avalon. It is time that you took your proper place at my side." Avalon smiled as he clasped her shoulder in a tight squeeze. With nothing more to say, King Birch turned and Avalon followed. They walked together out of the suite and along the corridors, and Avalon's heart raced in anticipation.

Avalon could feel the king's excitement as she accompanied him down to the council chamber. Although she had been in this room countless times, Avalon felt her nerves rise with each step. Within the immense oak doors, she found the king's councilmen standing and ready to take their places on long benches behind marble tabletops. She saw Counselors Nelson and Robert, their red and white silken robes bright in front of the oval windows that spilled light onto the tables. The room was large enough for all to sit, but small enough so that no man felt slighted in his proximity to the king.

Avalon smiled at Hawker who sat on a small, stone chair behind and to the left of King Birch who was seated in the pedestaled throne his father's grandfather had built. Avalon took the prestigious, ornate wooden seat to her father's right. Several of the council members were looking back and forth between Hawker and her, and she knew that this had been her uncle's seat until today. She glanced back at her uncle and he smiled easily back at her, his quick wink putting her at ease.

Counselor Nelson took a large, carved, wooden staff and pounded the floor at his feet twice, and the council came to order.

"I would like you to welcome my son to the council. As of today, Avalon is of age to take my place and to rule without assistance. This is a very proud day for me."

"Here, here," Hawker answered along with the rest of the council members.

When all eyes looked to her, Avalon's stomach jerked and she inhaled deeply to keep her face from flushing, but as she watched Counselor Glenn fold his arms and frown at her father, this time her face flushed pink. She could plainly see his display of disrespect. She was ready to stand and call out at Glenn's condescending manner, but her father said nothing, so in turn, she swallowed her tongue. Avalon didn't know how her father managed to restrain his temper in the face of such utter contempt. Avalon looked back to see if Hawker had noticed. Her uncle was usually aloof, but now he was eyeing Counselor Glenn, his squint of hatred likely to leave a scar in the center of Glenn's forehead.

"Thank you for your welcome, friends," King Birch pressed on, unfazed.

Avalon tried to listen to her father, but she couldn't bring herself to look away from Counselor Glenn for very long. He was still watching her, a half smile on his face. She felt a shiver up her back and tried to remind herself that she was a prince and he could not touch her. Her resolve weakened quickly. Avalon's most vivid memory of Counselor Glenn had come in her dreams half a lifetime ago.

It was her seventh birthday, and it was the first time Avalon had dreamt in her sleep. She saw Counselor Glenn standing over her, looking down into her eyes, his mouth drooling like a hungry dog as he half smiled. And then Avalon was falling, tumbling down, down, down. She'd fallen down the stairs, or Counselor Glenn had pushed her. In her sleep, Avalon had rolled over and over until she landed on the stones at the bottom. Instead of helping her, Counselor Glenn just watched with a horrified look on his face while Avalon lay on the brick, her legs and arms badly bruised, and tears streaming from her eyes. Her leg was aching and bloody, and Avalon couldn't stand up.

"You broke my leg!" Avalon cried up the stairs at the crows outline.

"You tripped," Glenn had responded, still hesitating to assist the young prince.

Then a familiar voice rang in her head. "Perhaps you were to meet your ancestors tonight."

Avalon had bolted awake screaming. The sweat clinging to her made her shiver, and the memory made her shudder even now. Under the blankets, Avalon had checked her legs, but they were not injured. She couldn't understand what was happening because she had been terrified of the thoughts she'd had in her sleep. Every other night's sleep was spent in peaceful darkness.

"What is it, my son?" her father had sounded more than concerned as he entered her bedroom followed closely by Myra.

Avalon told her story of the images, and then her father shared the Hall family secret of the dreams that became truth. He told Avalon that these dreams were understood as a warning, so that their owner's course could be changed, a lie told to try and calm his young daughter's fears. But knowing that dreams did become truth, Birch had his most trusted guard, Walthan, spend the entire next day with Avalon to make sure the young prince did not encounter Counselor Glenn.

Walthan was highly respected in Fontanasia as a great warrior. He was a bear of a man who was both enormous and swift, and Avalon felt very secure in his protection. They spent the day practicing with swords and hand-to-hand combat, and only when pressed did Walthan give the young prince his view of the kingdom's politics. Walthan gave her a tour of the fingers, which were almost fully complete, and schooled Avalon on Fontanasia's defenses. She could not tell at that age either who they would need defense against, but she listened intently. Avalon enjoyed spending a day in the shadow of this great man. Though her father was king, and she had always received her share of stares from the people as the young prince and the people's proclaimed "light of Fontanasia", that day she saw that Walthan drew more attention than anyone.

"Did you have a good day, son?" the king asked Avalon that evening.

Avalon remembered telling her father, "Walthan is the greatest! He taught me how to release my opponent's grip on the sword in defense. Want to see?" Avalon was only seven at the time, so she didn't notice that her father was not paying close attention to what she was saying. She could see it now as she remembered though.

The king was still worried for his daughter's health, so he declined the sword lesson that evening. He knew that in the nine hundred years his ancestors had ruled, from times even before Fontanasia, they'd had these dreams, and that the dreams had always come true on the following day.

King Birch stayed up until well after midnight outside Avalon's room, and when the morning came, he was baffled as to how Avalon made it through the day without breaking her leg. Four days later, he got his answer when Avalon fell down the stairs in the presence of Counselor Glenn, thus ending any shred of trust King Birch and Glenn still shared, and reigniting their game of cat and mouse. Of course King Birch threatened Counselor Glenn that day, but Glenn's few remaining allies in council quickly came to his defense, providing an alibi that they had witnessed Avalon tripping on her own. Even Hawker confessed to his livid brother and frightened nephew that it had looked like an accident.

Avalon brought herself back to the council room where Counselor Robert was reading out some small matters of policy. She noticed Hawker was barely paying attention, and that Counselor Glenn had finally turned his attention from her. She chided herself for her lack of interest as her father listened closely to each word in the decree, pursing his lips and nodding his head sincerely as it was spoken. The matters were soon closed, and Avalon took her father's lead when he stood.

"As you all know, we are having a birthday celebration for Avalon this evening, and it would be an honor if you would attend."

King Birch turned from his throne, and Avalon left the room in her father's wake, but not before she heard Counselor Glenn huff in disgust. The sound bothered her, but either her father didn't hear, or he was pretending not to, because he didn't lose stride. Avalon longed to turn back and teach Counselor Glenn a lesson in manners and obedience, but she held her breath as she followed her father down the corridor.

Chapter 3
A Gift from the Guides

The Hall of Kings was an immense, long room that set itself apart from the rest of the castle because it was constructed entirely of marble. There were six pairs of large pillars down the center of the room, four with a statue likeness of a former king posted in front. The ceiling was high and half glass, allowing in the glorious, black, starry sky and full moon shining like diamonds at its bright pinpoints of glittering spots. Several blue banners had been hung along the pillars announcing the prince's coming of age. By the time Avalon entered, most of the King's Council had arrived along with the Hall extended family of cousins. Even Myra George, who as a proud servant did not attend parties, was enjoying herself as a guest at this once in a lifetime occasion.

Horns sounded and Avalon heard, "Make way for King Birch's son, Prince Avalon Hall, on his fourteenth and most significant of birthdays!"

The crowd cheered and Avalon held her breath. All eyes were on her tonight. She managed to hold her head high to the staring faces, but she was nervous. Avalon's position had always drawn her attention, but this many eyes on her at one time made her self-conscious. She was proud, royalty, and every bit the light of Fontanasia at this moment, but part of her couldn't help but wonder if anyone knew that she was not a prince at all. She tried not to make eye contact with the onlookers as she walked through the parting crowd and finally reached the far side of the room. Her father clasped her shoulders with his bear claw hands. His eyes twinkled into hers as he turned to the room.

"Now I have a true heir of a man's age, with the ability to take the throne without advisors," King Birch bellowed, "to rule as he pleases upon my death." No one cheered at the thought of the king's passing. This was not a typical announcement at a prince's fourteenth birthday, but King Birch had a point to make to the council: that the Hall family remained as rulers, and would continue for the foreseeable future.

King Birch turned to Avalon and held out his hand. "Congratulations, Son." The guests did cheer then, as the king lightly embraced their prince. Soon music was playing and over two hundred voices could be heard sharing in the moment. A line formed for those who wished to present the prince with a gift. Zaria glided past Avalon first and curtsied with a wink. She touched her hand to her dark blond hair to remind Avalon of the gift of their mother's comb, and Avalon returned her bow in recognition.

Hawker was next in line to greet Avalon, and he hugged his nephew with one arm while Hawker's assistant passed forth a flawless, silver sheath, the ornately carved handle of a sword protruding from the end. Hawker beamed as he presented Avalon with her gift. Avalon pulled the one of a kind sword from its sheath and her mouth hung open as its detail awed her.

"I had it made just for you." Hawker's pride showed as he patted Avalon on the shoulder.

Avalon moved the sword professionally over in her hands taking in every detail from the jeweled handle to the carving at the base of the blade. The inscription read: *The sun may rule, but it is the moon that guides us to our true destiny.* Avalon wasn't sure what that meant, but she loved the gift.

"It's magnificent, Uncle Hawker," Avalon sang before remembering herself and clearing her throat.

"That's not all." Hawker leaned down like a giraffe plucking from the lower branches to meet Avalon's eyes. He smiled broadly and spoke loud enough so those who stood near could hear. "I know it is no longer tradition, but you shall have a suit of armor. Just see the blacksmith and he will measure you. It is all set." Hawker patted Avalon's shoulders in congratulations and then looked to those watching, pleased with himself for presenting this gift.

Avalon was beside herself. She had been learning sword fighting and combat since she could remember and had always been excited when the army ran large drills where Walthan dressed in full armor. None of the other soldiers still heaved the heavy battle garb preferring lighter body armor, but to have a suit of armor of her own made Avalon feel that she might become a great warrior like Walthan someday. She could practice harder, become stronger, and maybe persuade her father to have Walthan teach her some of his strategy. He was undefeated in tournament competition, and although Gamon was a great instructor, Avalon was sure that he wouldn't be able to train her how to fight in a full suit of armor.

Avalon's smile met her ears as her insides soared. She grabbed her uncle in a strong-armed hug and patted him on the back. She was much shorter, but his rail thin frame made it easy for her to get her free arm around him. "Thank you, Uncle Hawker."

"It is my pleasure," Hawker smiled as Avalon sheathed the sword and turned to the rest of her guests reluctantly, not wanting to put her gift down. She grudgingly handed it aside to the staff that was prepared to attend to her gifts.

Avalon accepted several more gifts before noticing her father's absence, and was surprised to see him standing off to the side of the platform with a small group of Guides. It was as though they had appeared out of nowhere. The Guides stood out among the other guests in their long, dark robes, with their olive skin a great contrast to King Birch's white. She had seen men like this in the throne room a few years ago and remembered the long symbol on their left wrist that her father had said marked them of the tribe. Just now the crowd was beginning to notice the Guides, and their natural party tones were traded for the whispers of gossip. It was strange to see the Guides even shopping in the Fingers, but for them to be in the castle speaking with the king was a very strange sight. King Birch noticed Avalon was watching, but instead of having the Guides move center floor to her, King Birch waved her over.

Avalon's heart raced as she excused herself from the waiting guests and went to her father. The Guides simply bowed their heads in a short nod as she approached. Her father had often said that most advisors had their own political agenda, while the Guides were more interested in the balance of the wind, the sun, and the moon, and the true needs of the people. He had said that she would gain their confidence when she became king and that they were a wise race and to treat them with respect. Remembering those words, Avalon approached humbly, but it was difficult to focus as she noticed the other guests watching intently to save notes of the interaction for later conversation.

"This is my son, Prince Avalon," King Birch proudly told the small group. He didn't introduce the Guides to her, and Avalon wondered if the Guides were so mysterious that even the king did not know them by name.

"I would like to present you with a gift," the eldest Guide told Avalon. She was surprised at how soft yet strong his voice was. His black hair was streaked with gray in small spots although the lines on his face painted a much older man.

"This gift is one of a kind in Fontanasia, and I have been keeping it for you." The elder smiled at her. "I could see that it should belong to you."

Avalon was mesmerized by how calm their presence made her now. Of all the adults participating in her life as a prince, only Myra truly made her feel at ease, like she was allowed to relax and just be herself. Everyone else came with some sort of expectation. Even Walthan anticipated that Avalon would be king one day, which added an underlying reserve from the warrior when King Birch allowed Avalon to ask Walthan about battle. But now, each of this tribe of Guides was looking upon her with grace and Avalon felt an automatic reverence toward them.

"You saw it should be mine?" she asked. "Do you dream too?"

"No," he softly chuckled. "We are not as gifted as the kings." He nodded to King Birch who was not put off by Avalon's slip although Avalon's face burned red.

The Guide handed her a small wood carved box that had many small holes around the top and sides.

"This is a jakkow, and while it looks harmless, it changes on either side of the window."

Avalon didn't understand at all what the Guide meant, but she didn't want to seem foolish, so she accepted the box tentatively as she glanced to the nearest window. The box was ornately carved with two moons on the top. Avalon recognized her moon, which was large with diamond like ornaments embedded in it, but the moon opposite was drab and consisted simply of a dark circle around shaded center. There were two different castles carved on either side of the box, and only one that looked like her castle. She appreciated the intricate woodcarving that had been done by a very talented craftsman.

"It is very beautiful," she remarked, and the Guides all smiled to each other sharing looks of amusement.

"That is not the jakkow." The Guide reached forward and slid his hand over Avalon's. She felt his warm, soft touch and tried not to blush. He moved her finger to a groove on the bottom of the box and they both pressed together as the Guide touched the drab moon on top of the box causing a lid to open. Avalon's hands jumped at the motion, but the Guide gently held her hands steady in his warm, level palms. He pulled the small lid aside exposing a tiny, red creature that had been trapped on the inside. Avalon's eyes bulged. She had never seen anything like it.

"Be very careful at first," the Guide told her. "The jakkow is a very loyal creature and will grow to be yours, but right now it is loyal to me."

As if on cue, the tiny red lizard sprang from the box and crawled onto the back of the Guide's hand, sitting itself on the intricate tattoo near the Guide's wrist. Avalon looked closer and noticed it was not really a tattoo, but more like a deep scar made from a very sharp blade. She flinched at the thought and then redirected her attention to the pet. The lizard had a pointed nose and long body that tapered out into a tail, which curled and moved like a cat's tail. Avalon had never had a pet before, and she was excited to have a one of a kind. She reached out for it.

"Wait," the Guide told her. "I must give him over to you so that he will come to understand where he belongs." The Guide gently lifted the red lizard from his wrist and placed it on Avalon's forearm. Its entire length was the size of Avalon's palm and she gently stroked its back with one finger as it waited to be retrieved by its former owner.

"You must keep him in this box for one week when you are not attending to him. After that, he will do well out on his own."

"Thank you," Avalon said, barely looking away from the lizard.

"Happy birthday, Prince Avalon," the elder said with a smile.

As though an unspoken command had been given, the five men bowed their heads in unison and turned from the Hall of Kings and moved toward the throne room where King Birch escorted them out of the party. Like the rest of the crowd, Avalon watched them go, wondering how they'd been allowed to come in that way. She dismissed the thought as she placed the jakkow back in the box and did not put it down for the rest of the night.

Avalon Hall was groomed and polite and mimicked the manners of her father, but even as a teenager, she was still a child behind closed doors. In her family's castle suite, she was allowed to sit on the floor and play marbles and Verticks, which was a game of carved sticks. Sometimes her father would sit next to her and play, stacking the fat, jagged sticks on end, higher and higher, until it spiked out like the branches of a tree, and the pile fell. Avalon could never beat her father at Verticks, and the king never let his daughter win outright.

"No concessions here, son," King Birch now remembered telling Avalon. "You must learn as a prince that you cannot trust those who would let you win. They are playing a different game altogether." He could see that Avalon was not sure what he'd meant by that, but the king assured her one day it would become clear.

He was proud of Avalon. He saw how hard she studied class work and swordsmanship, and how she'd learned to hold her tongue and study the character of those around her before making judgments. In public she was serious most of the time, but she also enjoyed a laugh when she let her guard down. Her father had been preparing Avalon to succeed him as King of Fontanasia since the day that she was born. His heart burst with joy knowing that she was attentive, knowledgeable, kind, and a teenager well beyond her fourteen years. She would be ready for the crown when her day came.

King Birch rarely spoke of the queen to Avalon, but when Avalon had asked what her mother looked like, King Birch, with a lump in his throat but satisfaction in his words, told Avalon that while the queen looked exactly like Zaria, she was a lot like Avalon: as approachable as an old friend, but as beautiful and hopeful as the morning sunrise. He thought that perhaps Avalon posed the question to remind herself that there was some of her mother in her. King Birch let out a deep breath. He was waiting, alone in their suite, to tell Avalon that she was more like the queen than she could ever have known. He had never discussed Avalon's gender with her, but now, at her fourteenth birthday, and with all of the responsibilities that came with her age, he needed to have the talk. Her body would be changing soon with all of the trappings of womanhood, and she deserved a chance to know what lie ahead.

The king was both proud and troubled by his daughter. He shivered, feeling that the fates were having their way with him in making her save his legacy by being born a girl, when she was more a boy than he could have ever imagined of a son. He often regretted forcing his young daughter into being a boy, and he was sure that someday he would suffer repercussions for his lie.

Myra George entered the suite and crossed the dark room, pulling Birch from his reverie. She didn't see him at first, and he addressed her as she crossed the room.

"The moon is full and sparkling like diamonds, just as they were the night Avalon was introduced to Fontanasia."

He'd startled her, and Myra grabbed her chest and held her breath for a moment, relaxing when she saw him alone in the large, stuffed chair.

"King Birch, are you trying to give me a heart attack? What are you doing sitting here in the dark?"

"I am waiting for Avalon."

"He's still at the party," Myra told the king. She always addressed Avalon as a 'he' to the king, and they had both kept up the charade since the day Avalon had been born.

"I can wait," the king said heavily. "I have been waiting for fourteen years."

Myra had been passing through to her chamber, but noting the heavy tone in his voice, she decided to sit with her old friend.

"And what do you mean by that?" she insinuated as she settled her bulk on the edge of the chair opposite King Birch.

"It's time to tell him. This is long overdue." King Birch cleared his throat, "I mean to say, it's time to tell her."

Myra understood at that very instant what the king intended, and her belly started to roll with laughter although she kept her face in check for a moment before bursting. King Birch wasn't expecting mirth in this most significant of moments, and he immediately became angry. His face reddened and he squeezed the arms of his chair until his knuckles turned white. Myra tried to stifle her laughter into a giggle so she could explain herself, and one look at King Birch's dead straight stare sobered her reverie. "But she already knows, Birch. You can't think someone as bright as Avalon made it to fourteen without figuring this out."

King Birch's anger turned to embarrassment, and his face stayed the same shade red as he felt his heart accelerate. The room seemed to spin around him. He had been dreading this conversation with Avalon for most of the year, and Myra had him dumbfounded. How could he have not known? Why hadn't his daughter approached him? His head filled with countless questions.

"Oh, Birch," Myra empathized. "But how could you know? She came to me about seven years ago. I watched her so closely, but I think it was my nephew Connor who gave it away to her."

The king now looked petrified. He knew Connor as the baby he had used to ruse all of Fontanasia fourteen years earlier.

"No, no. Connor doesn't know, nothing like that. They were out climbing one day, and Connor..." she looked for the right word, "well, he relieved himself in front of her. He was standing up, and Avalon was baffled, so she came to me." Myra sighed heavily and reached out to touch King Birch's hand. Her old friend's shock melted away with her touch, and she could see him taking in her words.

"It took some time, but Zaria and I were able to explain it all to her." Myra released Birch's hand and looked around uncomfortably, truly sorry that this was hurting her old friend. "I didn't know how to tell you. I'm sorry."

King Birch turned his head up to the panoramic window and gazed at the moon. It was his turn to sigh heavily. He still wasn't sure how he would have approached the topic, and after his failed attempt this morning, he was worried that he would let it go another year. But it was done, and deep down he was relieved. *She is fourteen, how could she not know by now?* He thought. Still, it was his lie, and he needed to talk to his daughter to make sure she truly understood.

Myra wasn't sure about Birch's silence, so she continued on, hopeful that he would not be too angry with her when she confessed the rest. "Truth be told, I've had her dress in Zaria's clothes now and then, so it might be easier to understand when she blooms and her figure flourishes."

This revelation stunned the king, and his face turned beet red again.

"We can't keep this secret forever," Myra pushed. "Zaria has grown into a beautiful woman, and Avalon is soon to follow. She prefers to be a boy, if you must know. She will only wear a dress once a year on her birthday, and does not like to be reminded that she is not a true prince."

Birch closed his eyes and let his chin fall to his chest. This startled Myra who quickly slid off the chair and knelt down, but Birch raised a hand to her. He let out a long hiss as though he was trying to remember how to breathe. When he looked up, tears pooled in his eyes, and Myra quickly looked away. She had been with Birch for almost his entire life, and this was only the second day she had ever seen him cry.

After a long silence, Myra reasoned, "Well, maybe what I have told you will make things a little easier between you and Avalon."

"It won't!" King Birch snapped. "She prefers to be a boy because that is what I have made of her, and that is all she knows." He clenched his teeth but tried to relax, not meaning to snap at Myra. "Avalon is like her mother, Myra. She has set her mind on this and won't lose focus. It won't matter to her if there is a better way for her, because her mind is set."

Myra didn't respond to King Birch until she was sure his temper had receded, and then her voice came out as a whisper. "Avalon is strong-willed like her mother, you're right about that. But she is not so single minded as the queen was. Avalon uses her mind and her determination because she is smart, but she will follow her heart because, boy or girl, that is Avalon. And yes, we both conspired to tell everyone that Avalon is a boy when she is a girl, and that has put a pressure on her that we will never comprehend. But she has handled knowing it for seven years already, and hasn't ever questioned what her future might hold, because Avalon is a prince and is your true heir to the throne." Myra reached out to put her hand on Birch's knee but thought better of it. "Maybe it is not Avalon that needs to come to grips with her future." She smiled softly and stood to leave, but Birch grabbed her hand.

"Myra, what would I do without you?"

She smiled broadly, her eyes warm with affection. "You can find out now," she said as Avalon entered the suite. Myra gave Birch's hand a squeeze and let go, leaving him alone in his task.

"Son," King Birch called, startling Avalon in the dark. "Let us finish the conversation we started this morning."

Avalon was not startled by her father's presence as Myra had been, but she hesitated. She still didn't want to have this conversation, but she respected her father and did as she was told. Crossing the room and sitting opposite her father, Avalon felt trapped waiting for the words she didn't need nor want to hear. She stared down at the box in her hand which held her new jakkow lizard, and her nerves were calmed by the barely noticeable shifting weight as the lizard moved about inside.

Avalon looked to her father and waited for him to speak. His face changed many times, and he seemed to be on the edge of tears. His hard features softened as he readied himself. He was looking at Avalon as his daughter now, she could tell that. He had always sat tall and broad in front of his son, but Avalon recognized his now tender countenance. She'd seen her father this way with Zaria before when they spoke of Queen Samantha. Avalon moved the box to the side table and felt the jakkow scuttle within. She looked out at the moon to distract her thoughts. No matter what her father said now, she knew who she was meant to be.

Finally, he spoke. "Your mother would not have liked this, Avalon. She wanted a boy more than anything, it is true, but she would not have liked this." Birch could not bring himself to look at Avalon, and she could see him biting his lip. She knew what he wanted to say, and she knew in the moment that his words would not change her. So she gently took her father's chin and pulled his eyes to hers, melting away the internal conflict she'd been having about the impending conversation.

"Father, she is not here to say what she would have or would not have liked."

Birch took Avalon's small hand from his chin and held it in his immense palm. "Son, you are growing up so fast. I know you think that you know what is best, but soon you will be Zaria's age, and I fear that you will want a different life for yourself."

"I am a prince. What could I possibly want? I have everything that I need."

"Ah, so wise at such a young age." Her father's lips curled up at the edges. "But you don't know yet what is to come. You might want your own family someday."

Avalon pulled her hand away and stood. "There is no way I will ever like boys," she insisted, laughing out loud at this thought.

"Never?"

"Never! I'm friends with a couple of Myra's nephews, and they are disgusting! They belch and hit each other and are unruly, and there is really nothing to like about them."

After having spent the past two hours in darkness and misery, King Birch was able to smile the tears out of his eyes.

"Father, know this," Avalon decreed as she snapped to attention in front of King Birch. "All I want in life is to follow in your footsteps."

He could see himself in her, his assuredness and determination, and he wished it was enough. Birch's shoulders squared for a moment, but Avalon could see them soften again. She picked up the box that held her jakkow lizard and bid her leave before her father could press the conversation further.

When Avalon slipped into bed that night, she could not find sleep. Although she meant everything she had said, her father's talk had her wondering for the thousandth time what would become of her in the years to come. She lay in the dark and remembered the day she had discovered that she was a girl.

She had been startled to see Connor relieving himself while standing up, and when she looked closer, she knew immediately. Myra was astonished when Avalon told her more than asked whether she was a girl. Her sister, Zaria, wasn't being raised as a boy, but at seven years-old Avalon didn't know any other way, and her life had seemed normal to her. Still, it was confusing to Avalon to find out she was not a true prince, and although knowing didn't change her every day life, she began trying to hide in plain sight so that no one would guess that she was a girl. Myra noticed the change immediately when a typically outgoing Avalon became shy and withdrawn.

One afternoon, Myra sat Avalon down and asked, "Do you believe that your father loves you?"

"Yes." Avalon was sure of that.

"Then as long as you know that, you will understand the rest one day." It wasn't much of an explanation, but Myra had always said just what she wanted, so Avalon didn't question her.

"It isn't that," Avalon confided. Myra had misunderstood Avalon's certainty for confusion. "I just need to make sure no one ever finds out that I am not a boy. It's too important."

Myra couldn't hide her tears as they spilled over, and she was astounded at Avalon's insight and determination at just seven years old. For the first time Myra really believed that Avalon would be king. "You will make a wonderful king, Avalon."

"It is my decision now, not my father's," Avalon pronounced.

Myra had hugged Avalon then, squeezing her tighter than she could remember.

And now, finally of age and secure in her future as king, Avalon touched the jakkow's box, pulled her covers tight, and fell into a dreamless sleep.

Chapter 4
Playing with Fire

Spring was soon summer, and Avalon spent the days engrossed with her jakkow lizard. She was fascinated as it moved about the box, crawled onto her arms, and ran about the room until Avalon was able to chase it down and place it back in the carved, wooden box that was its home. She'd come to call it Jackie, and just as the Guide had predicted, in a week's time the jakkow had taken to Avalon and had started responding to her. Avalon now kept the tiny lizard in her inner breast pocket as she strolled about the castle. She'd almost lost it once when the lizard crawled out during council, and Avalon dared not to jump and grab at it. She couldn't afford to seem erratic under Counselor Glenn's constantly watchful eye, but Jackie was a one of a kind, and Avalon had only shown it to Zaria and Myra so far.

When Jackie encountered different objects, its red scales moved to and fro as though the lizard's skin had a life of its own. The Guide had instructed her to feed it leaves, but she found that the lizard especially liked nuts, and its midsection had grown considerably as Avalon appeased its appetite. While the lizard slept, Avalon studied the intricate carvings on the box that the Guides had given her. She studied her castle and moon on the box wondering who had carved the odd moon and other castle and what they could possibly mean.

Her little, red pet was a fun distraction, and it was the day before the Festival of Fontanasia when Avalon finally remembered the suit of armor that her Uncle Hawker had promised her. She had spent the past week using her new sword as she trained with Gamon, but the rest of the time she was holed up with the jakkow watching its every move. She had gone down for her first fitting the morning after her party, but was supposed to return to check the progress. Feeling guilty that she had forgotten Hawker's gift, she tucked Jackie into her pocket and went to the armory in the basement of the castle for her fitting.

"Jackie," Avalon complained as the lizard climbed out of her pocket and scrambled down her pants to the brick floor. Weaving through the large items stored in the basement hall, the lizard ran behind a bin full of scrap metal and out of Avalon's sight. Avalon hurried after, worried that the tiny lizard might find a mouse hole to get lost in. She crouched down to scoop the lizard up when she heard her uncle's voice behind her. She stood up in a rush to meet him and promptly hit the back of her head on a metal pole that protruded out of the scrap bin. She was about to let out a protest as she grabbed the back of her head, but she heard voices that startled her into silence. It was the low scowl of Counselor Glenn. Out of sight, Avalon froze in place.

"Don't walk away from me, Prince Hawker! You will back me on this. You have to get him to understand." Avalon forgot the splitting pain in her head. She was terrified that they would see her hiding as they passed, but Hawker must have stopped to address Glenn because their voices did not move any closer. She tried to hold her breath as she held her head with one hand and squeezed the jakkow in the other making sure he couldn't escape.

"Please, Hawker," Counselor Glenn asked more congenially this time. "You need to come speak to the council members. They need to hear from you. You need to tell them."

"I won't do it," Hawker answered jovially, and Avalon could almost hear his smile.

What could they be talking about, and here in the basement? Avalon wondered. Her Uncle Hawker spent time researching in the subterranean archives and was more knowledgeable about Fontanasia than any historian. But Avalon had never seen Counselor Glenn in this part of the castle.

"You must!" Counselor Glenn pressed. "You must come forward."

He was threatening Hawker now, and Avalon held her breath.

"I don't have to do anything," Hawker answered calmly. Avalon didn't know how her typically outspoken uncle could remain so reserved in the face of their rival. She would have demanded Counselor Glenn remember his place, if she were given the opportunity as an adult. Although, her father would never condone it of her.

"You seem to understand little of politics, Prince Hawker, so don't insult me. You can see what your brother can't. You must recognize that all of the council's planning for the people is ready for implementation." There was a pause, and then Avalon could hear the beat of a fist rhythmically mashing into a palm to prove a point. "The people deserve to be protected!"

Avalon's blood boiled and even in her crouched position her chest roiled outward. "Counselor Glenn," Hawker merely sighed, "I will not come forward. I might not understand politics the way you do, but I know that you don't have the full council behind you, and I have to consider my brother's position. He is family, you are not." Then Hawker continued, pushing his point home, "He is the king, you are not."

Avalon wanted to see if Hawker's barb stung Counselor Glenn, but she didn't dare move a muscle. As royalty, she should fear nothing, but Counselor Glenn scared her. The way Glenn held her stare when most looked away in deference, and the way he challenged the king when others who might conspire still bowed, it gave Avalon an unsettling feeling.

"The plans of the council include…" Glenn started, but Hawker cut him off.

"Life is good for the people, Counselor. They have the luxury of a blind eye. But you see, I don't have a blind eye." Hawker was lecturing now. "You are trying to upset a very fine balance, but you will never be the people's true leader."

"How dare you!" Counselor Glenn spat. Avalon dared to peek over the edge of the bin before ducking back down. She had seen the side of Counselor Glenn's face turning red around his crow's nose and his shoulders rising as he searched for something more to say to Hawker. His mouth opened and closed several times with no words coming out. He was flustered, and Avalon wished she knew what they were discussing.

"All right, I will talk to him," Hawker conceded calmly before letting out a laugh. "You shouldn't get so worked up, Glenn. Everything has its time." Avalon could still hear her uncle smiling, and she couldn't understand why he was taunting Counselor Glenn. But Hawker was a Prince of Fontanasia first and foremost, and he always showed self-pride in his family's crest and bowed to no one.

"Of course you will, you have no choice but to talk to him, or I will," Counselor Glenn said sourly. "You will be his great protector." Glenn's air of confidence brought no reply from Hawker.

Avalon again poked a sliver of her face around the metal bin and saw the tall lean figure of her uncle standing over the shorter heavy frame of Counselor Glenn. Hawker, eyebrows raised, was making an easy appraisal of Glenn. Avalon watched as her Uncle Hawker bent down and snatched up a wandering mouse by the tail, lifting it to Counselor Glenn's face. Hawker poked at the mouse a few times, and it wriggled and squeaked. He grabbed its body firmly with his free hand, and in her own hand, Avalon felt her jakkow's skin twitching with the mouse's discomfort. Then Hawker struck a match, and to Avalon's horror, her uncle lit the mouse's tail on fire before dropping it to the floor.

Hawker's nose twitched like a rabbit as he looked into the sickened eyes of Counselor Glenn. He leaned down into the older man's bunched up face. "But I will talk to him in my own due time because, as you know, haste makes waste."

The mouse, shrieking in terror as the flame worked its way up its tail toward the grey fur, darted past Avalon who had shrunk back into the wall. The jakkow continued to squirm at the sight of the flames, and Avalon squeezed the red lizard tighter. She could hear the mouse's screaming stop and hoped that it had found its way to the sewer water. She heard footsteps in retreat, and she let out her breath. Then she heard footsteps coming toward her, and Avalon pushed her back into the brick wall using the metal scrap bin for cover. Her Uncle Hawker swished past without seeing her, but Avalon didn't stand up right away. She sat in the shadows holding the bump on her head until she was sure that she was alone. Myra George had mentioned Hawker's love of fire before, but Avalon had never seen him do anything like that. She wondered how such an intelligent and loving person could treat any animal so horribly. She also wanted to know what it was that Counselor Glenn needed Hawker to make her father understand. It was difficult to concentrate with the jakkow's squirming, so Avalon stood and brushed herself off.

"It's all right, Jackie," she said to comfort the lizard, but she shuddered herself. It was nearly impossible to erase the image of the mouse on fire, but Avalon tried to shrug it off as she arrived for her armor fitting. Jackie was tucked into her waist pocket, and Avalon hoped the fitters wouldn't squish the lizard with their pushing and pulling.

The metal workers were muscled men who wore a constant coating of black grime from the fires on their skin and clothes. The lead ironman wiped his hands as clean as they would get when he saw the prince enter. Without a word, Avalon stepped onto the small metal platform that she had been fitted on before. The ironman bowed as he approached and Avalon felt a pang of fear as he began to fit her with the chest and arm plates. He was trying to treat her gently, and he only looked into her eyes when he thought he had pushed or pulled too roughly, but Avalon wasn't used to being touched. She recounted trying on dresses with Myra and Zaria, and she worried that the armor wouldn't fit her properly for very long if her body was going to make the changes that she couldn't stop from coming.

"How long with this armor fit me?" she asked aloud.

The ironman looked back into the red of the fire before answering. "We are making it large for you, Prince Avalon, so that you might grow into it. You will be able to wear it right away, but we will tailor it as you grow."

"Thank you," she replied, a half-smile on her face. They would never tailor it, she knew, because she was almost at an age when she could not afford to be approached so closely by anyone but her father, Zaria, and Myra George. "Please finish the armor assuming it will be complete this first time with no future tailoring required," she told the ironman.

"Yes, my Prince," the gritty man responded without looking up or stopping his work.

"Young Prince Avalon," she heard behind her. She couldn't turn around while in the clutches of the fitters, but she could not mistake the deeply confident voice of Walthan. "It is surely too late to be fitted for tomorrow's festivities." As part of the show, Walthan would without doubt be the only soldier dressed in full armor. It was out of date and too heavy for anyone else to even walk around in, much less wield a sword accurately. But Walthan's massive frame would easily hold the heavy armor.

Walthan stepped in front of Avalon as another metalworker fetched Walthan's equipment. A huge pile of armor and swords was wheeled into Avalon's view. "It is good that you have armor though, in the case we ever have to see battle." Walthan wore a jovial expression, but his size and the way his eyes appraised everything around him gave him an air of acute intensity.

Walthan continued to talk as the helpers assisted dressing him in his entire battle uniform. "Of course, no Fontanasian of our time has ever seen battle, but we must stay vigilant. Butchers drove our forefathers from their home, and although we are safe here, it is easy to forget the bad times in the good times. Of course many here don't understand the difference," he added.

"You see unrest then?" Avalon asked Walthan, still engrossed in what she had overheard Hawker say to Counselor Glenn. "Do you think that when life is good, people can't see how good it is?" She wanted to ask Walthan what he thought about Counselor Glenn and his growing agenda, but she didn't want the fitters to hear her questioning the throne's vulnerability.

"That is a lot to think about for a boy of your age, my Prince."

When she didn't reply, he could see that Avalon was serious.

"Prince Avalon, you are wise beyond your years, but your depth still surprises me." Walthan contemplated the question another moment before answering.

"I think that there can be unrest in peaceful times. When you have everything that you need, and no fear to contemplate, it is easy to find yourself wondering if there is something better. But I also think that no matter how much people allow their suspicions to rule their behavior, hope lies at the root of every soul. And hope is the root of all happiness."

Although she didn't fully understand it, Avalon thought this was the wisest answer she had ever heard. "Walthan, I'm not surprised at your depths."

Walthan belted another laugh that echoed in the brick chamber, but he settled himself quickly, concerned for his king's son. "Are you not happy?"

"I am happy, for myself, but I can't answer for the rest of Fontanasia."

Fully suited in polished armor, Walthan stepped forward and clapped his swelled hand on Avalon's shoulder. She almost crumpled to the ground, her shoulder stinging even under the protective armor. "We shall see tomorrow, then, out amongst the people at the festival. I am sure you will find smiles abound."

Avalon's fitting went well, but she would have to wait a few more weeks for her suit of armor to be finished. She walked to the southern fields where the Festival of Fontanasia would take place and watched the staff setting up the areas of play and booths for food. Before sunset, she worked some sword drills for her competition. Although her father did not approve of her competing, she was determined to prove herself. Her trainers had assured her that even if she was not as large as the other competitors, she would be quicker than any other in her age group, and that would give her an advantage.

At the start of her workout, it was difficult to concentrate with the continuous thought of her uncle burning the mouse repeating in her mind, but as her heartbeat increased, she let herself go and soon forgot all else. The exercise relieved her mind so much so, that when she took her place at the dinner table that evening and she saw her Uncle Hawker was joining them for dinner, Avalon felt at ease.

"I thought you would be with your sister this evening," King Birch announced as Avalon took her seat at the table opposite her Uncle Hawker. She couldn't stop herself from glancing, as she always did, to the bare end of the table where her mother should have sat. No one had taken that chair for fourteen years.

"Your sister is having a celebration for the festival. Your cousins will all be there."

Avalon had been at few of her sister's parties, but they were never very fun for Avalon. She had grown up keeping her distance from everyone who didn't know her secret, and that meant keeping cousins and almost everyone else in Fontanasia at arms length. "Zaria's gatherings can be entertaining to watch, but I need to rest for tomorrow."

King Birch made a sour face at Avalon but did not respond.

"You are competing then!" Hawker announced. "That is wonderful. The festival is a great proving ground."

"He has nothing to prove to anyone," King Birch disagreed.

"Of course not, no prince does," Hawker said with an air of supremacy. He had not competed a day in his life. His lanky frame did nothing for his balance, and as a prince he abhorred proving anything to anyone as he already considered himself elevated above everyone else. Hawker was jovial and loved to talk, but was often absent minded and gave the impression that he was never really listening as his mind kept leaping from topic to topic. He was a bookworm, a historian, and had spent years combing through the archives of the history of their people. Avalon had never seen her uncle raise a sword.

"Still, it is good that Avalon be out amongst the people whom he will one day inherit. Counselor Glenn will surely have a parade of his own, and it will be good for him to see a strong, young, Hall prince take the field."

Avalon's ears rose at the mention of Counselor Glenn, and she waited impatiently for her father to respond, but the king sat silent and rang the bell for the first course to be served.

"Brother," Hawker leaned sideways across the long table toward Birch, "you know that Counselor Glenn won't rest until he has made this a people's democracy."

"I already work for the people," Birch reminded his younger, half-brother.

"Well, that is a waste of time," Hawker added nonchalantly.

As Avalon listened to their opposite opinions on the matter, she watched the brothers' expressions. They could not look anymore unlike. They must have each taken after their respective mothers, because they differed in both sight and speech. Her father was burly, active, and confident, and an open book; Hawker was pale and lean, and although seemingly outgoing, he was very private. Avalon marveled that the two were related at all.

"The power with the people is an ignorant notion. Kings are meant to rule outright. You should hear me out, brother. Disband the council and take back full control of your kingdom."

Her father's face reddened, and Avalon stopped pretending to eat her dinner and watched open mouthed. This could not have been the message that Counselor Glenn was bidding Hawker to convey to the king. Avalon was proud of her uncle for not buckling to Counselor Glenn's pressure, and Hawker was doing his duty to his brother by warning him. It was all Avalon could do to keep silent. She wanted to tell her father that Counselor Glenn had cornered Hawker, and that Hawker was wise in worrying about the council's intentions.

"Perhaps that didn't come out right," Hawker conceded as he watched his brother puff up on the verge of explosion. "I'm not very tactful, brother, you know that." King Birch let his breath out and Hawker waited a moment before continuing. "Of course, you are king and in turn have full power, but are you willing to chance Counselor Glenn's intentions? You used to be friends, brother, but you don't know him anymore."

King Birch took another deep breath and let the blood run back out of his face. "We were the best of friends. Glenn and I grew up together, and we were friends until he got these silly notions in his head. He changed." Birch looked remorseful. "But all he really wants is the best life for the people of Fontanasia, which is a goal that we both still have in common."

"Birch, he is pushing for your demise. I am advising you to open your eyes."

"Nothing has come of his wishes, Hawker, and nothing ever will." Now back in control of his senses, her father calmly returned to his meal as though he had been talking about a selection of flowers.

Avalon sat back in her chair feeling Hawker's defeat, and she wondered if she should have a talk with her father privately so that he would be adequately warned in heeding Hawker's advice.

"All right, I'll let it go." Hawker's nose twitched as his hand flourished his knife in the air to further his point. "But he's had these ridiculous notions for almost twenty years, and although you don't want to face it, he has become a threat."

King Birch grunted but didn't answer Hawker. Hawker looked at Avalon and raised his eyebrows, chuckling as though he was trying to lighten the atmosphere, but he was unsuccessful.

Chapter 5
A Warrior's Fortune

Avalon was surprised to find herself in a forest in the dark of night, but she wasn't scared. There was a light blue glow about the woods that filtered through the trees, but it didn't come from the moon above. She walked on between the massive tree trunks, and when she came to a clearing, she was astonished to see a bright, blue sea. It wasn't the Helon Sea that bordered Fontanasia, but some unknown body of water that rolled in front of her eyes almost blinding her.

Avalon squinted as she put her hands up in front of her face to block the light, but she couldn't see past the blinding, blue reflection of the water. Then Walthan stepped in front of her and waved her into the blue glow, and although confused, she was not scared. She followed him into the writhing liquid and felt a strange sensation as tiny fish tickled her legs. The rush of adrenaline was fantastic and made everything seem so real to her that when she awoke from the dream, she was reaching down to her legs to touch the water below.

Myra greeted Avalon that morning with a "pish posh" as she pulled open the blinds. Avalon rarely slept in and was usually gone to training by sunrise, but when she entered to a dark room, Myra assumed the prince was still sleeping. When light filled the room, Myra turned to the bed and sucked in her breath. Avalon was sitting in the dark, fully dressed for competition. She wore long, white shirtsleeves with a dark gray chainmail vest embroidered with the Hall family crest. Her boots were pulled high over pant legs and a leather skirt protected her thighs. "King Birch won't allow it," Myra said sternly.

"He won't stop me," Avalon declared as she stood and swiftly buckled her sword to her hip.

"He shouldn't have to," Myra scolded. "You should do as you are told."

Avalon could tell by Myra's sing-songy tone that this chiding was rudimentary to their relationship, and that no matter what she said, Myra expected nothing less from Avalon than to compete in the games this day.

"I am of age this year, and I do not wish to sit out and watch the games."

"The fact that you would deny your father's wishes so soon after your birthday is not a great example to be setting," Myra rang out as she picked up around the room.

"Well, then, as I am the youngest in the family, I hardly have anyone to set an example for."

Avalon bolted for the door, and by some miracle Myra's large yet swift and graceful frame beat the young girl to it. Before Avalon could protest, Myra simply put her hands on Avalon's shoulders and pecked a kiss on her forehead.

"Be careful, child. And good luck!" she yelled as Avalon ducked out of the suite.

The arena for the Festival of Fontanasia had been constructed on the south hills with a magnificent view of the mountains to the west. Avalon watched the small waves roll on the Helon Sea and tried to picture them in a bright, blue, blinding light, but they did not roll the same as the waves in her dreams. This puzzled her since her dreams always came true, and she wondered what other body of water she could possibly be standing in front of in the next week. She smiled in wonder that the dream hadn't frightened her before the day's competition enveloped her mind.

It was already hot this early in the day, and it would be scorching by the time the sun hung well over the grounds. Avalon hated the summer, which was to say that she loved the sun, the breeze on her face, and the bright green in all of the nature around her, but she hated sweating in her long sleeves. When she realized that she was a girl, she had started wearing long sleeves exclusively in an attempt to hide her skinny arms. Suffering the heat was a small price to pay if it meant keeping her secret, but she didn't have to like it.

The smell of meat filled the air as the food stations prepared a huge feast. Fortunetellers set up small tents, and musicians and carnival gamekeepers arrived to fill in the entertainment. It was soon afternoon with the sun high in the sky before the teens completed their games, making way for the grown men who would be the day's true entertainment. King Birch had watched eagerly as Avalon worked her way through round after round and won the close combat sword fighting title. She'd had butterflies in her stomach before the first match, but her confidence rallied. As her trainers had assured her, Avalon was smaller than most, but was swift and sure in her movements and easily took most of the points. Myra's nephew Connor, who was a head taller than any other boy their age, won the hand-to-hand combat, and another whom Avalon did not know took champion of targeting with arrows and knives.

They were supposed to gather as three on a center platform, but Connor would not step up behind Avalon out of respect for her rank as prince, nor would he let the targeter step up. So the awards were handed out, Avalon on the platform and Connor and the other boy on the ground. The gesture confirmed Avalon's suspicions that Connor didn't compete with the sword that day because he would not fight the young prince. She wondered if his Aunt Myra George might have had some say in that, but Avalon could see at the award ceremony that Connor's deference spoke for his own intentions. When it was over, they all shook hands, and Connor patted Avalon so hard on the back that she had to let out a cough to catch her breath.

Avalon brought her award to the king's podium and, although her father preferred she didn't compete, he was proud of Avalon and happy to show off the award to all of his party.

"Nicely done," Princess Zaria called as she moved to Avalon's side.

"Don't tease, Zaria. I know you don't care about the games."

Zaria tousled her little sister's sweat soaked hair.

"On the contrary," Zaria said, adding with a whisper, "I take greater pleasure than anyone here knowing that you are a girl and yet you were able to win."

Avalon shushed her sister immediately and looked around to make sure no one had overheard her. In an effort to ignore Zaria, she stepped forward in the king's box to watch the tournament, which had resumed play. There were ten pairs of young men competing with swords and the round was quickly finished, the winners of each competition to move on and the losers to be eliminated. Her eye fell on one of the young men who had advanced, and she found herself unable to look away. Of all of the people competing, he was the only other person aside from herself on this grueling, sunny day, who was wearing long sleeves. She noticed the long, white cotton shirt sticking to his body from the sweat on his neck down to the armor ringlets protecting his wrists. The air was full of humidity and the sun baked everything it touched, and Avalon was stunned that someone aside from herself would purposefully wear long sleeves in the sweltering heat.

"Look at his curly black hair," Zaria remarked as she followed Avalon's stare. "He's handsome."

"He's out of his mind to be wearing long sleeves in this heat," Avalon barked.

"You're wearing long sleeves," Zaria whispered slyly. Thankfully, her sister moved on after only one remark, and Avalon was left alone to watch.

She watched him lunge, twirl, defend, and strike, a lean and graceful competitor. He won his division's title for close combat sword fighting, a feat which peaked Avalon's attention since she had just won the same category for her age group. When the hand-to-hand and targeting competitions came to a close, the curly haired man took the platform and was invited to approach by the king. The three category winners walked purposefully forward, and when they reached the king's platform, they bowed.

Avalon noticed that the swordsman's face looked much younger than she had expected. She thought that the winner would have to be older to be such a practiced swordsman, but he was obviously the youngest. Avalon was preparing herself to meet him as the king commented that his own son had just won in the same category. Avalon smiled and contained her nervousness when he approached, but the swordsman only made a short bow to Avalon, his attention already aimed at Princess Zaria. When he was introduced to her, the young man smiled like the sun for a brief moment upon seeing Zaria's face and then bowed again gracefully.

"Who is this fine swordsman?" Zaria actually managed to blush on cue.

"This is Taggerty," the master of ceremonies answered.

The swordsman made an embellished bow this time, and while Avalon respected the ability he had shown in competition, she felt a rising hate in her gut, and her instinct begged her to punch him in the face. She actually curled her hand into a fist before exhaling some of the fury out through her nostrils.

Although this Taggerty looked to be a couple of years younger than Zaria's usual suitors, the princess gave him her full attention. Zaria could never leave the moment to Avalon, and the princess gushed a river of complements over the champion. It was all Avalon could do to stand still.

Avalon was the prince and heir to the throne, yet this commoner found it easy to ignore her. Avalon never liked people staring at her, but now she couldn't help but feel in competition with her older sister. It wasn't the lack of interest that bothered Avalon, that couldn't be it. But the fact that she received somewhat curt and meticulous treatment from people because she was to be the next king, whereas Zaria received more gracious smiles and cordiality, did bother her.

She hated feeling envious of her sister. They had been the closest of friends, but the years between them caused a rift as Zaria's changing interests altered their relationship. These days

Zaria cared more about her attire and her hair than her studies or playing games, and Avalon sometimes felt left behind, a reaction that both confused and angered her. What was there to be jealous of? Zaria would not become ruler one day. She would never be King Hall of Fontanasia. She would find a suitor and have a family, and that would be her position in life with no opportunity to rise.

Avalon took a deep breath and found a proud smile for the black haired boy still talking to Zaria. Zaria could have all the parties and friends at court that she wanted, but Avalon meant the attention of the day's competition to be her own. Any feeling of earlier triumph had already run out of her. Her stomach swirled and, for the first time in her life, she wondered where she would fit into the world socially. Because she was a boy, but she was a girl.

"And my brother, Prince Avalon, won in his division too," Avalon heard Zaria saying to the curly haired young man. Avalon straightened up and felt flustered. He looked straight into Avalon's eyes for a moment, and her face flushed pink.

"Ah, yes, Prince Avalon," Taggerty bowed, this time a little lower than the first. "I saw you draw your sword, and when I managed to look back, you had already won. But I am sure it was a thrilling battle for you." Taggerty smiled as Avalon tried not to grimace.

She let it sink in. *He hadn't watched her fight.* He couldn't find the time to watch the prince fight, and didn't even care enough to lie and say that he had been impressed. Avalon was not used to bold honesty, and she was appalled.

When King Birch gave leave to the winners, Avalon gladly parted Zaria's company and lost herself in the crowd, trying to put as much space between her and the formalities as was possible. Zaria could linger with the pompous, black haired boy if she wished; it was her time to waste.

An hour passed as Avalon stood with the crowd and watched the real warriors compete. Walthan won two of the three competitions losing out to his friend and equal, a veteran soldier nicknamed Brick, in the targeting category. The whole crowd now watched intently as Walthan and Brick teamed up with each other to battle hand to hand against a mob of soldiers. Loud cheers mirrored Avalon's emotions as she tried to keep the composure of royalty while watching the two work as one in the mock battle. It was amazing to watch Walthan move so quickly while still wearing most of his suite of armor. They slashed, punched, parried, and in the end were the last standing.

The crowd roared with pleasure, and King Birch awarded both Walthan and Brick with life sized gold swords. Up on the platform, they held the swords up in victory and received deafening cheers. When the crowd had finally had enough, they embraced in a manly half-hug before going their separate ways. Brick retired to clean up, but Walthan, sweaty and proud, made his way among the people and accepted their congratulations. He towered over everyone and easily spotted Avalon as he slapped hands with those brave enough to offer theirs up to him.

"Prince Avalon!" Walthan exclaimed. Many people in the area who hadn't noticed Avalon were surprised and immediately craned their necks to see. "What are you doing on this side of the field?" Walthan asked, glancing back across the field to the king's platform.

"Just getting some air," she told him as he stopped in front of her. They were both dirty with the job of the day still on their clothes. Walthan gave Avalon a pull and she easily hopped over the small makeshift fence that signaled the arena for the day's festival.

"You were fantastic!"

Walthan beamed at the compliment. "There is no one else I would rather have at my back than Brick. He is an excellent warrior and friend to boot." Walthan moved ahead and turned back to wave his young companion forward, and at that moment she remembered her dream.

"Walthan, can I ask you something?"

"Anything, my young charge."

"Have you ever seen a bright, blue sea that glowed in the black of night?"

Walthan looked back at her and then faced the crowd again, shaking his head. He didn't answer at first, still offering the wanting crowd his hand. He then looked back at Avalon, smiling and deliberating.

"Prince Avalon, you never cease to amaze me." He nodded his head to the young prince motioning for her to walk with him. Avalon barely kept pace as they continued around the arena accepting the crowd's adulation.

"You have then," she proclaimed when he didn't immediately answer her question directly.

"I have seen the blue glow that you speak of on the journey to Cormicks," he answered softly for her ears only.

"Oh," she said aloud as though that explained everything, even though Avalon had no idea what or where Cormicks was. But she didn't get the chance to ask. Hawker spotted them making their way around the arena and he approached from the king's platform, placing his hands on her shoulders.

"Would you like to become a warrior like Walthan?" he asked.

"No." Avalon had to turn her neck up to meet her uncle's face, and for the first time she realized that Hawker stood almost as tall as Walthan.

"Smart boy. Being king allows you to have warriors of your own so you don't have to become one."

"Thank you again for the sword, Uncle Hawker. Were you watching?"

"Of course, Avalon! I wouldn't have missed it for the world. And you, Walthan! Powerful as always!"

Walthan nodded a slight bow. "Prince Hawker, you are missing out."

"Me?" Hawker laughed. "Me fighting with a sword? Don't be foolish."

Walthan moved on to greet his admirers, and Hawker retired, leaving Avalon to move on alone. She was tempted to see a fortuneteller, but staying away from them was one wish of her father's she would obey. She found herself strolling up toward the castle, but instead of retiring, she moved through the fingers and enjoyed the solitude among the crowds of strangers. Still wearing soiled clothes, she wasn't dressed in her royal attire, and few people noticed that a prince walked amongst them. The feeling was strangely freeing as everyone around her simply moved about their lives.

She breathed deeply, the thick air a striking mix of roses and evergreen. Children were pretend sword fighting in the streets, and the adults were smiling and laughing in the wake of the festival. She stepped into a flower shop and a then moved along to a garment shop where the owners, instantly recognizing her, bowed. The woman dismissed herself to fetch a tissue package, handing it to the shopkeeper on her return. He presented Avalon with a magnificent blueberry-purple hooded cape. Avalon regarded the beautiful, yellow stitching and soft exterior before trying it on. She was surprised by the weight of its thin material and was not uncomfortable wearing the garment in the evening heat.

"I can't pay for this," Avalon explained. She wasn't carrying money while competing and hadn't changed yet.

"You cannot pay for that, Prince Avalon," the star struck shopkeeper told her. "Please, accept our gift."

"Thank you," she replied sincerely. She pulled the neck clasp closed and left the shop. She strolled up and down the residences until darkness began to settle, lost in her thoughts of a bright blue ocean, before she sensed anything was wrong.

"But who is this?" a rowdy voice called behind Avalon when she found herself alone on a quiet street.

She had been envisioning her dream and not paying attention to where she was going. She now looked up and down the avenue to see that the street behind her had no outlet. She looked for the brown brick wall of one of the fingers, but shops and houses she had never seen before surrounded her. Avalon swung around, squaring up to see three young men blocking her exit. She could feel her heart rate increase as she set her jaw. Now that they were face to face, she expected them to recognize her and bow, making way for her exit. One of the boys did bow, but he quickly stood erect again when he saw that the largest boy was not going to show the prince his due.

"Aah, it is the champion of the day," the huge, disheveled boy answered his friend. Avalon remembered the boy's face from earlier that day when she had disqualified him in the first round of play. She was relieved to find that at least one of the boys was her age, but the other two looked a few years older.

The three looked her up and down, and one staggered as if he was drunk. Surely, if there was going to be real trouble, she could take the scruffy boy and the drunken one, but their leader might be a different story. His face was young but his frame massive for his age, and Avalon decided to remain far enough away to stay out of his grip. She couldn't remember Connor fighting this boy in the tournament this morning and wasn't sure if he had skills.

Avalon tried to keep a cool appearance, but she could feel her legs weakening under her. She had trained since she could remember, but that was all it had been. Even the tournament had been by touch only and not full out combat. This was the first time she would ever face a true attacker if it came to that. It was chilling yet exhilarating, and as unsure as she was about the boys who slowly approached, she was sure of her ability to defend herself. But deep down she didn't believe that anyone would truly wish to harm her in a kingdom meant for freedom and peace.

"Why, it's Prince Avalon," the hefty young man called. "Care for a rematch?"

"Do you dare mock a Prince?" Avalon said in the sternest voice she could muster.

"I do whatever I please," the largest boy rebuked. At that moment the scruffy blond boy she had competed against lunged for her, and she had but a second to side step his advance as she drew her sword. She was relieved to find full control of her legs. Although sore from the day's events, Avalon found that her attacker was still no match for her. In the tournament, they were tagging with the swords to win a series of points. Avalon let her instincts take over and as he lunged, she sidestepped, the cape furling out behind her as she twisted her body. She again let the iron slap at her target instead of cutting him with the blade. She wasn't sure how long she could keep this up without hurting him, but he managed to stumble forward and ram his head into a stone awning pillar, instantly knocking him cold. What was left of Avalon's fear dissipated, and the young men looked to her like mere boys once more.

It was another boy's turn as he took up his friend's sword. Avalon's heart was racing from the adrenaline, but the workout was less grueling than her regular training regimen. The boy was older and taller, but he was drunk and staggering so much that he was hardly a match for Avalon who moved so quickly that she was never forced to fully defend against his lunges. After a full minute of watching, the largest boy ripped the sword from his friend's hand and threw the staggering boy out of the way. Avalon knew deep down that she could take him, but his size and the scowl on his face shook her confidence. She unclasped the cape and tossed it to the dust of the street.

"Now that you are warmed up…" he said to Avalon as they circled each other. She thought of running away when the open street was at her back, but wasn't seriously considering it. It was the smart play, to get back to the castle, but it would do no good for her ego or for the name Hall if she did. Her resolve set in as she looked up into his massive face.

He came at her several times, and Avalon was able to throw off his blows with her sword. She could feel his superior strength and began to question her own talent. This would be the true test of her abilities.

"I wonder what the king would pay for the safe return of his precious son," scoffed the young man.

Avalon gulped hard.

"Not so much as you will pay if you threaten Prince Avalon again." Both Avalon and her enemy were surprised at the sure voice that had interjected as the tip of a sword crossed over her shoulder and touched her attacker's throat. Avalon hadn't even heard her rescuer's approach, but she was relieved to find someone had finally come upon them.

She backed away a few steps in the confusion but held her sword at the ready.

"Taggerty," Avalon's attacker announced coolly without turning his head. "This doesn't concern you."

Her relief turned to frustration as Avalon recognized the name. She now took a moment to look from the corner of her eye and noticed the long sleeves with metal wrist guards. He was close enough for Avalon to see that the crest on the sword matched the ones on his wrist plates. Taggerty glanced at Avalon and then turned his glance to the two buffoons who still lay sprawled on the ground. They each stood up quickly and retreated down the street.

"It seems your friends are still smarter than you," Taggerty said congenially.

"I said this doesn't concern you."

Taggerty's sword pressed harder still against the chubby skin on the boy's neck. "You know it does concern me."

"I see your new lodgings are suiting you." The young man was stalling, and Avalon could read panic in his eyes although he tried to cover it with a smirk. But when Taggerty's sword angled up and pinched the skin on the young man's throat, he immediately dropped the sword that was still raised in Avalon's direction.

"You are learning fast, but not fast enough."

Avalon could see Taggerty's cunning smile as he swung his body in between the two. Avalon moved her sword to the side, but kept on guard. It was ridiculous that even with her heart pounding, and confronted with the worst danger she'd ever been in, she could only wonder why he would still be wearing long sleeves. She would never wear long sleeves again if she could help it, but the blouse covered her slender wrists and the vest contained any curve of her body. Avalon would wear long sleeves for the rest of her life if that would help her keep her secret.

"Are we finished here?" The huge frame was backing away slowly.

"Hear this, and let your thug friends know: if you ever threaten so much as a hair on Prince Avalon again, I will kill you."

Avalon's chest filled with anxiety as she had never heard a direct threat like this in her life. She was used to the subterfuge of politics, but politics would have no part on this rocky street.

The adrenaline continued through her blood as she found Taggerty's words ominous but also thrilling.

Taggerty lowered his sword and nodded his head, and just like that, the young pack leader backed up a few steps and then turned and ran away. Avalon took a deep breath but was forced to hold it in as Taggerty turned to face her because she didn't want him to see her relief.

"You are safe now, Prince Avalon," Taggerty said formally with a bow.

"Thank you," Avalon managed, "but I didn't need your help." She was short with him and couldn't help herself. "Taggerty, is it?"

Upon hearing his name, he bowed again to her the same way he had done to Zaria.

Well, Avalon thought, *not the exact same way*.

Although he remained courteous, she could see a slight sideways smile on his face, and this took her already boiling blood to its limits.

"I am surprised you found us," she said indignantly. "It is amazing that you were able to pull yourself away from Princess Zaria." Even though hours had passed since the festival, Avalon knew her sister liked to take compliments for as long as they would be bestowed upon her.

"Even a prince should not take on so many at one time."

"I can take care of myself," she replied resentfully.

"Your lip is bleeding," he told her evenly, and his salty green eyes became serious for a moment.

She couldn't remember having been cut, but Avalon pulled the back of her sleeve to her mouth and saw the red stain. She scowled, and he stepped out of her way bowing his head and holding his hand out toward the street's exit. Avalon made her way to the end of the cross street but then realized that tangled this deep in the city, she didn't know which of the fingers she was in, and didn't know her way directly back to the castle. The mountain sprawled in front of her, and she could only guess which way was home. Taggerty stopped just behind her and waited, and Avalon's ears burned.

"To the castle," she ordered him.

Taggerty smiled wryly and stepped directly in front of her taking his time to look up and down the cross street. He was toying with her, and she knew it. Avalon considered punching him in the face, but decided that could wait until she was safely back home. He held his arm out to the left with a slight bow again, and Avalon stormed past him. She could hear his footsteps behind her keeping time with hers as they weaved downhill through the streets.

He had saved her tonight, she was pretty sure of that, and he was ensuring her safety by following her back to the castle. Why was it that Avalon still felt as though he hadn't noticed her at all, and that he was doing this duty as a citizen and not for her alone? She didn't know if she was angrier that he was here with her, or that she felt safe now because he was. Three more times she came to a turn where she did not know the right way, and three times he stopped behind her and waited for her to ask the proper direction. He deferred to her when it was convenient, but his pretension made her anxious. Avalon was educated, she was able, and she was a prince, but there was an air about Taggerty, something within him that made Avalon feel that Taggerty thought he was her equal in some way, and she was not used to that.

Avalon found the first cross gate closed, but when they crossed under the arch of the wall further down, she turned the last corner and saw the familiar shops that she passed in the mornings. To her left was the sprawling stone castle, reassuring her in the looming darkness. Confident of her direction, she turned back uphill and picked up her pace. She could hear Taggerty keeping step with her, but she refused to turn around or to slow her pace so that they could walk together.

Dusk had become dark when she entered the castle, the young man still on her heels. She wished that the soldiers at the gate would have questioned the intruder or stopped him from entering, but realized too late that they must have assumed the young man was entering with the prince.

Assuming that the grandeur of the king's domicile would be intimidating, she waited for his footfalls to slow when she turned the corner to the royal suite, but he continued on behind her.

Avalon had stewed long enough, and she swung around to face him.

"Taggerty?" She knew his name very well but asked again as a jab.

"Yes, Prince Avalon." His sincere answer made her jaw clench harder, and even more so when he held out the blue-purple cape that she had forgotten in the street. She ripped it from his hands.

"You may go now. If you are looking for my sister, Princess Zaria, you won't find her here." Her voice was louder than she had intended, and she checked herself.

He remained where he stood with his brow curled up and subdued a smile. She hated that he smiled in moments of discomfort. She tried to stare him down, but still he didn't move. Avalon refused to be treated like a child.

"You can see I am no longer in danger. Now go!"

"Danger?" Avalon heard her father's voice boom from inside the suite. She closed her eyes slowly and pursed her lips before King Birch stomped into the hall.

"Why should you be in danger?" The king started when he saw her bloody lip. "You're bleeding, Avalon!"

"It's nothing, father." Without addressing Taggerty, Avalon pushed past the king but stopped inside the door when she heard the men continuing the conversation.

"What is the meaning of this?" her father bellowed. The king's ferocity would frighten even the heartiest of men, but Taggerty didn't budge.

"Sir, you might remember me from the competition this afternoon."

"I do not!" King Birch bellowed immediately without giving Taggerty even a small once-over.

"What is happening?" Zaria whispered, startling Avalon.

"Your boyfriend is back," Avalon mocked, holding Zaria behind her and listening to the conversation in the hall.

"I don't know what you mean?" Zaria feigned.

"You don't know *who* I mean," Avalon retorted and looked at her sister's disapproving face.

"It is the boy from today, at the competition."

Zaria shrugged.

"Yeah, well, there is something really wrong with him, so it is probably best that you don't remember." Avalon turned her back on her older sister to concentrate on her father.

"It's Taggerty, sir. I had the fortune of being introduced to you as one of the tournament winners this afternoon. I am one of the king's guard, sir."

Avalon flinched. He was in the guard, which seemed impossible to her. And he had not come to her aid today out of interest, he had protected her because it was his job.

"You are too young to be in the guard."

"I have always looked young for my age, but I was just eighteen last week. I was trained by Brick, himself, and he recommended me for the position."

Zaria pulled on Avalon's ruffled shirt. "Oh, yes, Taggerty," she said slowly. "I think I do remember."

Avalon's heart stopped as King Birch roared, "What happened to my son?"

"He was cornered in town by three young men."

"Cornered? And you came to his aid?"

Avalon almost burst out of the room before suffering Taggerty's answer, but she held herself still when he didn't give her away.

"He was holding his own, sir. But my presence seemed to tip the odds until the boys ran away."

King Birch was stunned by this news. He couldn't believe Avalon was attacked; it was unfathomable in a city such as this. "We have no crime in Fontanasia," he said unconvincingly to himself, and Avalon could hear the uncertainty in her father's voice.

"No, sir," Taggerty readily agreed. "I am sure that the boys were drunk and must have been playing with your son in a more forceful manner than they would have intended if sober. Out on the street alone, they undoubtedly didn't recognize the prince at all, and must have thought they were playing games with a commoner."

Avalon's stomach turned. She hated that Taggerty was covering for her more than she hated the lie itself, because ever since Counselor Glenn had tripped her down the stairs when she was seven years old, Avalon understood that there really was a small measure of danger in Fontanasia. Her father had never accepted that fact.

King Birch looked at the floor, all of his years of certitude being questioned at this moment. Perhaps his position as king was not as secure as he had assumed. Still, he could not believe that this would have been a coordinated attack. It was most likely just as the guard recommended.

"Thank you, son," King Birch told Taggerty. "In the guard for only a week and already you have performed a greater duty than any other."

"It was my honor, sir." Taggerty bowed and left the king in the hall.

Zaria and Avalon scrambled away from the door and deeper into the suite, but Avalon knew that she would not avoid being questioned.

"Avalon," her father heaved just inside the sitting room.

She knew that her father would get angrier at each passing minute, so she didn't make him wait. Zaria grinned at her little sister and made her way to her own room.

"Yes?" Avalon asked her father from her door. She had tried to clean the blood from her lip and took her blood stained vest off.

"What were you doing alone in the town today?"

"Nothing. Just walking."

"Just walking?" he mock reiterated her words as only a parent could.

"Yes, I was just walking around and enjoying the evening."

"And who were those men who attacked you?"

"They were boys, father, barely older than me. I don't know who they were. And I'm fine," she protested.

King Birch crossed the room and was having a look at Avalon uneasily. "How could it come that you could be in any danger?" he said more to himself. Avalon could see sadness in his eyes, and his unapproachable hulk of a frame slumped low into a chair.

"I'm all right, father. I won't go off alone again." It was painful to see her father show any weakness. She had been seeing his tender side too much in the past month since her fourteenth birthday. She tried to change the subject. "I just needed time to think something through, and now I need to ask you a question."

King Birch looked up.

"Where is Cormicks?" Avalon wasn't sure what his reaction would be, but she was glad that she had asked the question because the distraction immediately returned her father to life.

"Why do you ask?" he growled.

Avalon tried not to smile. "Because I saw it in my dream last night."

King Birch's face turned bright red.

Chapter 6
Blue Heaven

King Birch's face stayed bright red for several minutes before he decided how to reply to Avalon's question. "What makes you think you saw a place called Cormicks in your dream?"

"Well, it wasn't Cormicks I saw, but that was where I was headed. I was with Walthan, and we were walking into a bright blue sea together." Glad that she had distracted him from her bloodied lip, Avalon spoke quickly as she didn't want to lose momentum. She didn't mention that Walthan had told her the name of the city Cormicks.

King Birch was now pulled forward, his bulk perched on the edge of his seat. He waited, deliberating in his mind how much to tell Avalon. He wasn't planning to have this conversation for a while, although he was younger than Avalon when he'd first heard the stories, but his daughter was of age now and would become king one day. He couldn't put it off any longer.

"Shall we play Verticks?" he asked Avalon, in an effort to stall the conversation. It was a child's game, but King Birch to this day never let too much time pass between games. He felt that it kept him young.

"Dad," Avalon moaned, "I'm not a child."

"Perhaps I am." Her father smiled while Avalon squirmed impatiently.

Although he knew she would play the game, King Birch gave her a stern look, and Avalon pulled a box from the end table. They each took a stack of the jagged sticks and played, Avalon losing once because her jakkow had scrambled from her room to greet her, rustling up her arm as she tried to stack the small branch.

"Jackie," Avalon moaned as she scooped the lizard up and placed it in her pocket, separating out the wood pieces for the second game. Avalon lost this game to her impatience.

"No concessions here, son," King Birch said in his gravelly voice. "You must learn as a prince that you cannot trust those who would let you win. They are playing a different game altogether."

Her father had said this a lot over the years, and Avalon wasn't sure yet what he meant by it, but she nodded in agreement as she always had in order to move the conversation along to the topic of Cormicks. After they each played a few pieces, Avalon purposefully knocked a lower piece out and collapsed the small tower. She was through with this game, and her father did not chide her for her edginess.

"Father," Avalon tried to keep her voice level, "I don't want to play games."

"Avalon, my child, you are to know of Cormicks, but it is too early for you to see it."

Here Avalon took the upper hand in the conversation as she had been rehearsing his denial in her head. "Father, I had a dream of it."

King Birch was silent.

"You know that I go, because my dreams always come true."

King Birch was well aware of Avalon's ability to see the future in her dreams, and he didn't need reminding. He was proud of what a proper young man Avalon had learned to become, but time was passing too quickly, and he wanted her to stay innocent of the truths of the world for as long as possible.

"When you were born, you were a tiny speck of a baby."

Avalon's irritation was becoming more apparent, but she knew that she should not rush her father when he became reflective about the past because it would only make him linger in his own thoughts for a longer period. Her foot had been bouncing her left leg, and she quickly held herself still and set in for the coming conversation.

"Everyone tells me I was a plump and massive baby without a wrinkle anywhere on my body." Avalon was well aware that Myra's nephew, Connor, had sat in for her on that first showing. Their difference in size remained to this day.

"No, you were so very little, but alert and aware." Her father's eyes twinkled but were sad at the same time. "Only myself, your mother, and Zaria saw you for the first month. And Myra of course..."

With the shrinking and defeated look on her father's face, Avalon couldn't help but feel at this moment that she had murdered her mother with her own two hands. Her mother's death was the one thing that had been out of her control, but the one thing she truly blamed herself for. Her father must have sensed her reaction, because he forced a smile and continued his explanation in a pleasing light.

"You were a miracle to your mother, and hope for this family. Your birth alone quieted any of the council who were feeling discontented and restored the natural order of things."

Avalon couldn't conceive that her birth had anything to do with the nature of the people nor the will of the council, and she hated the fact that it was mentioned. Her innocence in her mother's death was a lie her father must have told himself, a just clarification for the loss of his queen.

"You are the promise of Fontanasia, the promise of the people. They trusted in you before you could even speak."

Avalon's leg twitched again and she looked away. She hated what he was saying, that there could have been an order in anything, that events were preplanned, and that she should be some knight in shining armor in a land where no one wanted for anything; a savior in a land that did not need saving.

There was silence for a few long minutes until Avalon could no longer hold still. "You should approve of the journey, father, or I will have to make it on my own. It is already a fact, that I will see the bright, blue water and wade out into it. Where is Cormicks?" she pressed.

King Birch knew the power of the Hall family's dreams, and he couldn't deny Avalon's request. It was an argument he could not win. Walthan had not been to Cormicks in over a decade, and King Birch knew that if Walthan was with Avalon in her dream, it was because the king himself had ordered his most trusted guard to look after the prince on the journey. Still, he played with his daughter for a second.

"Maybe you are starting to dream years into the future."

"Please," Avalon told her father, pushing her point now while her ears burned.

"I will give my permission," her father smiled reluctantly. "I won't have you running off on your own like you did today."

"Will you tell me where Cormicks is then?"

"You already know of the city."

"I do?" Avalon asked. She had been rolling the name around in her head since Walthan had spoken it, but nothing named Cormicks came to mind.

King Birch stood and prompted Avalon to follow him down the hall and into his private study. When they entered, he closed the door and locked it. Avalon watched intently as her father removed a picture of a small pool surrounded by tall grass that was mounted in a gold frame. She knew the picture well; it had hung in that spot her entire life. Her mouth opened involuntarily when she noticed her father removing a brick behind the picture and pulling a long parchment from the small hole. The king unrolled it on his worktable and held the corners down with polished stones. It was unlike any parchment Avalon had ever seen. It was a thick, weighted cloth with heavy gold braids around the edges that helped the document from unraveling over time as it was undone and rolled back up. The king pointed at a city on the map named "Hawkerness".

"That is Cormicks," he told Avalon, whose mouth was still open.

She collected herself and took her father's side at the table but did not speak as she took in the map. She knew Hawkerness from old tales her father had told her when she was a child, and because it was the place that her uncle had been named after. The city had lost its meaning over the generations. Old stories changed as they were told to new children and the true history was slowly erased. It was the city that her people had fled from as a warring people decimated it. She was surprised to find that the city still existed.

"Hawkerness is now called Cormicks?"

Avalon collected herself and studied the map while her father stood soundless next to her. She recognized the part of the map that was Fontanasia as she had seen maps of the country before, but never with any other countries named on it. Hawkerness, or Cormicks as it was now known, looked very close, and Avalon could not believe that in two hundred years, they had not received any visitors nor repelled any enemies. Her father read her face.

"Yes, Avalon, it is that close. A mere journey of five days would put you at their gates."

"It isn't possible," she told her father.

King Birch had felt the same way when he had first learned of the city's proximity to Fontanasia, and he was patient with his daughter.

"When our people lived in Hawkerness, it was a peaceful place, and much like life in Fontanasia. We lived there for hundreds of years and even made an agreement with the Runners whom are settled here." King Birch pointed to another small and archaically drawn village that was over a mountain range to the east of Cormicks, marked with the words "Runners Village".

"The Runners?" Avalon asked.

"Yes, Avalon. Our people called them that when we first became aware of their people. Decades before we came to Fontanasia, we tried to befriend the small groups of animal like men who would run up to our walls, and then when hailed, would run away. It took a long time before we were able to open up a dialect with them. They were a very strange people."

"How so?" Avalon asked drawn in. She tried to remember the stories of Hawkerness from when she was a child.

"The Runners were much less developed and were often violent."

"Toward us?"

"No, they were peaceful toward us, and over the decades they traded with our people without conflict. They were violent toward each other, though. It was said that their leader forbade any outbursts toward our people because we were more advanced and taught them how to dig wells for water. We also showed them how to work metals for utensils and…"

"And weapons," Avalon concluded, cutting into her father's speech.

"Yes, very good, son. They had clubs and rocks when we met them, and we showed them how to make weapons to make hunting easier for them."

Avalon shook her head.

"I know, son, in hindsight it doesn't seem smart, but the Runners were so under developed, our people viewed them no more a harm than you would view a young child. And even though we had the Anthracite's on our side, when their leader died, his son violated the pact and raided Hawkerness. He declared himself monarch of all the land and allowed the Runners to become bloodthirsty. When they slaughtered our ancestors and drove the rest into hiding, they renamed the city Cormicks after their new leader. It remains today a dark and terrible place ruled by evil people."

"But didn't we have weapons?" Avalon asked, imagining her ancestors fighting for their lives.

"Yes, we had weapons and a guard, but we had never been attacked and weren't prepared for their viciousness. The Runners were a savage people, and we underestimated their willingness to slaughter outright. They would kill two of their own if it meant killing one of us. We also weren't prepared for their numbers. Their women and children attacked as well, and our guards were not ready to kill children." King Birch hesitated, and his own reluctance to send his daughter to Cormicks resurfaced.

"They were not gentlemen, Avalon. After decades of trading with the Runners, our people had forgotten the suspicious and uneducated people that they had first come upon. They had gotten used to their presence and forgot their true nature."

Avalon felt a growing concern for Fontanasia now, and her father recognized the look.

"That is why we send out two men, a Guide and one guard, twice a year, to travel to Cormicks and spy, and to make sure we are still safe. The next expedition is set to leave at dawn the day after next. In your dream, Avalon, you placed yourself on the path four days from now, on the next full moon." They both stared at the map, Avalon studying it for the first time, her father not seeing the diagram in front of his face.

"I don't want you to go, son." His eye twitched at the word, but he quickly regained composure. "But if you are to be king some day, then you need to know where we came from, and I need to teach you everything I can for you to keep Fontanasia safe."

They talked into the night, King Birch telling Avalon truer stories than the childhood fairy tales she knew, stories that had been passed down from his forefathers. "Cormicks was ruled by a ruthless man who in turn bore ruthless men. After Hawkerness fell and our people fled, none of our enemies ever tried to cross through the dense forest to find out where those who had escaped slaughter might have settled. Since none of those fleeing had ever returned from the forest, it was assumed everyone who had survived the attack had walked to their death. But it was in that forest that our people found hope for survival.

"My father's great, great grandfather was the third cousin to the king and eleventh man in line for the throne when he was put in a position he had never thought possible. The people followed him out of the rubble, through heavily forested area, and across uninhabited country. Our ancestors were a defeated and scared people trying to stay together, too willing to follow any heir to the throne no matter how far down the lineage, because no one really knew where to go. After many weeks, we found the safety of the mountain and the sea where we now stand, and our people actually felt safe with so much distance placed between them and the Runners. Our people didn't forget the history for many years, but when no armies came for them, they relaxed. There are only a few of us who remember our true history anymore. If anyone speaks of Hawkerness, it is through the fairy tales that you learned as a child."

King Birch stretched and yawned after their long talk, readying himself for the many questions that were sure to come.

Avalon's adrenaline had her attention piqued. She could see how the people of Fontanasia, safe in their kingdom, could live in peace and blissful ignorance. She had herself done it until this night.

And now she knew the truth. Twice a year on the full moon, an envoy of two men traveled back to the outskirts of a city now called Cormicks to track any possible movement and make sure that Fontanasia would not be disturbed. It had remained so for over two hundred years, the kings of each generation gratified for their tranquility but not quite trusting that they were truly safe from their past.

"How is it that I have not heard of this before? No one in council has mentioned it, and I am sure Counselor Glenn would have brought this up to upset the people and use it against you."

"You are to speak to no one about this map. As of now, there are only a few alive who have seen Cormicks, including myself. A small handful of the Guides know the way, and only Walthan and a few of the most trusted soldiers have taken the trip. It is a well-kept secret for a reason, Avalon. As King, it is my duty to ensure the welfare of the people, and part of that is making sure they lead happy lives. We have not been found in all of this time, but I am sure that if this got out, there are some who would want us to lead an offensive into Cormicks to destroy the monarch, and wage a war against the Runners. As king, I can not condone war for my people, and my silence protects the status quo."

King Birch's words went straight to Avalon's heart. It would be her duty some day to keep the same promise. She didn't plan to tell Zaria, Myra, or any other living soul of Cormicks. She returned her attention to the map, taking into memory every stroke of ink before her father returned it to its hiding place in the wall.

"I need to see Cormicks," she told her father. "I need to know what is out there." Her heart beat as though she had seen first hand the battle and escape from Hawkerness and already sensed the evil ruler of Cormicks bearing down on her even though she was not yet king.

Her father rested his large palm on her shoulder. "I will allow you to go so that you can begin to see the reason we keep a guard here in this peaceful city, so that when I am gone, you do not let down your watch. For your protection, I will send Walthan and Brick and another guard on this trip with you, and I won't rest until I see you return safely."

"I am sure it will be a successful reconnaissance trip, father, and I don't want to make it more trouble than it is worth."

"Nonsense," King Birch remarked. "My father sent me on an expedition of five men the first time I went to Cormicks, and I will do the same for you. I have to protect my heir, you know." King Birch turned to his daughter and hugged the back of her neck, pulling her head to his immense chest for a moment. "I am proud of you, son," he told Avalon. He grinned at her and sighed in confidence, not knowing that five would set out in pursuit of the full moon, but only three would return.

Chapter 7
Abyss

They saddled up just before dawn. It was four days to the full moon and the start of summer. Dew hung thick on the fields of grass. Avalon was nervous, but not about sneaking into enemy territory. She was worried that on a trip lasting almost a month, one of her companions would find out that she was a girl and expose her as a fake. She rubbed her hands on her trousers and checked her breast pocket for her pet, Jackie. "It will be all right," she whispered to herself as he rustled inside.

Two men emerged from the stable side of the castle as six horses were brought forth at the first sign of light. Avalon saw Walthan first, his stocky, muscular mass plain to recognize even in the gray light of dawn. Avalon had always looked up to Walthan and was pleased to be going on an outing with the senior guardsman. Walthan had never been in a real battle as Fontanasia hadn't ever been at war, but he had destroyed any opposition in the Fontanasia games for twenty years straight. He was taller than almost any man, and his body mass made contenders shudder at the beating their bones would incur under the bulldozer's strength. His life had been spent studying the art of defense, and he proudly served the king, creating mock battles and filtering through every scenario possible if an attack should ever occur on Fontanasia.

It was under Walthan's prompting that the king had reinforced the outer wall and commissioned the construction of a new, higher wall that circled the castle. The new wall did not take away from the open estate in the front of the city, but reinforced the king's home and last resort for the people if the city was ever over run. Now that Avalon knew of Cormicks' existence, she regarded Walthan with even more esteem, if that was possible.

Behind Walthan came Brick whose appearance was just as recognizable. His short muscular mass lumbered forward. He and Walthan clasped wrists, and then he nodded at Avalon in a silent greeting. Their expedition was covert, and not a word had been spoken yet.

A tall, thin figure emerged behind Brick appearing waif-like next to the beastly warriors. At first Avalon didn't know the soldier escort, but when the gray orange light of dawn caught his face, she knew him immediately. It was Taggerty. She was glad that the sun was emerging slowly and no one noticed her blushed expression. She was petrified that Taggerty was here to tell Walthan about her being attacked and the fact that he had stepped in to defend her. She was mortified though when Brick quietly introduced the young man.

"Prince Avalon, Walthan, this is young Taggerty of King Birch's guard. He will ride with us."

"It is a great honor to meet you, Prince Avalon," Taggerty answered the introduction sincerely with a proper bow, and Avalon felt her cheeks burn again but regained herself. He was probably saving the story of their real meeting as an anecdote for the campfire.

"Are we ready then?" Walthan asked softly.

Three of the horses held heavy packs, but Avalon was directed to her unburdened white mount. She placed her foot in the stirrup and easily pulled her frame onto the magnificent animal. She looked around for the Guide who would surely be riding with them, but none was to be seen. When they had all mounted,

Walthan raised his hand in a silent command to move out but was interrupted by Hawker who had materialized from inside the castle.

"Prince Hawker," Walthan greeted evenly. "What are you doing out so early?"

"I was walking to the archives, and you were making such racket. I thought I'd come out and see what was going on." Hawker took a moment to look at the men and then back at his nephew.

Walthan's eyebrow lifted because the party had been purposefully quiet and there had been no noise, but he nodded in agreement. Walthan did not dispute royalty.

"Avalon!" Hawker approached but stopped short of her horse. Avalon knew that her uncle reviled horses, and his shoulders curled up in aversion when the animal turned its head into his chest. Hawker took a step back and his tall frame brought his head above Avalon's mount, and he didn't have to look too far up to meet her eyes.

"You are off so early, young Prince."

"I am going to see…"

"Hunting," Walthan interrupted.

"Yes," Avalon did not miss a beat as Walthan caught her eye, but Hawker was a scholar and not easily fooled, so Avalon pressed on. "We are going hunting, Uncle. Care to join us?"

"Really?" Hawker asked intrigued, making Avalon regret the invitation for a moment. But she knew that there was nothing Hawker liked about the outdoors, and he had not hunted since he was a child.

"Hunting, you say?" He wasn't accepting the invitation, but rolling the word around in his mouth waiting for Avalon to offer more. When she didn't, he pulled his lips back in a smile and let the skin on his rabbit's nose bunch up. "I see, I see. Keeping secrets from your uncle. I just hope that you have not deceived your father."

"It was his idea," Avalon offered. She didn't like lying to her Uncle Hawker, but her father had told her of Cormicks in the strictest of confidence, and she dared not discuss it in the open.

There would be plenty of time to talk with her uncle in private when she returned.

"Very well, then off with you! And good hunting." Hawker smiled and reached out short of slapping Avalon's horse. Walthan did not hesitate, and the instant he nodded to Brick, the party of four was off.

Avalon looked back when they reached the courtyard wall and could see Hawker slowly turning back to the castle. There was a cloud around her heart knowing their relationship had just taken a turn. She had lied to him for the first time. *Well, not the very first time*, she thought, remembering that her Uncle Hawker did not know she was a girl. But that lie was really her father's.

She put the thought behind her as the group moved along the castle wall. Avalon thought they would leave through the burrows, but Walthan led them off to a small, gated arch. Two of the king's own guard crowded the doorway, and when they saw Walthan approaching, they unlocked the thick, steel door and pushed it aside. The group had to slide out of their saddles to the ground and walk their mounts through the opening, which was just large enough to fit the horses and packs. Avalon heard the gate clang closed behind her with the sound of finality, and she remounted her horse. They walked their horses down the hill along the huge, stone, city wall. The going was easy enough and Avalon was surprised to find a beaten path in the dirt. At first, Avalon thought that her father must have placed soldiers outside the wall to walk the area as a patrol, but when they reached the bottom of the hill, her throat closed tight to the truth.

When they reached level ground, Walthan picked up the pace, and they trotted past low rows of grass roofed, stone huts. A small village opened up in front of Avalon's eyes. It sloped down into the trees where Fontanasia met the mountain. Avalon saw children's eyes peeking at her from inside the huts as she passed. It was a village she had wondered about but had never seen, and she was shocked that in her fourteen years, she had never picked it out from high up in the castle.

Avalon hadn't noticed the two olive skinned Guides who were silently waiting with their bridles pointed toward the open prairie. Walthan met the Guides with a nod, and then they began at a gallop out of the small village and onto the plains. The brisk morning air on her face was exhilarating, and she turned her attention away from the village as her horse accelerated. Walthan rode next to Avalon, and Brick and Taggerty followed. Once they hit the open field, they rode hard the ten minutes to the city's outer wall where they reached a dead end and came to a stop. Avalon noticed that the wall had been built on a downgrade so that it looked smaller and décor-like from inside the kingdom, although she remembered it appearing immense and intimidating from the outside. The wall was constructed with perfectly squared stones that were arranged in a way to play tricks on the eye. She concentrated, looking for the way out, but there was no way to see the break in the wall.

"Can you see it?" Walthan asked Avalon.

She squinted as she looked down the line of bricks and should have known the secret, but her father had only shown her once how to find it on her own, and she could not find it now. Only the hunting parties went beyond the safety of the walls, and the design allowed those who knew where to look to enter and exit. Avalon noticed that Taggerty's eyes didn't seem to be struggling with the proper location, and she tried staring in the direction that he seemed to be looking, but she could not find the break.

When she didn't answer, Walthan pointed to the right.

"Look at the bottom row and keep your eyes steady."

Embarrassed, she squinted along the bottom row, and then Avalon saw it. Once she knew where to look, she could make out a small defection in the pattern. The Guide led, and they paced over to where the wall opened up into a small corridor that led them single file thirty feet along the stones before letting them out on the other side. When all six horses emerged, they began their run toward the southern forest. The Guides led, while Walthan and Taggerty took their places on the outside and a little behind Brick and Avalon. She knew that they rode in this formation to protect their prince, and Avalon was glad that Brick was next to her, but she felt a little disconcerted that every time she glanced at Walthan, she couldn't help but catch Taggerty's eye.

They rode this way through the expanse of low grass for over an hour giving their horses little rest, and Avalon was surprised at how hard the men pushed forward. The Guides stayed out front, and Avalon watched their black hair wave up and down in rhythm with the horse's gate. Avalon recognized one of the olive skinned men from her birthday party. Avalon understood that his job had been handed down for five generations, and her father had hand picked this Guide for this trip as he had hand picked Walthan. She already respected the Guide, surmising that he must have been the most knowledgeable of Cormicks out of the entire tribe. The only person Avalon couldn't place was Taggerty. She didn't know how he'd made this group, and she was almost afraid to ask.

They reached the edge of the forest and took to foot just as the sun's heat sapped their strength. Avalon was relieved to be off of her horse after the long, tense ride. She patted her horse as she straightened her sword and checked on Jackie who was tucked safely in her shirt pocket. The second Guide, who did not carry any packs, collected the reins. He would stay back with the horses, rest them, and slowly make his way back to Fontanasia. He would be back and waiting with the horses at the edge of the forest on their return in four weeks.

A whole month, Avalon thought with an excitement mixed with dread. She had been away from the castle for exactly four nights before, when her father had taken her on one day hunting trips. He would always keep the hunting party at one day's ride when Avalon was with them, saying he had business to attend to and couldn't make it a full range trip. But Avalon knew that her father was afraid of her secret, and one night was all he would tempt.

The four men with Avalon each carried a pack of provisions on their backs and small weapons on their sides. Walthan's pack was enormous, but he didn't seem to have any trouble as they moved through the dense foliage on the outer edges of the forest. Avalon insisted she carry something more than her water canteen and sword, but the men would not allow the king's son to bear any weight, and they did not want to risk the prince slowing them down as they had a lot of ground to cover before the full moon.

She watched Taggerty's hair curl tighter in the humidity as he lifted his pack. He was barely four years older than her and was allowed to share in the burden while she traveled empty handed. It had always been this way for Avalon, but this trip was different, or at least she expected it to be.

She tried to let go of her grudge before moving on and was excited as she stepped into the thick growth of the forest. She had never been in this area of the forest before, and she wondered if it would be any different than the parts she had visited. So far, it looked much the same. The dense underbrush thinned out as they moved below the tree cover where the sun didn't penetrate as well. She followed the Guide with Walthan right behind her, his sharp eyes equally watching the forest and the king's son. Before she'd left, Avalon's father had told her to stay behind the Guide and listen to anything Walthan told her to do, no matter how strange it might seem. He had said that in the area they would be traveling through, there were poisonous plants that could kill a man in moments. She tried to notice anything that looked out of order and immediately became paranoid, realizing now that her few hunting trips had little prepared her for this journey.

They walked at a brisk pace. Walthan knew the Guide and trusted him, and there was no one he'd rather have with him to protect the prince than his old friend, Brick. But the other soldier, the young Taggerty, was an enigma in that he was neither a Guide nor a seasoned soldier. Walthan tended to know all of the king's guard, and he had never met one who had not searched him out to introduce himself on the first day of service. Walthan was not insulted, just curious about the youngster. And yet Brick had recommended the young man for this journey just as King Birch had insisted Taggerty go with the group. Walthan couldn't figure what pull this unfamiliar soldier could have, but he put it out of his mind when Avalon stumbled over a tree root.

For her part, Avalon had sometimes forgotten that Taggerty was even with them. She watched Walthan and tried to copy his large, swift gate while she intensely wondered what Cormicks must look like. But when she tripped over the tree root and Taggerty reached out to right her with a smile, she brushed off his offered hand and concentrated on how much she disliked his furtive manner. He was turning up any time she stumbled, and his presence aggravated her.

They walked without rest for hours, and lost in the forest, Avalon wondered how their direction could possibly be clear to the Guide. There was no trail discernible in the dirt, and although the route took them away from the heaviest growth and made travel easy, she could not tell where they might be headed from one moment to the next. The Guide stopped to get his bearings next to a leafy boulder that was shaped like a thumb, between two tall, snaking trees, and then an hour later under a brown, rock overhang. He moved forward, slowing his pace and sweeping his head back and forth. Everything the tall, dark man did was deliberate and methodical. He seemed to be looking at the ground instead of ahead, and Avalon wondered what landmark could be showing in the mossy dirt.

Walthan was ever watchful, and Avalon wished she could talk as they walked, but the men were quiet on their mission, and she needed to fit in. She looked back and noticed her burly, longhaired guardian had stopped sweeping his eyes and concentrated to the left. Under the thick canvas of trees, the shrubs disappeared altogether and now they walked on red dirt that stuck to their pants as they kicked it up. It was half an hour later that Walthan stopped in his tracks, a full five seconds before the Guide stopped, and Avalon could see that Walthan knew better than anyone the way to Cormicks.

"We will rest here," the Guide announced.

"We're stopping already?" Avalon asked puzzled. She was exhausted, but it wasn't dark yet, and the trip to Cormicks and back took three weeks. No matter how close the cities had appeared on the map, they had a lot of ground to cover.

"Patience, Prince Avalon. We stop here for the night," Walthan said.

It was then that Avalon realized how tired she was after hours of long, steady walking. Walthan sat after Avalon, and bringing up the rear, Brick and Taggerty sat near but not too close to the king's son. The Guide moved away from the others and perched himself up on a huge rock. They each sat in silence for some time catching their breath and swigging from their canteens.

Taggerty rubbed his shoulders where he had been holding a large pack, but he didn't complain.

Avalon stood. She needed time alone, but she didn't know if the men would let her go off on her own. She was confused at what to say, but Walthan read her movement and stood up, his arm extended to the thickest part of the forest.

"Prince Avalon, we have to travel light on this trip and will not be able to set up a tent for your privacy. Please, take your time, but remain within ear shot." Walthan winked.

Avalon wondered how much instruction her father had given. Could Walthan know that she was a girl? She set out into the woods, thankful that she didn't have to make excuses to find privacy. Brick rolled his eyes at Walthan's grand gesture and stepped just away from where they were sitting to relieve himself on the closest tree.

Avalon made her way toward a cluster of six trees that would block her from their view. "That was close, Jackie," she whispered to her jakkow lizard who, for the first time, popped his red head out of her hip pocket. Avalon brushed him back and then fed him a few leaves. Even though he was trained to stay with Avalon, she didn't dare let him out for fear that he would run away in the forest and be lost forever.

That they should be stopping to camp already gnawed at Avalon. She tried to retrace in her mind the map her father had shown her. Knowing now that the journey past the big rock took only one day, Avalon realized that the city Cormicks must have been even closer than she'd originally thought. Since their city had not been attacked, nor a foreigner appeared in over two hundred years, she had assumed that they were alone in their country. But the men had covered what had looked like an endless expanse on the map in a very short time. She tried to find something that looked different in this deeper part of the forest, some plant or animal that would tell her they were headed to a different land. But aside from the red dirt caking her boots, the trees were still the trees, and the brush was still the brush.

When she returned to the campsite a few minutes later, Taggerty and Brick were already helping the Guide with the fire, which had been scratched together in no time. Walthan rose when he saw Avalon approach, offering another wink as he did so. Avalon's heart raced but she couldn't guess what Walthan knew. She would have sat close to him, but her paranoia carried her to the opposite side of the campfire. She tried to watch Walthan through the flames, tried to deduce the thoughts in his mind, tried to tell if he knew her secret. He caught her staring and she looked away quickly, the rest of the party settling in for the night, no one choosing to sit very near Avalon.

"I know you," Walthan told Taggerty. Walthan waited a moment for a response, but the soldier did not offer their connection. "Where have I seen you?"

Avalon watched Taggerty shift in discomfort, and she could only assume it was because Walthan was intimidating, even unintentionally.

"I have seen you in the castle lower halls. I have helped with the armory on many occasions," Taggerty offered.

The answer satisfied Avalon as Walthan slowly nodded. But the warrior's eyes were squinting still, and Avalon could see that Walthan didn't believe Taggerty.

"Maybe that's it," Walthan granted not wanting to play his hand too soon.

"You might also recognize me from the festival. I won my division in combat." Taggerty was obviously proud of this accomplishment, but Walthan and Brick quickly clasped hands in triumph and laughed at the young soldier.

"And we won everything else!" Brick snorted as Walthan grit his teeth in a menacing smile, shying Taggerty away from any further discussion. The warrior would have continued to challenge his young companion, but the Guide was up and unpacking their dinner.

Avalon slept well that night. The tree cover blocked out most of the moonlight leaving her to sleep in a gray haze. They took turns at watch, and Avalon was supposed to stand guard sometime in the night with Walthan, but she woke as the sun rose, her head heavy. She realized that the excitement of the journey had taken a mental toll, and her leg muscles felt sore from the hours of walking. Before Avalon stood up, she listened to the sounds of the forest. Birds chirped their song, and the leaves moved in the breeze so that there was never quiet around them. She looked up into the trees swaying in the wind and held fast by their massive, brown trunks crafted into the earth.

Jackie had been tucked in close to her body and eating leaves on the ground, but he scurried back into her front pocket when he felt her move. As she sat up, she noticed Taggerty standing below the large rock that the Guide, who had not moved position since Avalon had fallen asleep, was still perched on top. Avalon immediately imagined the Guide dropping a rock from the boulder onto Taggerty's head. She shook her head clear of the image and wondered why such a thought should occur to her.

Avalon had been the last to stir, and Walthan gave her a hearty pat on the shoulder as he walked past.

"You were supposed to wake me," Avalon protested.

"And so you are awake!" Walthan answered with a smile.

Avalon tried to lift one of Walthan's packs, but it was too heavy for her to even pull it off of the ground.

"No you don't," Walthan told her as he lifted the pack with one arm easily onto his shoulder. He winked at Avalon before turning away, causing her to begin again her internal line of questions from the previous night. *Does he know? Does he not want me to carry a pack because I am a prince, or because he knows I am a princess?* The unanswered questions were a slow torture as they got under way.

They walked under the tree canopy the entire day, resting in the sun at the edge of a small valley before taking to the woods on the other side. Avalon's questions soon melted away in the labor of the day. All of the men carried two packs, but Avalon had only her canteen and sword, and she complained several times that she could at least take one pack off their hands.

"Why do we need all of these blankets, anyway? It's summer."

"You will understand when we get there," Walthan simply replied without giving a true explanation.

"You, Taggerty," Walthan's voice boomed in the peaceful wood.

Avalon watched as Taggerty's eyebrows responded, but he didn't speak. They were all laboring, even Avalon with no extra pack to carry, but not once did Taggerty take off his long sleeves or even roll them up. His shirt was stuck to his skin with sweat, the same as the day of the festival. This trait annoyed Avalon. She was boiling hot too but was forced to wear extra clothing to fill out her slender waist. There was no reason for Taggerty to suffer in the heat too.

"Have you ever taken this trip before?" Walthan continued.

Taggerty shook his head. "No, this is all new to me."

"Are you not wondering anything then? Do you have no questions?"

Taggerty smiled. "I have many questions, Walthan, but I am of the king's guard now, and I do not complain."

It seemed Taggerty's comment about complaining was directed toward her, and Avalon tried but failed to ignore the rest of the conversation.

"Very good," Walthan complimented. "It's just that no one has ever gone without asking at least one question about why they have to carry so much for this journey in summer. Do you not wonder about the blankets like Prince Avalon?"

Avalon noticed the Guide who glanced back at Taggerty and Walthan. This was the first time Avalon saw the deliberate man react to anything, but the discreet leader didn't speak.

Instead of feeling challenged, Taggerty flashed a smile. "I guess I am just more man than most."

Walthan guffawed at that, and Brick patted the boy on the back.

"I really like this young man, Walthan," Brick declared.

But Avalon remembered the same cockiness from the street fight he had pulled her from, and all she saw in the curly haired boy was a pompous fool.

To put Taggerty out of her mind, she listened to the bird's chirping, and Avalon soon lost track of time. Just as the sky was darkening, they came to the edge of a deep ravine, and after the Guide took his bearings, they moved only thirty yards up the edge of the steep drop and stopped.

"We camp here tonight," the Guide said just loud enough to be heard. They each sat down slowly, their legs tired from a second day of walking. Only Walthan remained standing as he heaved his packs off and moved back into the trees.

"I've got this one, boys," he said heartily.

Avalon could feel small blisters forming on the sides of her toes, but she didn't complain. She kept her boots on knowing that if she took them off now, her feet would swell and her boots would be hard to get back on. Now that she was still, she could feel her jakkow stirring in her pocket, and she quickly stuffed a couple leaves down to keep him busy.

Walthan returned from the trees with his arms full of firewood. Although she was sore, Avalon rushed to help him. She was the only one without a pack, and she wanted to carry her weight. She diligently stacked the wood for a fire and Taggerty stuffed dry leaves and sticks underneath for kindling. She lit it with a match, trying not to meet Taggerty's gaze. They were soon eating bread and the little fruit that was sent along.

Before they had set off from Fontanasia, Avalon had imagined that there would be robust conversations around the fire. But the Guide was always off on his own, she didn't want to talk to Taggerty, and even Walthan and Brick didn't talk much. She had come to realize that the brevity of the words between the two great warriors did nothing to dispel the fact that they would really do anything for each other. When she sighed and stared into the flames, chewing her plum slowly because even moving her jaw was an arduous task, she realized they were all too tired to speak even if they'd wanted to. They were dozing off one at a time.

The Guide took the first watch with Avalon who had decided on her own that she was going to have to force her way into helping since they did not want to push their prince. They sat along the ravine where the moonlight was brightest. It looked like a full moon, but upon further inspection, Avalon could see that there was still a sliver of the moon in shadow. The white crystals on the moon's surface gleamed like the reflection of lights dancing on flowing water. It was a beautiful sight in the blackness of the woods away from the lamplights of the city.

"It will be full tomorrow," the Guide told Avalon who almost jumped when his voice broke the silence. "You should rest, Prince Avalon."

"We are walking up along the ravine tomorrow?" Avalon asked the Guide without really expecting an answer. She thought she could see his white teeth in the moonlight and realized that his name had never been offered to her as introduction, and she didn't know what to call him.

"We climb down into the abyss tomorrow, and if we are lucky, we climb up the other side."

Avalon looked down the face of the cliff and tried to make out the bottom, but the darkness prevented her from seeing how deep of a chasm lay before her. She remembered thinking this would be a river by the way it was noted on her father's map, but now she understood why it was labeled "Stranger's Pass". It had been marked as a simple irregular line with an arrow and the words 'The Way Down'. Avalon wondered if her descendants had been playing a joke when they wrote that modest statement. She recounted the map's markings and tried to remember the entire route they had taken, but even for a sharp girl, the dark of the forest erased most of the journey. She closed her eyes and remembered the markings at Stranger's Pass, and she couldn't remember seeing 'The Way Up'.

Avalon soon learned that there was no specific way down into the ravine. Walthan's pack contained just enough rope to tie off on a tree, and one by one, they lowered themselves down to the bottom. Avalon had a lot of experience climbing the mountain that contained one side of Fontanasia, and she performed better than the others had expected a young boy to. On the way down, her feet walked on a hard, black rock that reflected light in places, but at the bottom, the earth below their feet was dusty and crunchy. The rope chapped her hands, but she hardly noticed as she was thrilled to have made it to the bottom. Walthan lowered the packs, and he and Taggerty climbed down last.

"Stick to the rocks, and keep up," the Guide said before turning and beginning the trek across the bottom of the ravine.

Avalon watched as the Guide took a few steps in the loose dirt before placing one foot on a small rock. He paused to look at the ground before taking another step in the dirt.

"Do as he says and stick to the rocks," Walthan added as he set out. "Stay close, Prince Avalon."

Avalon felt like a fool perching with one foot on a small rock and trying to keep her balance. She looked at the ground like the Guide and Walthan, but had no idea what to look for. "Just stay close," Walthan reminded her when he turned and noticed a gap between them.

"What are we looking for?"

"Sand eels," Walthan told her as though she should naturally know what those were. "Just don't step in anything soft."

Avalon hesitated and it was Brick who set her straight. "Just watch out for any loose ground."

She moved ahead slowly, staring at her feet. She had to move quickly to stay out of Brick's way, but it was difficult to move fast because she was beginning to fear each step. What did soft ground look like? She stuck to the rocks as much as she could, but Brick had been moving fast and was outwardly annoyed at Avalon for slowing him down. Taggerty came up behind them and didn't speak, but he looked to be in a hurry as well.

Avalon lost sight of the Guide who had climbed through some debris, and Walthan was way out in front of the group beckoning them forward. Avalon took three quick steps and tripped, falling over a branch.

"Prince Avalon, you mustn't dally." Brick stood with his legs wide on two rocks next to Avalon. "Let's move!"

She stood up and brushed herself off and was forced to walk in the dirt until she could get ahead of Brick who was still standing on the most immediate rocks. Her right foot began to feel heavy and she stepped forward lifting her knee as hard as she could. She must have pulled a muscle because each step was more difficult. There was a sting on her shin and she started to feel dizzy but kept trying to catch up to Walthan.

"Get a move on, Prince Hall," Brick egged. "We have a lot of ground to cover and I don't want to be down in this ravine any longer than necessary."

But Avalon couldn't move her feet anymore, and now both of her legs were tied down with large weights. She tripped over the next rock and landed hard, her jakkow scampering out of her front pocket and into the back of her shirt collar just before being squashed by her weight. Avalon saw the ground rushing toward her face, but she couldn't make herself react. The smashing ache that she expected against her face never came as firm hands grasped her falling body.

"Prince Avalon!" she heard a faraway voice yell. Someone's hands were gripping her chest in a bear hug and rolling her over. Arms were around her waist now as the dizzying feeling encompassed her body. "Help!" The voice called out. It was Taggerty lowering the rest of her to the ground.

"Don't put him down on the ground!" Walthan called back.

But Taggerty couldn't hold Avalon up while simultaneously trying to hold her as far away from himself as possible like she was a leper. He could see three sand eels engulfing both of her feet and slowly making their way up her legs. It looked like the ground had risen up like a snake and was trying to swallow her whole.

Taggerty scooped Avalon up under her arms and dragged her toward Walthan who was running back along the rocks toward them. Walthan was back quickly, and he took Avalon by the arms and wrested her straight up in the air. She hung vertically now; her legs limp as the sand eels sucked the energy out of them. It wasn't an uncomfortable feeling for Avalon, more an annoyance that she couldn't think straight. She wanted to go to sleep, but Walthan's arms shook her as he held her off the ground.

"Hey," she protested to Walthan who kept shaking her awake.

"Hold still," an unfamiliar voice demanded. The Guide was excited now, and Avalon didn't know what his problem was because she was now sagging perfectly still in Walthan's grip.

But the sand eels had done their job, and not being able to feel anything, she didn't know that her legs were convulsing under their electric shocks. One of the eels made its way up to her thigh, and Taggerty, who was on the edge of panic, began to rip Avalon's boots and pants off. Walthan almost punched the young soldier until he realized that taking Avalon's pants off was a way to get rid of the sand eels and could possibly save her life. Taggerty threw her boots and pants well away from their path, which accomplished getting rid of all but one of the flat, scaly creatures who slithered up. Luckily, the prince was wearing a second pair of pants underneath and it kept the slimy eel from touching bare skin.

Avalon followed Taggerty's wild gaze and looked down at her legs horrified at the flat, foreign creature that was attached. The lower half of her body was jerking fitfully, but she couldn't feel it. The Guide quickly pulled a pouch from his hip pocket and tossed its contents of a flaky dust onto Avalon's leg, which caused the sand eel to melt away and drop back into the soft ground. Avalon's legs finally stopped jerking. Walthan breathed easier under the still weight but did not set the prince on the ground. The rest of the men balanced their feet on the closest rocks and looked for more soft, moving sand, but there was none.

"What is that?" Brick asked the Guide.

"It's keeley dust, repels the sand eels. It's like salt."

A faint stinging returned, and Avalon felt limp. She wasn't sure of her senses yet, but she knew that the dust was nothing like salt because the sand eel hadn't simply fallen off, but more dissolved off of her leg.

"I don't know who would wear two pairs of pants in this heat, but it saved your life," Brick told a semi-conscious Avalon. "You are very lucky."

"Sand eels tranquilize and then suffocate their victims." The Guide took a moment to catch Avalon's eye. "Stay on the rocks," he finished sternly before calmly turning his back on the group and heading forward into the brush.

"I have spare boots," Taggerty told Walthan.

"No time," the warrior replied. His massive arms pulled Avalon over his shoulder and he carried her like a sack of potatoes.

They climbed over the remaining dead tree limbs and other forest debris and finally made their way across just as the sun rose high enough to reach the far side of the crevice. They set their packs on a small rock shelf where Walthan gently placed Avalon.

"Excuse me, my Prince," Walthan said as he rubbed her legs.

"I'm fine!" Avalon protested again. She was still wearing the thin layer of pants, but she was all too aware. She brushed Walthan's hands away.

"Lay still, Prince Avalon. I've seen what those sand eels can do, and believe me, you need the rest."

Avalon laid back and watched from the ledge in amazement as the Guide began to climb the wall with no safety line. He had a rope tied to his waist, and he pulled himself up one cleft after the next leaving the rope to dangle down behind his ascent. Avalon was used to the solid rock of home, and the vine covered, stony surface looked durable. Yet as the Guide slowly pulled his body into different holding positions, dust-covered clay seemed to move beneath his feet. Vines helped him steady his steps, and sometimes he remained still like a spider on a wall, deliberating his next move. Within an hour the Guide had reached the top. Walthan waited with his hand on the limp rope that the Guide had dragged up, and once two short pulls came, Walthan let his huge mass hang a foot off the ground to test the rope's strength.

"Brick," was all he said, and the shorter warrior grabbed the rope, his beefy arms pulling him up one hand over the other without help from his feet. His aging body caused the need to catch a large gulp of breath halfway up, but that was the only weakness Avalon had ever seen out of Brick. What took the Guide almost an hour took Brick ten minutes.

"Stand up, Avalon," Walthan encouraged his young prince.

Avalon stood, but much slower than her mind wanted her to, and she could feel her leg muscles still twitching.

"Okay, rest," he commanded. Walthan placed a huge hand on each of Avalon's legs. "You'll be fine. You're better already," he reassured her. Then he leaned in so only she could hear him. "I don't know this Taggerty, and I don't trust him, but I have no choice but to leave you alone with him for a few minutes." Walthan's eyebrows rose as he met Avalon's gaze, and then he stepped away.

"I will go next," he announced. As he tied a large loop in the bottom of the rope, Walthan gave a cautionary look to Taggerty, even though the young soldier had just saved Avalon's life. "We will pull Prince Avalon up, and then the bags," Walthan told him, and then he was moving up the ravine. Where Brick went arm over arm, Walthan pulled with his arms and walked his feet up the side. Loose chunks of dirt fell from the ravine forcing Avalon to stand up and move aside. She took deep breaths and tried to hold her legs as still as possible, but she ended up taking a seat on a large rock making sure not to touch the ground.

"It's okay, Jackie," she whispered to her red lizard as he scampered out of her collar, down her arm, and into her palm. She had forgotten about him and was relieved he was all right. She rubbed his back and placed him back in her pocket. She looked up to see Taggerty preparing the bags, and he approached her after retrieving an extra pair of boots.

"The sand eels are impossible to see until it's too late," Taggerty told her as he gently pulled the boots on Avalon's feet. She was intently watching Walthan climb the rope, but her every attention was on Taggerty. No one but Myra and Zaria had ever dressed her before, and she was not used to the touch of a stranger. She held her breath as he laced up the boots. They fit so well that she wondered if he had brought the spare pair along just for her.

"They are on you before you know it, and they numb your senses and eventually sedate you and suffocate you." He spoke softly and easily about the sand eels as though he was discussing how to make a sandwich.

"It's keeley dust. It drives the sand eels off," Taggerty told her as he held out a small leather bag. Avalon took it and placed the small pouch in her hip pack. She tried to concentrate on slowly tying her hip pack so she wouldn't have to look into his intense, green eyes again. "You have to be aware enough to spread it on them while you can still control yourself. Next time we go through the ravine, have it in your hands."

Avalon couldn't remember the Guide giving the pouch to Taggerty, but she had no time to question him. Walthan was at the top, and Taggerty was placing the loop at the bottom of the rope over her head and under her arms. He gave two short tugs on the rope, and Avalon could feel the slack being taken up quickly.

"Mind the dirt," Taggerty said as Avalon was lifted smoothly off the ground. He was right to warn her because chunks of the ravine fell on her head where the rope rubbed against the edge. She was able to turn herself around to face the wall, and regained her legs as she used them to help walk up the side of the ravine. Brick and Walthan pulled her over the top and gently set her on the ground.

"No sand eels up here," Walthan reassured Avalon when he saw the panic on her face.

They lowered the rope twice to get the packs up, and then Taggerty appeared over the edge showing no signs of the wear that the climb should have produced.

Avalon was able to stand alone showing the barest of side effects still left over from the attack that occasionally made her leg twitch. She watched the men retake their packs, laboring under the weight. "We should construct a bridge," Avalon said helpfully as she looked to the other side of the ravine where they had camped the night before.

"No, we should not, Prince Avalon." The Guide eyed her warily but said nothing else, and Avalon immediately felt embarrassed.

"You don't think that would help?" Avalon asked.

Walthan placed his hand softly on her shoulder and winked. "It would help us reach Cormicks, but we don't want to advertise the path back to Fontanasia." His whispered words sat eerily upon her as they moved on into the forest.

Chapter 8
The Black Moon

Summer was upon them, and the sun made them all sweat before they took to the trees again. Avalon soon got lost in the continuous walking, often losing sight of where they were going, and in her mind was just out for a stroll. She found herself very aware of where Taggerty was in the group. And Walthan, the wise soldier guardian, constantly seemed to be noting Taggerty's position in relation to Avalon's in an effort to stay between the two young charges. Avalon had been saved once by Taggerty, and although she didn't care to be near him, she couldn't imagine why she would need protection from him, but Walthan obviously didn't trust the new guard.

As they made their way deeper into the woods on this side of the ravine, Avalon noticed a change immediately. The trees were much wider at the base here, and as they moved into denser areas, they seemed to be pressed closer together. She could no longer see a quarter-mile ahead as the tree trunks and massive exposed roots blocked her vision. They climbed over and under branches for two hours before the Guide suddenly stopped.

Avalon looked around to find the telltale sign they had reached another landmark, but she could only see this new forest around them.

They stood still for a few minutes, only the chirping sound of the unseen insects and wild life around them making noise until Walthan broke their silence. "We have three more hours before we move. Let's eat."

"Shouldn't we get moving while we can see our way?" Avalon asked. The huge trees had blocked out so much of the sunlight already, and Avalon knew that if they stayed here until dusk, the air would be pitch black and impassible in the darkness. Taggerty seemed to be waiting as well for Walthan's response.

"We don't travel past here in the light, boy," Brick interjected, and Avalon immediately wished that she had kept her mouth shut. She noticed Taggerty looking her way and turned her back on him. Avalon caught Walthan giving Brick a look of warning, but she hadn't minded the warrior's tone since his condescension meant that he saw her as an equal, and that is all she had wanted on this trip. She needed to be one of the boys.

"You'll see," Walthan smiled and winked at Avalon as he unpacked a roll of beef jerky and dried fruits.

Avalon was used to the tender and juicy cooking that the king's staff provided, and she had never eaten beef jerky before. She found it salty and the texture too course to be enjoyed, and she made a sour face causing Walthan to let out a hearty laugh as he watched his young prince reluctantly chew the dried meat. Avalon grit her teeth at the tell and swallowed the rest of the jerky whole. She was still sweating in her layers and noticed Taggerty's long sleeves again as she took Walthan's shield and moved into the woods for some privacy. She gave Jackie a piece of the salty beef, but he spit it out, so Avalon stuffed a piece of dried fruit and leaves in her pocket to keep him busy. Avalon let the lizard stretch his legs while she pulled on her spare pants before hiding him back in her pocket and returning to the group.

The Guide said very little, but as the men sat around the fire, he offered one detail. "Enjoy the warmth, men. This will be our last fire for two weeks." Avalon could hear laughter in his baritone voice, and she could only wonder about the quick smile the Guide shared with Walthan.

They each dozed off one at a time for a short nap. Then, an hour before sunset, Walthan extinguished the campfire and had the men clean the area. The Guide was still perched in a tree watching the woods to their left, and Avalon wondered if this man truly had such great concentration, or if he had learned to nap with his eyes open. As the sun fell, the gray light that filtered through the massive trees faded. The faction was quickly suited and ready to move, but all remained still waiting for the Guide's lead.

Avalon would have asked why they weren't moving if it wasn't for the expressed look of concentration on Walthan's face. The hefty warrior was staring toward the same section of the forest that the Guide had been trained on. Neither moved for thirty minutes as the woods grew pitch dark. The air was warm, but the energy exerted in their stillness caused a chill in Avalon. She kept herself from shuddering, purposefully straightening up instead. She grew slightly impatient and couldn't understand why they were just standing there, and then she saw the blue glow. And then she knew.

The canvas of trees overhead blocked the moonlight, but there seemed to be one area in the woods getting brighter as the blackness of night settled on them. The Guide stood and moved quickly toward the bluish glow. Walthan gestured for Avalon to follow the Guide, and then he and the rest followed. Avalon had to jog every few paces to keep up, and it was hard not to fall down in the thick brush as they climbed over roots and under huge fallen branches. She managed to stay on the Guide's heels as her heartbeat increased, and she remembered the dream that had brought her to this moment. The glow in the night had to be the bright blue sea.

They covered one hundred yards quickly before settling on the area of the forest that lit up in the night. It was a small valley that cut into the trees, and although she'd had this vision in her dream, Avalon could not believe what she was seeing. The ground was shimmering and swaying like waves on the sea. It was not water at all though, but thousands of tall glowing reeds of grass with tips like blue stars on a dark night; a million specs of light filling a black blanket. Avalon automatically searched for a pattern, but there was none. It was the most beautiful sight, and she felt a rising heaviness in her throat. Tears of joy crossed her eyes, and she was grateful just to have lived to see this wonderful enchantment. But she stopped herself cold and closed off the emotion that beckoned to swallow her. She was a prince and a man, and there was no time for tears.

An old bit of memory tugged at her, and Avalon struggled to bring it forward. Now that they were right in front of her, she recognized the tall, thin stalks of grass; she had seen them before when she was very young.

Everyone stopped walking at the edge of the woods, but Walthan plunged straight into the blue glow of the tall grass.

"No!" Avalon yelled.

"It's all right boy." Walthan moved deeper into the heavy grass and stopped to look back at Avalon as the Guide moved into the blue.

"It's elbagrass. I remember it now. My father showed me a piece of it once. He told me that it was poisonous." Avalon's eyes were wide, but Walthan remained in the grass.

Brick swept passed and followed the Guide further into the prairie, leaving Avalon and Taggerty waiting at the edge of the woods.

"It isn't poisonous in the moonlight, Avalon. When it is glowing blue, it is magic." Walthan's tone was filled with reverence, and Avalon knew he wasn't making fun of her. He waited hip deep in the field of glowing grass for his young charge to follow him, but Avalon was still hesitant as the memory became more clear with each second. "Your father was protecting his young son when he said those words, he was protecting his baby. But you are not a little boy anymore, Avalon, and it is time you learned the truth about elbagrass and the door to Fontanasia."

Walthan nodded his head and beckoned her forward with his hand just as he'd done in her dream, and although Avalon was still apprehensive, she knew that the warrior would do nothing to harm her. She stepped into the tall grass that quickly covered her up to her chest. Taggerty followed as they all tried to catch up to the Guide.

Walthan walked in a path behind Brick and just in front of Avalon now in an effort to press the thickening grass down so the young prince could wade through without getting stuck. Avalon could see that the field was made of tall, thick reeds that grew taller the farther in they went. Soon she could no longer see over the top, and she rushed to stay behind Walthan whose height allowed his head to stay clear of the grass.

"Elbagrass glows blue for only three nights each month, only in the full moon light and on the nights on either side of the full moon. If there is no full moon, there is no door to Fontanasia."

"I don't understand, Walthan."

"You will. This is not something easily explained. You'll have to see it with your own eyes."

Avalon felt a tickling sensation through her pants and her stomach tightened and her heart raced as she looked down at her legs for sand eels. Her hands were already reaching for the pouch of keeley dust before she knew what was happening.

"Ouch," she complained.

Walthan spun around but then laughed. "It's the alleya leaf poking you through your pants, kiddo."

Avalon noticed the crisp, green leaves growing low on the tall grass. They rubbed against her and poked through her pants before falling off to the ground.

"Eat these," Walthan handed Avalon three of the small green leaves as he chewed on his own bunch. The leaves were brittle and bitter, and Walthan explained as she chewed. "The alleya leaves grow green out of the elbagrass very fast, in one night only, when the grass is bluest. They are a cure for the poison."

Taggerty bent over as they walked and scooped up leaves to eat, and Avalon leaned down and picked up a leaf stuffing it into her pocket for her jakkow. She didn't have to encourage him too much since he'd eaten little on this trip missing the fresh fruits of Fontanasia, and he scarfed the leaf down quickly.

Avalon had to pull her knees up to her waist to step through the thickening grass, and she could hear the others laboring as well. Ever graceful, the Guide did not seem to be having trouble in the thick meadow, and it baffled Avalon that he could even follow a direction in the disorienting field of swaying, blue light. They had walked for ten minutes, each man staying in line with the Guide who finally stopped in front of a small pool of water that had been lined carefully with square rocks. To Avalon it was a startling find since she had not seen another man made landmark since they left the outer wall at Fontanasia. But something much stranger than seeing the landmark happened in the blink of an eye.

The Guide reached past Avalon and handed Taggerty three alleya leaves. Avalon was surprised at the gesture, and Taggerty shrugged at her in question as though he was confused as well. The Guide then stepped back to the side of the pool, looked to Walthan who winked, and then the previously tight-lipped, expressionless man smiled. He bent over to look at his reflection in the small pool, and disappeared. Taggerty, who was still standing behind Avalon, gasped. Avalon held her breath to keep from reacting and did not flinch, although she was terrified and her chest filled up with fear leaving her wanting to cry. So this is what her father had been protecting her from, and what Walthan had called magic. Avalon had seen magicians entertain the king, but instinct told her that the way the Guide had disappeared was different. It was real. She'd never seen anything like it before.

"Go ahead," Walthan told Brick who, as a well-seasoned soldier, knew what to expect because he had taken this trip before. Brick gripped the hilt of his sword and the strap on his pack before looking into the pool and disappearing.

"Avalon," Walthan stated as he motioned toward the pool and looked over her shoulder at Taggerty. Walthan clearly wanted Avalon to go before him because he did not want her and Taggerty, the other newcomer on this journey, to be left behind from wherever they were going.

Avalon's heart raced, but she took a step forward out of the grass next to the marker stones. She looked back at Walthan who was plainly visible in the light of the moon and bright blue grass.

"Did you eat the leaves I gave you?"

"Yes." Their bitter taste lingered on her tongue.

"Then just look at your reflection, it's that simple."

Avalon did as she was told. She stepped forward and bent over. The reflection of the moon in the pool was radiant, and then she saw her eyes. There was an immediate unsettling feeling in her stomach, slight yet world changing, like the first time she had dreamt in her sleep. A tingling sensation ran up her back and engulfed her skull. She didn't know if the sensation was some magic coming over her as she disappeared, or fear and excitement colliding within her.

But nothing else seemed to happen. She was still looking into the pool, only it was extremely dark now as the moon high above in the sky had somehow disappeared. The air emanated blackness, and it was impossible to see beyond a few feet. Avalon could hear the rustling sound of the tall grass blowing in the wind, but it no longer glowed blue. The other immediately noticeable change was that Walthan and Taggerty had disappeared, and the Guide and Brick had reappeared.

Before Avalon could ask what had happened, the Guide grabbed the young prince and yanked her away from the stone. An instant later, Taggerty reappeared next to the pool. He stepped away to his right, and then immediately, Walthan was there too. Taggerty and Avalon were both confused, but the Guide moved on before any questions could be asked.

The air had turned cold, and Avalon shivered from the cool sweat that had collected on her shirt. She had to blink to clear her eyes in the dark, and soon saw that they were surrounded by tall, unglowing elbagrass. She followed Walthan away from the pool and tried to keep her footing. The elbagrass was challenging enough to walk through when it was lit up but almost impossible in the pitch darkness.

"This is why we had to eat the alleya leaf, so that we wouldn't be poisoned on this side of the window," Walthan whispered.

"We should have saved some for the return trip," Avalon quipped. She was getting colder each second and soon began to shiver. She was starting to understand why they had brought packs of blankets on this early summer trip.

"The leaves turn brown in a day and are useless, which offers great protection for Fontanasia." Always the warrior, Walthan was thinking battle strategy as they walked. "But that also means that we will have to wait two full weeks for the full moon here to return to Fontanasia."

"It's really cold," Taggerty said. Avalon could hear him sloughing through the grass behind her.

"It's winter here," Walthan said calmly. "You'd better pray that there aren't clouds in two weeks, because we are stuck here until this elbagrass glows." It was two weeks away, but Avalon found herself already praying for clear skies.

This was the first time Avalon could remember being glad that she had to wear long sleeves. She folded her hands up into her cuffs for warmth and looked back at Taggerty. He was rubbing his arms for warmth, his large wrist guards keeping him from tucking his hands into his shirt as Avalon had.

Jackie trembled in her shirt pocket, and Avalon pulled the flap open to tuck a handkerchief in to keep his body warm. He wouldn't sit still though and Avalon knew immediately that his twitching was more than the cold. His whole body writhed, and his tail stung her chest like a whip. Avalon took him out of her pocket, but before she could see what was happening, the jakkow bit her and she instinctively dropped him. His small body should have been impossible to see in the dense grass, but his shape writhed as Avalon watched him balloon until he was almost her size.

Taggerty was seeing now, open-mouthed.

"Jackie!" Avalon begged. She didn't know what was happening as her jakkow grew larger than Walthan, and then larger than her horse. Now they were all staring back at her, and although the Guide couldn't see clearly in the dark, he could make out the form that had grown above the grass line.

"Command him!" he yelled back to Avalon.

But she was too stunned to answer.

"You have to take command on both sides of the window!" the Guide was yelling in a hushed tone.

Avalon backed away as her jakkow's giant, red tail whipped at the grass and his chest barreled forward into Walthan whom was knocked off his feet under the brute force. Then the red lizard ran off through the grass. The Guide tried to grab his neck and hold on, but the beast was too strong and easily flicked the man to the ground. The lizard continued his run, and Avalon watched Jackie's giant outline disappear in the darkness. Then there was a loud crunching and crashing of wood in the distance, which faded into silence. Avalon ran blindly through the grass out after him with the rest of the men in pursuit.

"What was that?" demanded Brick.

"Jackie!" Avalon screamed in a light, girly voice but then coughed deeper to cover it up. "Come back, Jackie!" She had long lost sight of his growing figure but continued to run recklessly through the grass, the tall reeds ripping into her face and hands. She blindly broke through the grass and instantly smashed face first into a tree trunk, falling back and slamming to the ground. Avalon held her chest where the wind had been knocked out of her, already tasting blood.

The Guide was the next out of the sea of grass, and he immediately ran to her side.

"Quiet!" warned Walthan as he emerged, looking around the small clearing toward the woods.

Brick chimed in again. "What was that?" he panted, catching his breath on the edge of the grass.

Avalon could not have expected what had happened to Jackie, and she wasn't sure what to say. She was stunned and disoriented. Her jakkow had somehow ballooned into a huge animal, and she wondered if he would ever stop, or if he would grow until he exploded.

Taggerty had silently emerged from the elbagrass, and he answered for her. "It is a jakkow lizard. They are good luck."

Everyone but the Guide looked back at Taggerty. "It's not mine, so don't look at me like that," he said defensively.

In any other situation, Avalon would have thought that Taggerty was being a pompous know it all, but she wondered how he could have even known what a jakkow was, if it was as rare as the Guides had said.

"I don't know what it is, but leave it. It's gone," Walthan told Avalon.

She propped herself up on her hands and wiped the blood from her lip, rubbing her forehead and hoping it wouldn't swell. The very air was pitch black, and she could hardly see any of their gray outlines. She watched as the Guide's figure snatched tiny, shimmering bugs from midair and smeared one of them on each of their backs. Walthan looked down at the Guide with a question on his lips.

"I don't like it either," the Guide answered him. "But this group is too large, and someone is bound to get lost. Move," he instructed as he stepped away from the elbagrass and into the woods.

"Stay close, everyone, it gets darker from here," Walthan added as he pulled Avalon up onto her feet. Avalon wondered what darker than black would look like.

"I'm okay, I'm okay," she reassured him. He held his hand out toward the tree that Brick had just stepped behind, and Avalon followed. As she walked, she moved her tongue around her lips to clean the wound hoping that the blood would stop soon.

Three steps into the woods, and Avalon had to struggle to see the tiny spot of light on Brick's back. Fallen branches cracked beneath her feet, and the trees had grown so close together that she had to squeeze around them. She reached around their tall, slender trunks having to find her way by feel. She felt like the air itself must have been black, each of them breathing it in until they became invisible shadows in the night. She shuddered at the thought and moved forward, staying on Brick's heels to make sure they did not get separated. Brick was short but wide and had a harder time squeezing between the trees with his heavy packs. Avalon matched his steps as branches scraped her legs, arms, and face.

They walked for a long time, and Avalon's thoughts turned to Jackie. He'd been with her for over a month, riding in her pocket, and sharing her journey. She was sorry that she had brought her pet along to this uncertain land, and she was distraught to know that she had most likely killed him in doing so. She felt a pang of sadness and guilt as she remembered something Myra George had told her when she was a very little girl. Myra had found Avalon crying about her mother and had curled up on the floor to hold the small princess. When Avalon was all cried out, Myra had whispered simply, "Nothing is ours to keep."

Chapter 9
The Charcoal Beasts

After thirty minutes of zigzagging, the trees finally separated and Brick sighed loudly. Avalon hadn't been aware of Walthan behind her until she broke through and stopped behind the Guide. She pulled her hands to her cheeks and felt the cold scratches, taking a deep breath in to relax her expression. Even out of the woods, it was hard to see any of the others in the dark.

"Stay close," the Guide stated simply as he turned to move on. They walked slowly in the darkness for a while, Avalon half crouched to keep her footing sure.

"We will sleep here," the Guide stated. "No fire," he told Avalon. Her neck curled further into her collar and she tried not to meet his gaze, realizing for the first time that the cold was seeping into her bones.

They were in a small clearing where huge boulders circled their group. Walthan unpacked five blankets and laid two out on the largest boulder. "We're over here," he told Avalon who was trying not to shiver. "We must sleep on the rocks because of the everreds."

Avalon didn't know what that meant, but she was beginning to feel that asking questions was belittling her to the group and she was becoming self-conscious. She hoped Taggerty would ask about the everreds, but he didn't. She touched the freezing rock and now understood why they needed to carry so many blankets. The rock was colder than the bitter night air.

Brick pointed Taggerty to the other largest boulder leaving the Guide to sit unaccompanied. Avalon could hear the lone front man grinding his teeth as they settled in.

"What's wrong," Walthan asked the Guide as he turned his head from side to side in the black night.

"We should never travel in such a number, it is too dangerous." Avalon felt the unintended sting from the Guide's words, as she knew there were five instead of two because of her.

"King Birch feels better knowing he has Brick and I protecting the prince." Walthan's massive hand slapped Avalon's shoulder, and she flinched. Then he added with a laugh, "But Taggerty could have been left behind."

The Guide did not respond.

"Very funny, Walthan." Taggerty was flexing his muscles before stretching out on the rock.

"You shouldn't talk back to your senior guard," Brick scolded Taggerty.

The young man huffed, and Avalon could see that he was not in the mood. It was the first time she'd seen him without a quick rebut, and she knew then that he must have been trying to fit in just as much as she was.

"I'll take watch," he announced as he stole his blanket from the rock and lithely climbed the nearest tree.

"Gone to pout, have you?" Walthan quietly sang after the boy, who this time did not respond. Avalon's eyes were adjusting to the darkness, and she could see Taggerty's gray outline getting settled on a low branch of the tree.

"Are you warm enough, Prince Avalon?" Walthan asked sincerely. She nodded, grateful that the others had carried the blankets. The steady wind whipped around her but could not cut through the thick fur.

They were silent for a while, but because of the cold, or the excitement, or the loss of Jackie, Avalon couldn't sleep. "I can't find the moon," she whispered into the night.

"It's not in the sky here right now, but we will begin to see a sliver of it in a day or two. It is nothing like our moon," Walthan responded in a low conversation as Avalon closed her eyes and recalled their white moon that shone with dazzling crystals every night that there was no cloud cover.

"And it's cold here," he stated the obvious. "We are on opposite cycles here. Summer at home, winter in the land of Cormicks. There are countless differences."

"Where there is good and light in Fontanasia, there is only evil and darkness left in Cormicks," the Guide whispered prophetically. Avalon was warming up in her blanket, but felt a chill from the Guide's words.

When they were silent for a few more minutes, Avalon asked, "What are everreds?"

"Don't you worry," Walthan told her. "Just don't sleep on the ground."

Walthan walked away before Avalon could ask any more questions. She remembered the sand eels and shuddered, pulling her blanket up tighter to make sure it was not touching the ground. It seemed that in this land, the very ground was not a safe place to stand, and it dawned on Avalon that she hadn't yet seen what the ground looked like here.

"Come down, Taggerty, I was just having fun with you," Walthan called. Avalon was absorbing the large warrior's sense of humor on this trip, and she could see why her father liked him. She could hear Taggerty coming down from the tree and then watched Walthan's large frame as he talked to Brick. She couldn't hear what they were saying, but the two men clasped wrists and Brick looked in Avalon's direction. Avalon guessed that Brick was to watch over her while Walthan was on guard, but as Brick approached, Taggerty slipped up onto the boulder with her.

"So, where did you get the jakkow?" Taggerty asked as he wrapped himself in his blanket.

"A Guide gave it to me for my birthday," Avalon answered. She wasn't sure what to make of Taggerty anymore, but Brick didn't seem to mind him sitting with her. "You knew what it was?" she asked.

Taggerty waited, leaving Avalon to speculate.

"You knew what it was," she stated again.

"I've heard of them."

"What have you heard?"

"That they are very rare."

Avalon waited for more, but that was all he would offer.

"We should rest." He rolled his back to her. Avalon stared up and tried to see the stars through the trees, but they had disappeared behind newly forming clouds.

They woke after only a few hours of sleep. It was dawn now, and Walthan had replaced Taggerty on the rock next to Avalon. She was well rested and quickly looked below the boulder in the light to catch a glimpse of what an everred might be, but there was nothing on the ground. "Thanks," Avalon motioned to the huge fur blanket that he must have placed on her in the night.

Walthan nodded and smiled. "Thank Taggerty."

Avalon bit her lip and removed the blanket, standing and stretching. The woods looked the same to her as the ones she had left behind in Fontanasia, but the large, green boulders that they had camped on looked out of place.

It was overcast, and Avalon wished they could have a fire and a proper breakfast. It would be a long two weeks surviving on the salty jerky that had been packed along with hard crust bread and dried fruit. Her stomach growled, and she wondered if they had enough to last the entire trip.

The Guide addressed her, "Come, Prince Avalon. We will search for something to eat." They had spent several days together on this journey, and yet Avalon didn't know any more about the Guide than she had when they'd started out. He rarely paid attention to anything but the forest, and the way he looked at her now made her feel anxious. She still didn't even know his proper name.

Taggerty climbed down from his lookout in a tree and followed them. Even though she was used to being treated like royalty, when she saw him shivering for lack of the blanket that he'd placed on her in the night, Avalon felt embarrassed.

They walked to a small cropping of bushes and Avalon watched the Guide who simply stared at the bushes without speaking. A few moments later, tiny white birds with red freckled wings descended on the bushes and pecked at small orange berries.

"They are the paiches, birds of life," the Guide whispered as he approached the bush. "There are many poisons here, but we can eat what the paiches eat." The little birds flew around them as they collected berries from the bushes to eat, and Avalon soon appreciated the innocence that the birds brought to this dark place. She and Taggerty knelt next to the Guide and collected the berries. It was a tedious task with few results, but Avalon didn't complain. They returned with the berries and placed them all together in a pile, and then Walthan's huge fingers split the cache into five tiny piles. They each ate in silence, Avalon glad that the berries offered a sweet taste.

They set out, and for the rest of the daylight hours, they walked very slowly and quietly, the Guide making them stop, look, and listen every hundred yards. No one spoke, and Avalon felt like they were moving in slow motion, but the time-consuming pace wasn't tiring and the cool daytime air was refreshing. Avalon wondered when the trees would break and tried to remember the map of Cormicks in an effort to prepare seeing her people's history for the first time. She was anxious and excited by the knowledge that she was in this foreign land, but she wasn't sure of what to expect of the mongrels that inhabited Cormicks. She held her chin up as fear of the Runners coursed through her.

Before sundown, they made it to the edge of the woods where the Guide stopped them again. He crouched down and stared up at three different ridges for a long time before pointing to the one on the left. "There, I know that one," he told Walthan. Walthan led as they scurried to the rocky range of hills and the Guide escorted them under a rock outcropping to sit. "We will camp here," he said.

"Sure is going to be a cold night," Brick said as he unpacked his blanket.

"No fire. It will attract attention," reminded the Guide ominously. This time he was talking to Brick. Avalon had noticed that the Guide had become more commanding since they had crossed over in the night. He was obviously not willing to chance anything.

They had traveled all day without seeing any people, and aside from the paiche birds, they saw no animals either. Avalon wondered just how close to the city Cormicks they were, and her question was answered immediately.

"Prince Avalon," Walthan beckoned her forward. She followed him, and they were led up the side of the ridge. The Guide's tall frame crouched and stepped even more deliberately as they approached the top. There were loose rocks mixed in with patches of grass, and Avalon stepped lightly, her breath coming fast from excitement. When they reached the peak, the three laid flat together just under the lip of the ridge, and then the Guide slowly stood and leaned forward. His head was perfectly still for a long time, and Avalon could see his piercing eyes scanning whatever lay below the other side. After a long time, he gestured Walthan with his hand, and Walthan did the same to Avalon. With a gulp and stunted breath, she stood gradually and looked over the top.

Beneath them lay Cormicks, a stone city in the near distance surrounded by the forest on three sides and an open expanse in front which led to three small ridges, one of which Avalon was crouching on now. Around the city, crude wall barriers had been built and destroyed and built again, and debris scattered the earth. Grime left by large, destructive fires painted all of the stone walls. It looked as though the attack on Hawkerness had just ended the week before, and the inhabitants milled about its dusty remains. It wasn't as evil looking to Avalon as the Guide had suggested. The city was dilapidated, worn down, and neglected. It was difficult to imagine that her ancestors had ever lived here, but the beauty of her home in Fontanasia was hard to see through.

They watched over the ridge as afternoon settled into dusk. Avalon looked for the sliver of moon Walthan had promised, but it was not there. Fires were coming up, strewn about the inner grounds of Cormicks.

"They have fire there," Avalon whispered, feeling the chill of the winter air creeping through her clothes.

"They are protected," Walthan answered matter of fact.

Once again, Avalon didn't understand. A million questions crept to the edge of her tongue, but she held, silently taking in every detail of Cormicks that she could.

They watched together for a while as the inhabitants went about their evening. Avalon took notice of the two smaller ridges off to the east. They were just shorter than the one she was perched on now. There was something strange about them; their dark and sharply shaped bumps gave the appearance of purposefully formed jagged edges even from this distance. They were small mountain ranges, but their silhouettes looked more like purposefully handcrafted fortresses. Avalon looked back to the fires in the distance, wishing she could sit beside one and warm her chilling bones.

Without warning, Walthan wrenched Avalon's neck as he tucked her head into his arms, shielding her from some unknown danger. She struggled to move, to be able to see, as the air came alive with a deafening cracking and ripping sound. It was the loudest lightning she had ever heard, and it sounded close enough to have been right on top of her, but Avalon never saw the flash of light. Her heart was struck with fear as she looked up at Walthan whose face was covered in shock. She pulled her head loose and tried to push away from his tree trunk hands, her attention turning her to the right where Walthan and the Guide were both staring. As she watched in awe, the earth shook apart and Avalon thought her eyes were playing tricks on her in the gray light as the two sharp edged ridges began to peel away from the earth.

"Move!" the Guide yelled.

Avalon's arm burst with pain when Walthan jerked her away from the ridge and yanked her down after him. They half ran, half fell down, and although the night was almost dark, Avalon heard another terrifying crack and watched in disbelief as one of the ridges tore itself from the ground. The sight was amazing and terrifying at the same time, and she felt a million needles poke at her skin as though alerting her entire body to the imminent danger upon them. She slid down the loose ground and tried to jet from rock to rock to steady her progress without tumbling forward. It was difficult going because her attention was split between her escape and the incredible ridges that were climbing alive in front of her eyes. She watched in disbelief as each rising heap of rock peeled apart and became three massive black, two legged towers which, impossibly, stood up and began to stomp toward them.

The giant rock legs with no torso bore down on them covering the distance in seconds as their massive stump legs crushed the ground in huge steps. At first they looked like two legged beasts with no real body, but as they closed in Avalon could see a large hump on the back that resembled a sort of face, like the rear legs of a cricket walking backward with a small amount of body in between as an afterthought. The legs and humps were rippled and scarred as though they were the remains of something that continuously exploded. And the forms didn't merely walk; they morphed from solid rock into thousands of moving rock pieces and seemed to ooze forward.

She was sliding and rolling in panic now, Walthan steadying her fall with his until they reached the bottom. Avalon jumped under the rock outcropping where they had left their belongings. She felt the slow, crushing cadence of the beasts approaching, and menacing black powder began to billow at her feet. The Guide pressed his body as close as he could to the crevice, and the rest of the group followed suit. Brick and Taggerty were standing close to the edge of cover and staring at each other in what Avalon mistook as wonder as to what was upon them. The beasts roar was more violent than that of a thousand frenzied pigs and more deafening than when they had first ripped out of the ground, and Avalon's heart pounded as her will shuddered. She clamped her hands over her ears and wished she could be back in the ravine with the sand eels.

Amidst the terrifying onslaught of noise combined with the choking black dust, the Guide pulled himself away from the wall and moved to the blankets. He picked up a long piece of burnt rope and looked at Brick quizzically. He didn't move to safety as the beasts began to smash the rocks over the outcropping. The ground rumbled and shook, and Avalon looked to Walthan for comfort, but the warrior was watching the Guide intently.

"It was Taggerty!" Brick pointed at the young soldier. Avalon now read their faces of fury and understood that they must have been in the middle of a standoff when the beasts had awoken.

"I tried to stop him, but he said that he was too cold and it would do no harm to have a fire," Brick yelled over the onslaught of noise.

"That's not true!" yelled Taggerty, the piercing slits of his green eyes aimed at Brick.

Walthan stepped forward and coiled his hands, his anger apparent on his reddening cheeks. He made to punch Taggerty in the face for defying the rules and threatening all of their lives by lighting the fire, but at the same moment he had stepped away from her, the outcropping gave way and large pieces of rock started falling down around Avalon.

Taggerty yelled, "Prince Avalon!" But she was gone.

Chapter 10
Betrayed By Fire

Rocks continued to rain down on them as the charcoal beasts raged over the protective ridge. They would all be killed if nothing was done. Walthan moved quickest and in a frenzy, he heaved at the pile of rock that covered Avalon. It was almost impossible to see as night settled over the rock outcropping. He blamed himself. He shouldn't have let his temper dictate his actions, and he should never have left Prince Avalon to be pulverized and buried under the rock. The thick, black dust sloughing from the moving mountain creatures saturated the air and made them all cough. Their eyes burned as they tugged at the rocks, pulling their way to the bottom of the pile. To Walthan's immense relief, Avalon was alive and still conscious. She suffered a few lumps and scrapes, but had managed to duck into a crevice before most of the rocks had fallen where she was standing.

Walthan grabbed Avalon's shoulders and looked her over. Even with the charcoal beasts continuing their stomping and smashing, he felt relief.

"They saw the fire, and they know where there is fire, there is man," said the Guide.

"They're moving away," Brick pressed.

"They are searching. They will not give up," the Guide stated ominously.

Walthan placed Avalon directly behind him but kept a hand on her wrist, not trusting the ridge's stability. He turned toward Taggerty. "You!" he accused.

"I didn't do this!" Taggerty took a few steps backwards to stay out of Walthan's reach. He looked to Avalon, then the Guide, and before anyone could make another move, Taggerty snatched the remainder of the burnt rope from the Guide's hand. He gave a quick look to Avalon again, and her heart leapt into her throat. Taggerty steeled his jaw and ran out from under the safety of what was left of the rock outcropping. Avalon squinted through burning eyes as Taggerty lit a match and caught fire to the rope. The air around him ate the flame and the black dust cracked and crunched like a million fireworks. Avalon immediately felt the ground shake as the charcoal beasts sensed the fire and returned their attention to the rock outcropping. Taggerty held the burning rope above his head leaving a trail of fire and smoke in the dark air as he ran toward the forest in retreat.

Avalon yelled, "Taggerty!" but Walthan shushed her. She had disliked Taggerty from when they were first introduced at the festival tournament, but no one deserved to be crushed to death by those mountainous animals.

"He'll be lucky to make the forest," Brick said over the pounding. The charcoal beasts were massive, and she could make out their awkward two legged frames as they moved away. Their bodies oozed rocks forward each step, like their limbs were made of thousands of rock snakes. Taggerty's flame trailed into the woods, and then it was gone. She felt the chills on her spine again as she wondered how Jackie was fairing on his own in this strange land, if he was still alive.

"We must leave." The Guide gave a last look back, turned in the opposite direction, and led them around the base of the ridge and into the darkness.

"Those were the everreds?" asked Avalon, her eyes still watering from the black powder.

"No," Walthan replied. "Anthracites. They despise fire. They could stomp out small fires if they had to, but large fires will destroy them, so they don't allow uncontrolled fire to burn."

Avalon remembered her father mentioning the Anthracites as allies when he was telling her about her people's history. He had said that the Runners must have made them allies because there is no way to defeat the Anthracites, and that was a big reason her ancestors lost Hawkerness to the Runners. She had assumed then that Anthracites were another people, and Avalon wondered how the rock ridges could come alive into thinking beasts.

"Isn't someone going to look for Taggerty?"

"It's way too dark to see anything, and we can't chance it," the Guide answered.

Walthan added, "Besides, you saw the Anthracites. Taggerty must be dead by now." He didn't trust the young soldier, but the warrior said this with no amount of pleasure.

A lump hung in Avalon's throat. A part of her regretted that their acquaintance was so short, and another part was angry with Taggerty for not following the rules. He had seemed to know what he was doing for most of this trip, and she was surprised that he would make such a deadly mistake as to light a fire when they were all strictly told not to.

They wandered in the darkness for a while; the only sound their slow, crunching steps. The Guide led them up a long, easy hill, and they ended up on a ledge where they could again look out over Cormicks while under the cover of thorny shrubs. Avalon could see from this vantage point that they had come around to the very opposite side of the city and were even closer to the city wall. She was struck now as to the city's defensive disadvantage being built near so many ranges. She could fully appreciate Fontanasia's location and understood why her ancestors had chosen to build a city next to a lake and into the side of a mountain. Once she was burrowed under the prickly bushes, she thought strategy until Walthan told her to rest, and she didn't argue.

It was afternoon before she woke. The toll of the previous night had left her with a headache and sore limbs, but her adrenaline soon canceled out any negative feelings when she heard strange voices. She had slept like a rock and luckily didn't have to untangle her clothes from the low, thorny shrubs she had been sleeping under. She crawled forward next to Walthan to watch the scene below. They listened closely as grimy people went about their menial tasks. They spoke her language very crudely, and Avalon could barely understand them. She got a good look in the daylight and could see shanty tents meant as living spaces lined up along muddy walkways. They lived scantily, dirt painting most of their clothing and skin as they dragged their feet like dirty dishrags being pulled about the garbage-strewn enclosure. They were a poor and hungry people.

"Why do they stay here? They look miserable," she whispered to Walthan who looked on with heavy eyes because he hadn't slept in over a day.

Avalon had never seen anyone live this poorly. Granted she was a prince and lived in a castle, still she had never seen anyone in her city in squalor conditions, and she couldn't understand why someone would simply accept living this way.

"Most people live what their parents live and never try to make a better life," Brick challenged. "They live what they know, and if this putrid poverty is all they have been exposed to, how could they dream that there is something better?"

"That is ridiculous," Avalon whispered.

"You have a young mind Prince Avalon, full of ideals. You haven't lived long enough to understand where the black and white turns to gray." Brick turned his attention back to the people on the ground.

"Brick has something there," Walthan agreed. Avalon held her tongue and her temper as she struggled to understand that foul living conditions for these people was normal. The Runners were ignorant, but did that mean they should be left in the dirt? Avalon took a deep breath and looked sideways at Walthan who eyed the scene with calculation. She realized that although it was generations before her time, the Runners did murder her people, and Brick and Walthan must have wanted all Runners buried to ensure the safety of Fontanasia. That thought returned Avalon to the reason they took this trip in the first place.

The three men and Avalon took turns carrying out the reconnaissance of Cormicks. At night, wrapped in blankets to ward off the chill, they shared the meat jerky and dried bread. Fires dotted the ground again and they watched the locals prepare cooked meals of water and greens with the occasional bird or rodent mixed in. They would take breaks away from their small camp one at a time to stretch their legs. Avalon was ready for her turn, but Brick had been gone for a long time. When he returned, Avalon moved over so the soldier could take his spot to look over the ridge. She watched the fires closely and tried to pull their heat into her bones to rid the constant chill she felt seeping through her skin. She observed the sky and studied the stars, looking for the same constellations that she would see in Fontanasia, but none were there.

She watched her breath getting thicker as the night got colder. Avalon was ready to settle in for sleep when, suddenly, Walthan and the Guide both tensed. All Avalon could hear was the chatter below, but the Guide pushed his body from under the thorny bushes and jumped to his feet. He frantically looked from Avalon to Brick. The night air between them was dark, but Avalon read panic on his face.

"No, no, no!" the Guide's voice shuddered prophetically. Then he looked at Walthan, and terrified Avalon when he whispered, "Run."

Avalon turned to Walthan and then back to where the Guide had been standing, but he had already disappeared. She threw her blankets off, but before Walthan could take her up and run, Avalon could hear the clatter of metal and rumble of footsteps. She couldn't see clearly in the pitch black, but men were already upon them with swords and spears. Walthan grabbed her arm and moved quickly to the left, but more soldiers were moving up the edge of the ridge.

"Follow me!" he commanded as he drew his sword and ran along the thickets. The soldiers saw their prey in the dark and made for Walthan. He stepped forward into the fray and fought fiercely, and his craft was no match for the first wave of fighters.

Avalon had never seen his feet and sword move so quickly as he cut down one after the next. Avalon had backed against the mass of thorny bushes. She drew her sword to defend against the few Runners who did get past Walthan, and her years of practice paid off. She slayed three easily, and she and Walthan pushed forward next to the thicket, Walthan stabbing and backhanding attackers, some falling where they stood, others careening into the thorns or over the edge of the ravine. Avalon fought at his back as the center force filled in behind them. She stood at the ready and waved her sword to all sides, but the mass of attackers held back, and Avalon could see that they were not out for blood.

Soon a second wave of larger, more skilled warriors was upon them, and there were too many to fight. They advanced on Walthan in unison, and he backed up closer to Avalon. Then the mass of men sprang forward at the same time Walthan's sword arced in a clean slice from the thicket to his left around to Avalon's right. His massive shoulder held his sword out and blocked Avalon from the advancing force. Walthan had cut the first row down, and Avalon felt a moment of hope, but twice as many soldiers stepped forward this time. They advanced as one, ready for his sword, and soon they had overwhelmed the huge warrior. They beat Walthan down, separating him from Avalon and smothering his final attempts for freedom. Avalon looked for Brick in the chaos, but she couldn't find him. The soldiers threw her on the ground and surrounded her, swords up, but palms out like they were trying to tame a lion that they didn't want to hurt. A man on her left stepped in and Avalon turned to defend herself, but she caught the solid hilt of a sword in the back of her head and was knocked into a place that was darker than that very night.

Chapter 11
The Conquerors

When Avalon came to, she didn't open her eyes right away. There was a beating pain in her head, and she listened to the churning sound of her pulse grating in her ears. When the only other sound she heard was the deep breathing that she came to recognize as Walthan's, she slowly opened her eyes. Avalon sat up and immediately regretted it. Her entire body ached, and she had to take a moment to move her joints to make sure nothing was broken. She cleared her head and looked around, trying to adjust her eyes to the darkness. She and Walthan had been left crumpled on the dirt floor in a cell of rock with only a tiny, barred window at the top of one wall.

Avalon leaned forward and slid her body over to Walthan who was beaten and bloody. She decided to let him sleep as long as he could knowing that if her body ached this much, his pain would be excruciating. She stood slowly and stretched trying to reach the bars well over her head, but it was no use. Unable to look out the window, Avalon had to settle with the knowledge that she could see light coming in and so she knew it wasn't night anymore.

"Where's Brick?" Walthan managed to say through his swollen face. Avalon was relieved.

"He's not here." She moved to Walthan's side and knelt over him, gasping when she saw his face. It had looked very bad when he was asleep, but Avalon's heart sank as he tried to open his eyes and move his mouth. He tried to play it off with a forced smile.

"I'm fine, Avalon. It's just my age catching up to me." Walthan actually chuckled to himself and Avalon gulped back her tears. "I'll be up in a minute."

She watched him crack his bruised knuckles, which were each swollen the size of Avalon's wrists. He was hurt but tried to hide his pain as he cringed silently with each movement. When he was upright, he checked his limbs and none seemed to be broken nor dislocated, although he had many welts built up on his head, arms, and legs where he had been beaten down. He also had some small cuts and scratches, but the fact that he was not bleeding from any severe open wounds was a testament to his ability as a fighter. Walthan smiled at Avalon, who was scared, and she wondered what there was to smile about.

"Well, we're alive and healthy," he told her as though he'd read her mind. "And that's a start."

"I guess so," Avalon hesitated. She looked around the tiny space, and she found herself ridiculously worried that Walthan would soon find out that she was a girl.

"How did they find us?" she asked as a distraction to her own thoughts. "We didn't light any fires or make any noise, and yet they seemed to come directly to us."

"I was wondering that myself," Walthan told her. He grimaced as he rubbed out some of the knots on his head. When he noticed her watching, he shot her another smile. Avalon knew that he was putting on a strong front for her, and as much as she didn't like to be patronized as the prince, Walthan's ability to seem nonchalant at this moment gave her hope.

"Do you think Taggerty was captured and gave our position away?" Avalon asked.

"No, I don't see how. He was running with fire, and the Anthracite's wouldn't have stopped to ask questions. And he's never been here before, so there's no way that he would have known where exactly we were headed."

Avalon tried in her mind to invent some way that would have had allowed Taggerty to escape, but the charcoal beasts were too big and strong, and the presence of fire pushed them over the edge. Taggerty had drawn them all to him in one heroic and reckless gesture. "Do they talk?"

"I don't know," Walthan pondered. "In a way, I guess. They're controlled by something in this castle, so they know how to communicate."

This surprised Avalon. "What controls them?"

"I don't know. Someone or something tells them what to do, and they do it. Maybe your father knows."

This intrigued her, communicating with someone or something that spoke a completely different sort of language. It would be like communicating with an animal but beyond mere gestures, and the thought fascinated her. She needed to know how to communicate with the Anthracites, and Avalon would question her father when they returned home. *If we return home*, she thought. She tried not to let the doom and gloom in, but it seeped into her through the dirt floor and tiny barred window.

"He who controls the Anthracites can control all of this land," Walthan thought aloud as he plotted battle strategy. "That's how our people lost this city, they lost control of the Anthracites, and it was no contest after that."

Avalon recalled the rubble of stones around the outer wall and wondered how many times the Anthracites had pulverized the castle in the past. The small cell brought her thoughts back to their present situation.

"So how did the Runners find us?" Avalon asked again. *And why didn't they kill us*, she wondered.

Walthan nodded his head slowly and became more certain of the conclusion he had been silently drawing. "I must admit, Avalon, it's very disturbing to me that someone knew we were here, and exactly where we were at that. In more than two hundred years, no one on this detail has ever been captured. No one has even been detected. This is very bad."

Avalon went two full days with no water and only a small bit of salted jerky to curb her growling stomach. She spent hours on end replaying in her mind the path to Cormicks and their capture, but inevitably her thoughts would move to Taggerty. She felt bad that she had disliked him so much without even really getting to know him, but she was resolved in that she wouldn't have liked him any better if he were here. She was pretty sure of that, but the fact that he died made her feel bad about it now. She spent hours deliberating a way to live her life liking everyone just to not feel this bad again. Was this the gray area that Brick and Walthan had talked about? Was it being resolved to a position one minute, and then caving in the next to alleviate the pain one felt in the center of their chest?

They slept in shifts and had plenty of time to talk. There was a shallow drain that ran across the back wall, and when Walthan was asleep, Avalon would crouch down and relieve herself. The lack of food and water depleted her remaining energy but also helped her keep her secret. Between thinking about Taggerty and the Anthracites, Avalon considered Brick and the Guide's fates and wondered if anyone had made it out. She hoped that they weren't trapped in this horrible place. Someone would need to warn her father. They heard wailing somewhere in the dungeons, but Walthan promised Avalon that it was neither Brick nor the Guide.

During daylight once, when he caught her looking at a large black scar on the far cell wall, Walthan had explained to Avalon that the everreds would have done that. He said they were tiny blood spiders that swarmed underground; a few on the skin was not a problem, but they were drawn to blood, and a swarm of them would suck the blood out and then eat the flesh to the bone. He told her that they were orange with a lot of legs, but miniscule and hard to see until it was too late. It was easier to see the swarm, he'd said, but then if you did, that was probably the last thing you were going to see. Then he stopped himself, but Avalon's imagination was already off and running. She wondered how a miniscule spider could leave such a huge, black mark on the wall. Every insect startled Avalon now that she knew what to look for, and although nothing entered their cell fitting that description on her watch, she spent hours feeling cooties up her back and frantically brushing her skin off at the slightest tickle.

Walthan's body was stiff, but he seemed relaxed in his surroundings. He spent time each day stretching his muscles and made Avalon do the same. She tried to copy his moves, but it was difficult because his massive frame took up almost the entire cell when he was in motion. He would do pushups, jumping jacks with his right arm only because his left arm was injured, and side arm stands on the one good side, whistling to himself all the while. They had rationed Walthan's meat jerky, and the lack of food and water made them breath heavily, but Walthan kept on her to continue. Avalon was anxious, and although the exercise took her mind off of their situation for a little while, there was plenty of quiet time to worry about whether they would leave this place alive. Avalon was able to guard her secret while Walthan was sleeping, although she wondered if it even mattered anymore.

On the fourth night of their capture, Walthan's arm had healed enough for him to boost Avalon onto his shoulders so she could try to look out the tiny window positioned in the top corner of their cell. The room was two times taller than it was wide, and when she still couldn't see out, Walthan grabbed her ankles and lifted her straight up over his head. She reached the bars and heaved herself up for as long as she could hold her weight. The window met the ground outside, making their cell completely underground, knowledge that made her more worried that the everreds would come in through the walls. Walthan asked if she could see the moon. Avalon pressed her face against the bars as hard as she could to get a look at the sky, and there it was: a wide sliver of white with a black ring around, hanging in the clouds.

"I think we have six days to the full moon," Walthan told her. As she lowered down to his shoulders and climbed down, her hope sank further. Their bodies were wasting away from the lack of food and water, and Avalon knew there was no way they would get out of this cell much less make it back to Fontanasia.

Depression took Avalon, and she lay on the floor in a heap not caring what happened anymore. It felt as though a solid pool of darkness had taken her chest hostage, and she allowed herself to swim in it without holding her breath. Walthan talked to her, but she couldn't understand what he was saying. It was over, any breath now would be her last, and she would not have a care in the world.

Avalon was unsure how much time had passed when a movement outside their cell door startled her, and Walthan rose quickly, stepping in front of Avalon. The door creaked and swung open slowly exposing three husky and fully tattooed men.

"Give us the little one," a menacing chain-clad guard demanded. He was big, but not as big as Walthan, and the other two guards leaned forward in warning as every muscle in Walthan's body tensed, ready to fight another army.

"We can take him now, unharmed, or I can have my men beat you again, and then beat him too. Your choice." The guard tried to smile, but Avalon focused on the hundreds of scars showing on the waste of his exposed flesh. She wondered if he was human after all. Weighing her options, she found that there were none. Their strength was depleted and there was no other way out but the door. She decided to take her chances.

"It's all right." She touched Walthan's massive arm and squeezed past. Walthan grabbed Avalon's shoulder. He didn't want to chance Avalon getting hurt, but he couldn't turn his Prince over to these ingrates either. With his ability to take care of his charge waning, Walthan's pride was injured. He pumped his arms and stepped forward, but Avalon placed her hands on his to release his grip, and the guards closed around her. The cell was locked behind them leaving Walthan powerlessly locked inside.

The burly guards escorted Avalon up a long ramp, their chain clad bodies jingling in time with their steps. Avalon couldn't help but find the irony in the fact that she was their prisoner, but they wore the chains. They went through two hefty locked doors and up a winding flight of stairs. Her body was wasted from lack of water, and she couldn't walk as fast as they did. They pushed her with the flat of their wide paddle like spears intending to move her along and intimidate her. It worked. Avalon kept her outward composure, but she was more scared now than she'd ever been in her life. She had felt strong when she had told Walthan to let her go with the guards, but now her entire frame was turning soft like jelly, and her teeth had almost started to chatter. Up and up the stairs they went. Her stomach felt as hard as a rock with butterflies still able to fly around inside, and she licked her lips several times to try to get her voice ready. Avalon had never felt so alone and unprotected before. She thought of Fontanasia and of Counselor Glenn and realized that her fear of him was a child to this massive growing fear of Cormicks, and of the unknown.

She inhaled short, stunted breaths as they entered a large hall that was built of gray stone on every side and flat stone on the floor and roof. Everything in this room made her nervous: the staring tattooed faces, the indistinguishable grunting of the dirty Runners, the metal hooks that hung down from the ceiling in places. This great hall must have been the highlight of the castle, yet it somehow emitted a shoddy quality. Avalon wondered if her people had even built this room, as it was not near the class of the Hall of Kings in Fontanasia. The fact that she was alone and unarmed in a foreign land scared her the most, but at least the rock room meant that she could forget the everreds for the moment.

Avalon tried to keep her breathing level and her shoulders back. She could see that there were clearly two different kind of people here. She had already noticed the larger, heavily tattooed men. Most of them looked exactly like the two guards who continued to paddle her in the back and the head as she tried to keep up. This burly sort left most of their muscle exposed, to frighten, no doubt. And now Avalon noticed slighter, sharper men who wore clean robes and held an air of ownership upon everything they viewed. And they were looking at her now.

She made herself look everyone in the eye, but only the cleaner, smaller men looked directly back at her. The slighter ones were each surrounded by some of the huge beasts of men, and Avalon saw that each of the smaller men had their own pack of bodyguards. As she tried to watch the men around her, she thought she could discern separate clans, and Avalon wondered about the hierarchy in this place. If they all had their own guards, then they probably needed protection from each other. She thought it ironic that although the burly tattooed brutes could have crushed the smaller men with their bare hands, they seemed afraid of the white robed men they protected. It reminded Avalon of mistreated dogs: beaten and neglected and yet starving for appreciation.

The guards stopped in front of a large stone platform, and her question of hierarchy was immediately answered. The whispering in the room was followed by a deafening silence as Avalon was placed in front of a large, hand carved, rock throne. The man who sat upon it was huge, with clever eyes that squinted but never seemed to blink.

"I ask you for our release," Avalon said loudly. She could hear breath being sucked in all around the room and knew that she had done something wrong.

"You will speak only when spoken to," she heard as one of the guards jabbed the blunt end of his spear into her gut. Avalon had miscalculated, and she doubled over in pain. She was royalty and, except when addressing her father, she always spoke first. But here, this monarch was royalty, and she was to wait for him. She heard laughter and then silence as she sucked in air and tried to stand up straight again.

The monarch watched her for a few minutes and then stood. He was huge, almost as big a man as Walthan was. He was clean, but the black tattoos on his face and arms made him look grimy. He stepped down from the platform and the flick of his hand caused the guards to retreat. The massive man looked into her eyes, and she held her breath but did not look away. He circled her then, and she got chills up and down her spine, but she held the shudder still.

"Who could possibly dare to speak to me, to speak before I have spoken?" he asked rhetorically as he paced the floor behind her. Her silence pleased him.

"Although, who but royalty dare address royalty?" he asked slyly. This statement confused Avalon as the monarch took the moment to circle around in front of her. She sensed his flare for an audience, and she waited.

"Tell me, Prince Avalon," he spat. "Tell me about your kingdom."

When she heard this stranger speak her name, an alarm sounded in Avalon's head and a blush ran into her cheeks. Her ears burned, and she held her shoulders down and breathed deeply trying to remove the color from her face without giving away her discomfort, but she was already given away. In these past centuries, no one from Cormicks had crossed over into Fontanasia. So how could he have known her name? These were the destroyers of her ancestor's home, destroyers of Hawkerness, and destroyers of her heritage. If they had known the location, they would surely already have wreaked havoc over Fontanasia.

"I don't know what you mean," was all Avalon could think to say.

"I hope you do," the monarch quipped. "The only reason you are still alive is because you are royalty, and you shall be treated accordingly." When Avalon remained silent, he went on.

"Tell me about Fontanasia, young man. Tell me about the rolling hills, the white mountain, the rolling sea, and tell me about all of its happy residents." He was mocking her, and she was trying not to listen, but her face reddened again when she thought of her people. Confused and terrified, Avalon's head was spinning. She couldn't think of any reason this bloodthirsty people would have never attacked if they knew so much, and the monarch was not guessing right now, which meant someone had told him about Fontanasia.

"I still don't know what you mean," Avalon shrugged bravely.

"No matter. I am sure that I can strike a deal with the king to ally with me and for Fontanasia to remain under my control, indefinitely. I think I would like it there."

The mention of her father incensed Avalon. "My father will never call you an ally!"

The hall built with laughter again: first the monarch and his white robes, and then their dogs all barking at Avalon with contempt. The monarch let it play out as he circled Avalon, savoring every moment he was allowed to toy with his captive. Avalon's hands instinctively balled into fists.

When the laughter subsided, the monarch stepped close enough for Avalon to inhale his repulsive burnt toast scent. He smiled coyly at her before speaking, "King Glenn will surely consider it." His words stunned Avalon.

"We overran this castle hundreds of years ago. We killed all of its inhabitants. Some tried to escape into the woods, but we hunted them down and slaughtered them. Imagine my surprise after all this time, to find that the job is not done."

Her fear pushed forward as tears, but Avalon gulped them back when the monarch stopped pacing and looked directly at her, his face inches from hers.

"I am more reasonable than my predecessors. I am offering a kind of peace. If you take the knee and vow allegiance, we will spare your people. Most of them, anyway." The monarch's laughter was contagious and the hall erupted once more.

She managed to keep her temper and spoke in a whisper. "You are lying."

"Care to explain?" He was looking at her with an evil smirk, but she could tell that he was not speaking to her.

Avalon turned on her heel and the guards closed in, but they didn't strike her. The monarch flicked his hand again and they retreated a few steps leaving Avalon to look upon Brick. She was at once filled with joy to see him alive, but her heart sank as her eyes took him in. He was badly bruised and swollen on the right side of his face, but he stood upright. She could see the beginning of a tattoo drawn on his left cheek that, together with the swelling on his right, made him look deformed. Brick stepped forward with a limp. She took a step toward him, but one of the guards lashed his flat spear into her stomach and batted her to the ground.

Avalon needed to get to Brick, to ask him what had happened to him, but as she sucked in her breath, she realized that he had been the one to give up their secret. Avalon stood up and looked over Brick's battered body, wondering if she would have been able to endure torture without saying anything, and she empathized. Still, he had given up Fontanasia and named Counselor Glenn as king. She speculated that he might have been protecting her father, but when she looked right at him, he stared through her, and Avalon's hope sank out of her. She could see now that she and Walthan would never be released.

Brick was uncomfortable as he looked around at everyone in the room. Avalon kept the bile from rising in her stomach and was smart enough to keep poised, concentrating only on Brick and the monarch. The rest mattered little at this point. They would do what the monarch told them to.

"The prince denies what you have told me," the monarch berated Brick.

"What I say is true!" the wounded soldier beckoned. "The king of Fontanasia is seeking an alliance with Cormicks."

"Liar!" Avalon yelled.

"It's true!" Brick yelled back, taking several steps closer to her. "By now Counselor Glenn has fulfilled his plans to kill the king and has found a way to take Fontanasia."

"You are a liar!" Avalon could not stay level headed anymore. She lost all composure at the mention of her father's death and stepped toward Brick to strike him but was cut down by the monarch's guard. Curled on the floor, she gasped for air, but was still able to push some words out. "Hawker would never allow this treason!"

She squinted up and saw Brick's mouth twitch, and through her anger and the puffed swelling on his face, she could swear that she saw him smile. Now Brick looked straight at Avalon and said gravely, "For some the road is long, but the winds wind it in the right direction. I am sure Counselor Glenn has already aligned himself with Hawker."

Avalon didn't understand what Brick was saying. She was quite sure that he was delirious. Tears waited in her throat, but Avalon swallowed them back as she stood erect. She wondered if any of Brick's words could be true, and needed to get back to Fontanasia now. But the next full moon was days away, and she couldn't even find a way out of her cell much less back across the elbagrass to the pond. She turned away from Brick.

"Sir," she beckoned the monarch putting a smile on his lips, "I don't know what lies this man has been telling you, but he knows nothing and is only trying to buy his own freedom."

"And how will you buy your freedom if you have nothing to offer?" the monarch responded. He tipped his head and the four guards immediately converged on Avalon, bruising her where they grabbed her arms tightly. They pulled her off of her feet and let her hang by her arms as the monarch approached.

He stared into Avalon's eyes. "You should worry less about your kingdom, and more about your own life." He had given her something to deliberate, and she didn't see the knife until it was almost too late. The monarch slipped back, and Brick came in at her from around the guards who held her tightly in the air. His arm was at the ready and the blade flashed upward. Adrenaline ripped through her body, and Avalon curled up her legs and kicked out as hard as she could, landing both of her feet in Brick's already swollen face. They both screamed, Brick falling back onto the floor, and Avalon jolting back to her suspended position.

The monarch's laughter led the crowd in a deafening frenzy. Avalon was surprised to see Brick writhing on the floor, her kick reigniting the pain from the beatings he had taken and the tattoos they had been inking on his face. She tried to think of something clever to say, something that would buy her time to make a plan of escape. But her head was filled with rage and hopelessness, and all words and common sense had gone before the guards had taken one step. They carried her from the hall, the roar following them back down to the dungeon. The soldiers tossed Avalon into her cell and she slid across the dirt floor. Walthan stuck his chest out at the guards who grunted as they relocked the door. Then he was beside her in a moment.

"I'm fine. I'm fine," she told him. "They didn't hurt me."

"They didn't hurt you!" Walthan exclaimed. "Is that someone else's blood on your pants?" Avalon looked down and noticed a growing red stain near the upper thigh on her left leg, and the moment her eyes saw it, the sharp pain jarred her. Walthan moved in and grabbed Avalon's pants, ready to tear them open at the top so he could look at the wound. Avalon slid back, shocked, the deep pain replaced with fear.

"Don't touch me," Avalon cried. Then she regrouped and tried to sit up. "I am royalty, Walthan." She felt horrible talking down to him, but she was terrified knowing that if he removed her pants, he would surely find out that she was a girl. She gulped back the lump in her throat and clenched her teeth to fight the growing pain. She could feel warm blood oozing down her leg.

"Prince Avalon," Walthan addressed her, his eyes not leaving her bloody pants. "I mean no disrespect, but we need to take a look at your wound and try to clean it as best we can."

"I'll be fine," Avalon said, holding her hand out in front of her. She was frantic, her eyes wide, looking around for an escape. He couldn't remove her pants to look at her leg. Then he would know. Avalon wished that Myra was here, she had tended to Avalon's small injuries over the years, and she had kept the secret.

Avalon held her leg propped out to the side, and when she looked down, she could tell that the cut went around the inside of her thigh to the bottom. The blood soaked her pants to the knee, and Avalon could see that the wound would need to be looked at. She met Walthan's eyes, the large warrior crouched at the ready, waiting for her hand to fall so he could help his Prince.

"It's fine," Avalon said through grit teeth, enormously self-conscious in this moment. But when she slid her leg over to close her knees together, the pain ripped through her, and Avalon thought she might throw up. Then Walthan's face crumpled into oblivion, and Avalon blacked out.

Chapter 12
Unveiled

There was no light when Avalon opened her eyes, and she took a few moments to focus in the dark before sitting up. She reached down and felt a lump of cloth over the inside of her thigh. The pain in her leg was gone, and Avalon bent at the knee easily. She sighed in relief only to immediately tense. He was sitting across from her, staring through the darkness. She sat still and looked back at him trying to pose carelessly, but she knew that a cover up was too late.

"My pardons, Prince Avalon, but I couldn't just leave you there to bleed out, what with the everreds..." Walthan trailed off. "I salvaged your pants, don't ask how, but your long pants had to go."

His words were apologetic, and now she knew that he had removed both pairs of pants, bandaged her wound, and redressed her in the outer pants. He knew. Avalon tried to remain casual, but her teeth were clenched and her heart pounded so loudly that she wanted to put her hands on her chest to keep him from hearing. He looked at her expectantly, but she couldn't find her words.

"I can't believe I didn't see sooner," Walthan mumbled as he continued to study Avalon's face.

Avalon couldn't meet his eyes anymore so she watched the floor but didn't answer. For once, she was thankful for the darkness because it kept Walthan from seeing the multitude of reds that must have been dancing in her cheeks. Her face was on fire now, burning the fourteen years of lies off and exposing Avalon for whom she was. Avalon expected outrage, curses, and damnation, but she received none of this from Walthan.

"Yes, I see," Walthan stated conclusively. Avalon heard the smile in his voice. He stood upright, towering over Avalon and shaking his head while she continued to squirm. Walthan reached his enormous hands out and took Avalon gently by the arms. He lifted her tenderly to her feet and squared her chin up to his gaze, and then lightly squeezed her shoulders. "I see," he concluded.

Avalon didn't want to know what he might be seeing. She didn't want to know what came next. She understood that he now saw a girl standing in her shoes, but she knew in her heart that she was a boy. She knew it in all of her upbringing, in all of her years of training, and in her title, Prince Avalon Hall of Fontanasia.

"I'll tell you one thing," Walthan laughed, "that explains all the crying."

"I don't know what you mean," Avalon's voice faltered.

"You're a girl!" he bellowed and then shushed himself before repeating in a whisper, "you're a girl." One side of Walthan's mouth rose up in amazement as the rest of his mouth fell agape. He was seeing Avalon truly for the first time.

"Boys cry too!" Avalon protested stubbornly. But the ruse was over, and there was no reason to lie to Walthan any longer. He had served her father, and would give his life this very moment if hers were in danger. If they were to die together, she owed him the truth.

"Yes," Walthan said, still staring at Avalon in amazement. "Boys cry too. But, you are not a boy."

She felt the energy wash through her as chills crept up Avalon's spine and over her head, as though an invisible veil was being lifted from her entire body. Walthan let her arms go and stepped away from Avalon, his huge frame kneeling gracefully in the darkness. Then he bowed his head.

Tears began streaming from Avalon's eyes. She could see in the shadows that Walthan had knelt and bowed before her, even though he knew that she was not a prince, and not a true heir to the throne. She had played this moment in her mind thousands of times, and she thought that if it ever came, if anyone had ever revealed her secret, she would feel panic and anger against them for knowing. Maybe it was her circumstances now, locked away in a dungeon on the other side of the world, not knowing if she was ever going home, not knowing if she would have a father to go home to, that brought relief in Walthan's discovery. Avalon took a deep breath in, tasting the tears that continued down her face, and told him the truth at last.

"No," she whispered, "I am not a boy." The secret she had guarded so carefully for fourteen years was lifted from her like a heavy weight into thin air. If she died here in Cormicks, it would be as a prince, but at least she had been afforded this final confession to clear her conscience. Avalon straightened up proudly and pulled her shirt taught. "Think what you will," she said defensively in her best male voice.

"I think you will make a wonderful king someday, Prince Avalon." Walthan's head was still lowered, and Avalon had to fight back more tears. He had accepted her as a competent heir to the throne no matter her gender. He had accepted her fully, and the gesture was not lost on Avalon. Aside from her father, Walthan was the strongest man she knew, and the fact that he might follow her without question, the fact that this future she had prepared for was exactly what was meant to be carved out for her, was exhilarating.

"Oh, get up!" She stepped forward and pulled on his shirt, but his huge frame did not move.

"I'm sure that King Birch is fine," Walthan said undecidedly. Avalon watched his eyebrows twitch, and she could see him calculating something.

"Stand up," Avalon said, impatiently this time. She needed his strength more than ever in this moment. He obeyed her this time.

"It's unbelievable," Walthan sighed.

"But looking back I can see the necessity, because I have never trusted Counselor Glenn, and now it seems King Birch didn't trust him either."

"It didn't start out as a plan or anything," Avalon backpedaled in defense of her father. "Myra George told my mother that I was a boy because she was dying, and then the lie swept out of control, and then it was too late to tell the truth."

Walthan was slowly and unconsciously nodding his head, but at least he was able to do so with his mouth closed now. "And that is the real reason your father named you S. Avalon Hall, after Queen Samantha," Walthan concluded. "Because as a girl your proper name would be Samantha."

"My mother named me Avalon, not my father," she said defensively.

"Yes, of course, Prince Avalon. I meant no disrespect."

Avalon was sorry for the comment, but she did not apologize. Walthan was pulling all of the pieces together and Avalon was sure he would replay all of their time together, searching for clues that should have told him earlier.

"And that is why King Birch lectured me on your need for privacy before we left for Cormicks," he stated in relief, smiling. "Who else knows?" he asked.

"Just my father and Myra George, and Zaria, of course." Walthan squinted in consideration as he watched Avalon. A month earlier she would have felt intimidated, but now they were more than a prince and her protector, they were friends.

"Amazing," he told Avalon nodding his head. "You're a good fighter."

"Thanks."

"For a girl," he jabbed. Avalon felt defensive again, but she held her tongue.

"And this accounts for some of the higher pitched screaming after your lizard, and the way I caught you looking at Taggerty a couple of times."

"I don't know what you mean…" Avalon trailed off, but she was glad that in the darkness Walthan could not see her blush. She was going to refute this comment, but the thought of Taggerty running into the woods with the Anthracite's crashing behind him, and sacrificing his life to protect them from Brick's fraud, left them both quiet for a few moments.

"It was Brick!" Avalon blurted. She put her weight on the bad leg and was surprised there was no pain.

"What was Brick?" Walthan asked.

"He was there, in the hall. He betrayed us, he betrayed my father." Avalon told Walthan what she had seen when they had taken her from the cell. She recounted the monarch and his people, and then told him that Brick had tried to kill her.

"I don't believe it," Walthan grunted in anger and punched the wall. Gravel crumbled under the force of his hand. Avalon had to move to the side when Walthan started pacing two steps at a time.

"I'm sorry, Prince Avalon. I was blinded by my friendship with Brick, and I should have seen this coming." Walthan was a pillar, and wise enough to admit that he had been a fool about Brick. Avalon wished her father had been wise enough to concede that he had been a fool about Counselor Glenn.

"You couldn't have know that one of your closest friends would betray you, just as my father couldn't see past his old friendship with Counselor Glenn, and that he would…" she trailed off unable to speak the words. If there was any chance that Brick was lying, then she shouldn't worry about her father, not until she was able to return and see him for herself.

"That he would what?" Walthan asked.

"Brick said that my father is dead. He said that by now Counselor Glenn…"

"Wait," Walthan said with finality. He shook his head for a minute and then slowly knelt in front of Avalon.

"No," Avalon told him, but he kissed her hand where the family crest would one day be placed.

"If the King is dead," he stated looking up in the darkness, "then long live the King."

Avalon pulled her hand away, not wanting to think about the possibility. She clenched her fist and put her hand in her pocket. Then she walked two steps to the wall and tried to think of something flip and impersonal to say, but the weight in her chest wouldn't let her speak.

Walthan rose but he remained silent, although Avalon was begging in her mind for him to speak so she wouldn't have time to think. Her thoughts traveled to Zaria and Myra, and she hoped that they were safe. Then, thankfully, Walthan complied with her silent wish. "I was a fool, too, now that I see you are a lovely young lady. I don't know how I could have missed it."

"I guess sometimes things aren't what they seem," she told him. "And I'm sorry about the crying," Avalon's embarrassment burned her cheeks. "I didn't know you could hear me."

"Not hear you? You were blubbering every night!" he teased and slapped her on the shoulder but then shirked back, unsure exactly how to act around Avalon now that he knew her secret.

Walthan didn't want to believe that Brick would betray him or the king, but Avalon's bloodied leg was proof that he had turned. Brick could have been lying about Counselor Glenn killing King Birch to throw them off, but why bring up Fontanasia in the first place?

"So then Counselor Glenn knows about Cormicks."

"It's possible," Walthan told Avalon. "King Birch saw this place when he was but a prince, like you. When he chose me to lead the soldiers after your grandfather passed, he sent me here along with a Guide so that I could see the true nature of the guard. Your father told me the stories of the slaughter that destroyed our people." Walthan looked to the floor as though he'd known personally each person who had been killed those centuries ago, and Avalon could see clearly now the path that had led Walthan to become the greatest fighter Fontanasia had ever seen. He was a warrior training for a real battle with an enemy others couldn't even imagine existed.

"Counselor Glenn has been on the council since I was appointed to lead the guard, and has been friends with your father longer than I have known either of them. I don't know for certain whether he knows about Cormicks, but it seems that is a great possibility."

They pondered this in silence, and Avalon hoped for a rescue attempt to be made. She knew her father would come for her and didn't want to believe that he might be dead, and if he was, wouldn't someone have to come for the prince? After a long pause she brought this possibility to Walthan's attention. "Maybe they will come for us. Does anyone else know about Cormicks and where it is?"

"The Guides know, but they are too smart to try a rescue attempt."

Avalon didn't understand, and they exchanged looks.

"If we are rescued, then the monarch will believe Brick, and he will know that there are more like us. He won't wait for an attack; he will go looking."

This weighed on Avalon. "Brick has told their leader about Fontanasia already. If they are aggressors, they will go looking anyway."

"Yes, but the Guides don't know that. All they will know is that we left and never came back. They won't know Brick talked." It hurt Walthan to say that, and he shook his head. Then he nodded, coming to terms with the fact that Brick had either broken under pressure of torture, or that he was part of a larger conspiracy. Walthan sat silent for a long time. "Hawker knows about Cormicks. Your grandfather showed King Birch the map, and also showed Hawker at least once since this city is his namesake. You were named for the star that led us to Fontanasia, your father for the protective mountain trees, and Hawker for your past."

"Maybe Hawker will send someone if Brick is right about my father." They were both silent in contemplation.

"Hawker saw the map, but there is no way that he will be able to find the way. Hawker was never allowed to take the trip here, and I don't think he knows about the window. As you now know, it takes more than the map to find Cormicks."

"Maybe Hawker would take confidence in the Guides." Avalon was reaching, but she was desperate for a shred of hope to hold on to, but hope was far reaching.

Days passed slowly with little to say. Both Walthan and Avalon were lost in their thoughts. Once a day their cell door would swing open and a basket of food appeared. The half cooked paste and thin crusts of bread tasted awful, but Walthan made her eat with him because it kept up what strength they had left. Avalon's leg was healing well, and the bandage had been removed.

She was under an abnormal amount of pressure, but Avalon worried that her overflow of emotion and growing need to cry was because she was a girl and not because she was locked in a cell on the other side of the world. Her body still looked straight like a boy's, but she had felt this emerging sensitivity over the months. She remembered how Zaria had changed as she blossomed. With all the time in the world to second guess, Avalon mulled over how she perceived everything in her life and silently berated herself for any emerging emotional changes.

She cried herself to sleep, hoping that Walthan couldn't see her shoulders shaking while she let the tears run silently across her face and into the dust. She cried for her father and his uncertainty, and her own inability to take action. Days passed, and Walthan continued to find the strength to push Avalon up above his head so that she could look out at the moon. It was close to full tonight, which meant they had two more nights to the end of the cycle and then they would be trapped in Cormicks for another month, if not forever.

Walthan seemed to be carrying a revived hope since he'd found out that Avalon was a girl. He found the energy to pace the cell, turning around in three long strides. It wasn't hope that was driving him though. It was his fear. He had been protecting the king's son, and now he needed to make sure that Avalon was not discovered as a woman in this place. He couldn't imagine the unthinkable torture she would have to endure and tried to put it out of his mind with thoughts of escape. Still, it seemed impossible. Even his massive hands could not break apart the door to their cell, and Avalon had not been able to loosen any of the bars on the small window up above. Walthan did not dare to dig for fear of the everreds. So now he paced and he contemplated how he would get them out of the cell, out of the castle, and out of Cormicks.

He still treated Avalon with the reverence he'd always held for his future king, but Avalon sensed the change that had taken place in his manner. He was driven more now than before, and although she didn't want to be treated as a girl, Avalon knew that this was the reason Walthan had stepped up his efforts to find a way out. That worried Avalon, and when she took up pacing, Walthan told her to sit down and save her energy.

"How can you expect me to sit still all the time? We've been here for two weeks, stuck in this prison, and tonight is the full moon!"

"This is not your end, Avalon," Walthan gently reassured her. "The beginning and the end are easier, it is the middle that is the most difficult." This comment again reminded Avalon of Myra George and the way she had always managed to speak in circles. Avalon had no idea what Walthan meant.

"Up," he said to her, prompting Avalon to climb up his limbs until she was standing on his shoulders. When she was ready, she let him know. She used her hands to steady herself on the wall as he pushed her up by her ankles until she could hold the bars above and pull herself up to look out the tiny window. Avalon watched the full moon move in and out of the clouds. She looked to the horizon for the glow of the blue elbagrass, but she knew she wouldn't find it. She used all of her strength to loosen the bars, but they wouldn't budge. When the muscles in her arms finally began to shake, she slid down the wall, onto Walthan's shoulders and then to the dirt floor. After tomorrow night, it would be another month to the full moon. She was distraught, and her hopelessness grew as she thought of her father, whom she hoped was still alive. She shook her head in anger, desperate to escape, but there was no way. Walthan had tested the door of the cell with his colossal strength and got nowhere. Full of futility, Avalon curled on the cell floor and cried herself to sleep.

Walthan had made it a habit to sleep against the door, and in the middle of the night the guards unlocked the cell with a clank and tried to push the door open. It took three men to get Walthan to budge, and the lead guard was not happy when they finally pushed the door open. The full moon gave Avalon and Walthan a little extra light in the dark, but there was nothing left to guess about in the small confined space. Three guards crammed into the cell with two torches, and Avalon squinted and put her hand in front of her face.

"Come," they demanded of Avalon. She took a step forward, but Walthan stopped her with an outstretched hand.

"The prince declines your invitation," Walthan answered politely as though he were announcing dinner in the court of Fontanasia.

The guard swung forward with a club, but Walthan was ready for a fight, and he easily stepped out of the way. The other two guards swept in toward Avalon, but Walthan stopped them by plunging his forearms into their windpipes. Avalon had to spin out of the way to avoid being burned by the torches as they ricocheted off the far wall. Both guards went down choking while the lead guard regained his balance and called for help. A fight ensued between Walthan and a troop of armed guards. He managed to duck, punch, kick, steal a sword, and cut several down while somehow keeping himself between the guards and Avalon. The reinforcements didn't fair well either. There were many of them, but the small confined cell only allowed two guards in at one time, and this helped Walthan keep control of the fight. He would cut one down and then another would come, but they never stood a chance under the warrior's blade.

Avalon knew this would be her only chance to escape through the open cell door, but she couldn't even move past Walthan's huge body much less get past the guards outside. If only Walthan could push them all back far enough, but the cell was closed and locked before they could take full advantage of the situation. They could hear the stampede of footsteps as the guards outside ran back up the ramp.

Walthan grabbed a fallen torch and searched the pockets of the five unconscious guards who had been cut down and were now locked in the cell with them, but none of them held keys. Avalon looked away when Walthan ran each of them through with a sword. She had seen many mock battles and tournaments, but she had not yet learned to deal with death.

"They'll be back," Walthan told her as he handed her a knife and a sword. He tore some fabric from his undershirt and Avalon helped him tie it around his bleeding arm. They didn't have to wait long before keys rustled the lock. Walthan held a sword at the ready in one hand, and a torch in the other as the door swung open.

"Walthan," Brick's familiar voice called in. "Walthan, we want to talk."

Avalon's heart was beating out of her chest with fear, but Walthan laughed as he crouched at the ready and turned the sword over in his hands.

"Sure, Brick, we'd love to talk." The sarcasm was easily read in Walthan's voice, but Avalon's shaky voice cut in.

"We will talk, Brick. Can we come out?"

"No," a deep voice called. Avalon recognized the monarch at once. In warning, she pulled on Walthan's arm, and they shrank back as a guard moved into the cell followed by Brick. They crowded in and pressed against the wall so the Monarch could enter the small space. The monarch stopped in front of Brick, but he kept his distance from Walthan who was holding Avalon behind him on the other side of the cell, dead bodies and a few small feet in between. Walthan looked the monarch over once, but after that his eyes didn't leave Brick. Avalon saw Brick's face in the dim torchlight. The right side of it was fully tattooed now, just like the other guards. Brick was an entirely different person than the one she had crossed over with, and the change in him was shocking.

"So, this is the man causing all of the problems," the monarch asked rhetorically as he looked up into Walthan's face. The monarch did not cower to Walthan's size, but Brick made sure to keep himself well out of reach.

"This is your best fighter?" the monarch asked Brick without facing him.

"Yes," Brick answered.

Walthan growled at Brick ignoring the monarch's appraising stare.

"We'll see how he stands up against my best." Avalon heard guards laughing from outside the cell. The monarch looked

Walthan up and down again. "Rest up, you will fight my best in the morning, if you are still here." The monarch glanced meaningfully at Walthan and then to the stain on the wall left by the everreds. It took Avalon a moment to remember what Walthan had told her about the tiny spiders, and then she realize that the bodies of the bleeding soldiers would eventually draw the everreds to their cell.

"What do I get if I win?" Walthan asked.

"Why, you get to live," the monarch heckled. They turned to leave, but Walthan wanted the last word.

"Traitor!" he yelled after Brick.

"You know nothing!" Brick managed to scowl. "You're done."

"Are you going to stay here then, and be his pet?" Walthan spat in Brick's face.

The monarch laughed as he swept out of the cell, the guards locking Avalon and Walthan in. Walthan grunted in frustration and paced for a moment, his hands to his head. When he noticed Avalon watching, he abruptly stopped pacing and forced a smile. This was the first time Avalon had seen him stifled and without a plan.

Avalon breathed in hard. She could clearly see why a peaceful country like Fontanasia, a country that had seen no war, needed great warriors like Walthan. That the king of Fontanasia kept such a powerful secret so that his people could lead happy and peaceful lives free of fear was a noble cause. Avalon pledged to get out of this cell and back to her city and her family. If she could protect the people from the fear that she was enduring now, the electric terror that spread through her thoughts and sent chills up her spine, it would be a just life. But her stomach dropped and she knew that the centuries of peace might now be coming to and end.

Walthan stacked the five dead soldiers' bodies in one corner. He took a second sword for himself and gave another dagger to Avalon. "You be ready now," he told her, and she nodded passively.

He squared up to her placing his heavy hands on her shoulders, his enormous fingers wrapped around her back, and his expression hardened. "Avalon, you be ready. When the time comes, you must get to the window. I will lift you up, and then you hold yourself to those bars for as long as you can." Avalon nodded at the great warrior although she had no idea what he was planning. The monarch didn't scare her right now, nor did the hoard of Runners waiting to kill her. What bothered Avalon at this moment was the sensation of all hope running out of her.

Walthan took a seat in the corner and tended to his arm while Avalon rocked side to side on her feet in the small space that was left. She racked her brain. Of all of the brutes she had seen in the hall upstairs, she could not choose who might be the best warrior among them. A long hour passed before they heard voices in the hall outside their cell followed by a loud thud. Avalon held her breath as the door clanked open.

"It's so dark in here. How can anyone see where they are going?" a familiar voice complained. The torches had long gone out, and they were left again in the small sliver of moonlight that made its way into the subterranean space.

Avalon squinted her eyes wondering if she was seeing the truth, because in her heart she was sure that the voice she just heard belonged to a man that was long dead. She steadied herself realizing that her mind had started playing tricks on her after two weeks of starvation and neglect. The soldier stepped into the cell and pushed the door closed behind him, jiggling the keys in the lock so that they were now all locked in together. He was smaller than the rest, and Avalon lifted her dagger and stepped forward before Walthan had time to stop her.

"If you want him, you will have to go through me," Avalon announced.

But before she could strike, the soldier removed his helmet, and to her astonishment and private joy, she saw Taggerty, alive, standing in front of her with his sly grin. "I don't suggest it, Prince Avalon. We both already know who the better fighter is."

Chapter 13
The Guide's Son

"There isn't much time. Walthan," Taggerty announced as he pushed past Avalon to help Walthan back onto his feet. The huge soldier gave Taggerty a squeeze and a pat on the back that nearly knocked all of his breath away. "Careful!" Taggerty told him as he removed two large black rocks from his vest. "Lift me up to the window."

Avalon stood with her mouth open. Her euphoric, puzzled state stirred confusing feelings around her chest. She wanted to throw her arms around Taggerty and choke him.

"You have the key, we can go through the door. The window is too small and barred," Walthan told him.

"We can't trust him, Walthan. He's the one who got us in here in the first place." Avalon wasn't sure why she had said those words, but they quickly blew out any emotion brought on by their reunion. Avalon felt sorry for a moment, but Taggerty ignored her.

"We can't go back that way, it is too dangerous." There were already faraway voices outside the cell sounding the alarm. Time was running short. "Walthan…"

With his bloody arm bandaged, Walthan easily picked the boy up over his head and let him do his few minutes of work. Avalon couldn't tell what he was doing, but Taggerty gave the signal and Walthan brought him down, Taggerty dragging a black rock like a piece of chalk along the wall.

"Prince Avalon, you should put some of the soldier's clothing on, to blend in," Taggerty commanded. There was no time to protest. Walthan helped her take some of the armament and, although he was obviously awkward because he knew she was a girl, he strapped the too big chest plate to her small frame.

"Quick, crouch down behind them," Taggerty instructed, pointing to the bodies of the soldiers that Walthan had stacked up. Walthan looked at Taggerty and shook his head.

"It's the only way, Walthan. I don't know what this stuff can do."

Avalon crouched with them behind the soldiers' dead figures. She frantically squinted looking for the first sign of the tiny everred spiders but was distracted when Taggerty lit a match. Before Avalon could protest the fire, he struck the flame against the black chalk he had drawn down the wall and a large flare burst forth. It crackled and popped and made its way up the wall. When the sparkler reached the top, Taggerty told them to close their eyes, and then a massive white explosion tore through the rock and steel. They all coughed as the dust settled, and then Avalon could clearly see the full moon.

"What was that?" Walthan asked.

"I took it from the Anthracites," Taggerty admitted.

"They keep explosives and yet they are afraid of fire?" Avalon asked.

"No, I mean I took it from their limbs. It is the rock that makes up the Anthracites." Taggerty pushed the dead soldiers off of himself and Avalon. Walthan was already standing ready at the large hole. He lifted them both up and out of the cell, and managed to stack a few rocks up high enough to climb out. Avalon and Taggerty pulled at his massive shoulders, and then they were all free. Avalon could see more tiny, barred openings in the rock along the building.

"I didn't know which one was yours from out here or I would have blown you out three nights ago," Taggerty told her before they started to run toward the castle's outer wall.

"Brick is dead?" Taggerty whispered as they ran.

"No," Avalon replied through gritted teeth.

"Then you are betrayed."

At the mention of Brick, Walthan put his large arm out and stopped Taggerty in his tracks. "You lit the fire, how do we know you aren't working with Brick?" Avalon had asked as much, but it sounded like a threat coming from Walthan.

"I did not light the fire. And, no, I am not working with Brick," Taggerty demanded impatiently. "Let's get out of here and I will explain."

Avalon found herself conflicted wanting to defend Taggerty to Walthan and argue at the same time that he couldn't be trusted because he had gotten them caught. It was ridiculous, she knew, standing in the castle yard, exposed to the enemy, and taking the time to think these thoughts no matter how fast and how random they came to her. She wanted to argue, to give each thought its due course, but the sound of pursuers coming from the castle cut short the time for any more questions. The low howling of the wind covered their retreating footsteps.

"He will lead them to the elbagrass and then to Fontanasia," Walthan told Avalon. "I have to stop him."

"Let Brick come to us," Taggerty answered. He led them to an opening he had dug under the wall where even Walthan could squeeze through. Avalon noticed the black scorched dirt like the stain from the everreds in her cell and she shot through the opening, patting her clothes off and itching from the mere thought of the tiny everred spiders. She was angry with Taggerty, but glad for his ingenuity. There would be plenty of time to hate him once they were free of Cormicks.

The wind bit at her skin, and she remembered how cold it was here, especially at night. She had been bunkered underground for weeks and their body heat had kept the cell at a bearable temperature. She wondered how Taggerty had survived all these days outside alone without the ability to make a fire to warm him. Avalon could see the full moon and dared to hope for the warmth of summer on the other side of the window, but her reverie was cut short by the grunting shouts of soldiers on the other side of the wall. Taggerty led the oncoming soldiers in the wrong direction, and doubled back once they got into the trees where Avalon came upon a wonderful sight.

"Jackie!" she almost yelled but stopped herself in time. She ran over but stopped short of hugging her pet. He had remained in his large form, and she had to look up into the lizard's eyes. Jackie nudged Avalon's shoulder with his nose, responding only when Taggerty drew near.

"I found him running himself ragged." The large jakkow lizard took two quick steps forward and rubbed his nose on Taggerty's neck. "I think he's taken a liking to me." In one swift motion, Taggerty pulled himself up onto Jackie's back. He reached out to Avalon, and she grasped his wrist. Walthan pulled Avalon up by the waist, and in an instant she was behind Taggerty on top of her jakkow and ready to ride bareback. There was no room for Walthan, but he was not climbing on board.

"Lead them out away from the elbagrass. I will double back and meet you where we first encountered the Anthracites. Go!" Walthan insisted as he cracked the jakkow in the back startling the lizard into a run. Walthan knew that Brick would try to lead the soldiers to the window, and he would have to start at the same location where they had first come out of the woods because he would not know the way by heart and would have to backtrack.

Taggerty slowed Jackie to a walk until he was sure the soldiers had spotted them. Then he kicked the jakkow and they rode with the foot soldiers in pursuit, off in the wrong direction. As the cold, night air washed through her hair, Avalon had to lean forward and hug Taggerty's waist. The jakkow's body slithered as it ran, and the undulating feeling was nothing like riding a horse. Avalon held tighter to Taggerty as they rode through the dark, her eyes easily adjusting to the simple moonlight. Taggerty rode into a grass clearing and found the moon. "We need to escape while the moon is still in the sky." He pushed the jakkow faster, and Avalon held on in awe of Jackie's size and power. It wasn't long before they were able to backtrack toward their predetermined meeting place with Walthan.

Walthan was at the ridge outcropping already, going through the packs that Taggerty had dug out of the rubble. The warrior tossed two small bags up at Taggerty who caught them and tied them off to the rope that held tight around Jackie's shoulders. Walthan led them just inside the forest and pulled out a length of rope to set a trap. He was sure that Brick would lead the soldiers this way, and he could only hope that his small trap would be enough to stop the detail of Runners. Walthan was sure that the Monarch would have believed Brick on some levels, because they were most likely the only race of people to be discovered in over two hundred years. He had to stop them, no matter how many came at once. Avalon watched Walthan work furiously, his rigid, marble expression full of concentration with the task ahead of him. He was steeling himself to slay his old friend. Avalon understood what Walthan had to do, and this made her angry.

"I have some questions for you," Avalon told Taggerty. He stopped what he was doing and looked directly into her eyes expectantly, which threw Avalon's concentration for the moment.

"I know, and I will answer all of them," he said sincerely, "just not right now."

He returned to work, and Avalon was ready to argue, but Walthan instructed Avalon to move any small boulders that she could carry out of the clearing. He wanted to make sure there was only dirt here. Her heart pounded under the exertion because her body was malnourished and worn out. She knew Walthan's strength must have come from his anger though as he and Taggerty moved like mad men setting traps with the rope and harnessing them to the trees. When the trap was set, they chose a spot out of sight among the boulders that Avalon had stacked, and they waited. Taggerty reined Jackie in, but the large lizard heeded no warning. The lizard sniffed at Avalon for a moment, and then like all animals that can sense danger before humans, Avalon saw the lizard freeze when she herself could hear nothing.

"They're coming," Walthan whispered soon after.

All Avalon could hear was her heart pounding. The forest was discernable under a full moon, and in the gray light Avalon could see how spent Walthan was becoming. Just then her stomach growled, and Taggerty looked up at her. Avalon's face burned, annoyed with her stomach and embarrassed. She wanted to growl at Taggerty.

"Just hold on a bit longer," Taggerty whispered close to her, his breath warming the biting cold on her ear. She heard the concern in his voice and was aggravated with herself for constantly feeling so defensive toward him.

She turned her attention to Walthan. She wondered if he was as hungry as she was, and she was worried about his bleeding arm. He looked strong and determined in the moonlight, and Avalon knew that there was nothing that would stop the greatest warrior in the world. Her breath was labored now from the strain of her weak state, but she was bolstered by the excitement running through her veins.

"There are only six," Walthan whispered again. "It seems their monarch doesn't trust my old friend or he would have sent an army."

They had set the trap too close to the edge of the woods, and Walthan swore under his breath when the first two Runners were snatched up in the ropes, allowing the last one to turn and run for help. Taggerty started to move, but Walthan held him with a touch and a look. Brick laughed, but it was a nervous laughter.

"Come out, old friend," he baited Walthan. Two of his guards hung upside down at the edge of the clearing, hindered by their protective gear and unable to reach up to cut free. Brick made the tactical mistake of hesitating to cut them down.

"Stay here, Prince Avalon," Walthan instructed. Then he and Taggerty doubled around to where Brick had entered the clearing.

"And where is Prince Avalon?" Brick asked turning to meet Walthan.

"Prince Avalon is safe now, back in Fontanasia. We stayed behind to clean up your mess." Walthan and Taggerty simultaneously drew their swords and lunged forward. Brick drew his sword but stood back and watched as the other two Runners flung themselves at the attack.

Avalon watched through the heavy bushes, and she could see Walthan and Taggerty pushing the Runners back. She also noticed in the slight reflection from the moonlight that Walthan's bandage was now soaked with blood and was becoming worse, but his enemy could not have known the damage as Walthan and Taggerty ran the two guards through.

"He's mine," Walthan seethed through clenched teeth. Taggerty moved out of reach behind Brick to make sure he couldn't retreat.

"With pleasure," Brick told Walthan. Any fear for Walthan that Brick had been harboring was shed that instant, and he stepped forward to meet his old friend.

Avalon and Taggerty had seen the seasoned soldiers duel in festivals, but the match before them paled in comparison. Brick had an advantage because he still retained control of both of his arms and was able to switch sword hands, but Walthan's size and the fact that he was the better kept Brick from taking full advantage. Both men were sweating and bleeding before long. Just when the duel seemed to be going in Walthan's favor, his arm came down in a swinging arc and he stabbed at the air and missed. Brick danced to the side, swinging his sword down into the back of Walthan's legs. The giant toppled over in an instant. Then, Brick foolishly leaned in for the kill, and was run through by Walthan who rolled to the side and let Brick's weight fall cleanly onto his sword. They were inches from each other, eye-to-eye, Brick's limp figure crumpling onto Walthan as his last breaths came and went.

Avalon could hear Walthan's gravelly voice. "I don't forgive you, Brick. I will never forgive you for what you have done here, and I will make Counselor Glenn pay. "Walthan pushed Brick's limp figure off of his own and managed to pull himself up to a sitting position. Avalon could see the ground under his legs turning red as she ran from her hiding place and took his side. He grunted as he stood slowly, using Taggerty's shoulder for support

"You are hurt!"

"It's a scratch," Walthan told her without looking to see the blood that had soaked his clothing and was beginning to drip on the ground. He picked up his sword, walked to the edge of the clearing, and ran through the chests of the two soldiers who were still hanging upside down from the trees. Avalon watched in horror.

"They are killers, Prince Avalon," Walthan told her when he noticed her incredulity. "You cannot view them as reasonable people who are captured now and deserve to live; that is the same mistake that our ancestors made. We need to make a clean escape with no one following us."

Avalon did not have time to respond because just then, Walthan collapsed. She ran to his side, his eyes fluttering open and closed.

"Stay awake!" Taggerty ordered the senior guard. "I have to get your jakkow," he told Avalon and raced back to the rock outcropping. Avalon held Walthan's hand and tried to keep him awake. She couldn't help but cry this time, and she let the tears clean streaks of dirt off her face.

"Stay with me," she begged him. She was thinking of her father now, wondering if he was still alive. The despair almost drowned her, but then Taggerty returned, and she allowed the anger to sweep over her. She was angry at Brick and Counselor Glenn for their merciless betrayal, and angry with Taggerty for being here to see her cry. Yelling at him would have been easier than crying in front of him.

Taggerty knelt down beside Walthan, and Avalon stood, cleaning her face and hugging Jackie for support.

"Get up, old man," Taggerty razzed Walthan up into a sitting position. "Let me get you onto this jakkow and then we will be home free."

"Just let me rest here one more minute," Walthan wheezed.

"No can do." Taggerty tried to lift Walthan, but the warrior was too heavy and would have to stand up on his own. "There's too much blood here, and we cleared the boulders, remember?"

Avalon's anger at Taggerty subsided long enough for her to look around for the everreds.

"That's right, that's right," Walthan breathed slowly. "Come, Prince Avalon, help me to my steed." Walthan's attempt at a jovial front hid nothing from Avalon and Taggerty. He was bleeding badly and his paling face looked worse every minute.

Avalon came around Jackie and crouched on Walthan's opposite side. After much effort he was able to stand, but his weight was unbearable. Taggerty tried to take most of it, and he clenched his teeth when they wrenched Walthan's limp bulk up.

"Up you go, old man," Taggerty squeezed out as they managed to get the huge soldier onto the bulging back of the red lizard. Taggerty took the rope that was tied around Jackie's neck and walked forward, and the lizard obeyed without needing even a slight pull from the rope.

"We don't have much time to make the window," Taggerty said, encouraging her to follow. But Avalon was unraveling, the past two weeks and hours caving in on her mind. She was angry and ready to burst. And what was worse to her was that she was to be king. She was to be the strongest person, the light of Fontanasia, and she was breaking. And then there was Taggerty: a pompous traitor turned hero, now ready to lead as she was falling apart.

"Walthan is hurt!" she yelled at Taggerty. "We haven't eaten in two weeks, and we are exhausted. And now you want me to just trust you and go where you say without question?"

Taggerty kept moving ahead with Walthan on the jakkow.

"I demand your answer!" she yelled at his back, immediately embarrassed that she had. Avalon was surprised by the energy running through her, and she wanted to apologize, but it was too late. Taggerty turned, and she was sure even in the darkness that she had made him angry.

"Okay, I'll tell you anything you want me to," Taggerty yelled back at her. "Just move over here for a minute, okay?" Taggerty had situated the jakkow on the rocks that she had pulled from the clearing. He instructed Avalon to stand on the rocks as he tried to bandage Walthan. "Now, what would you like to know?" His voice was soft, but he didn't look at her.

To her increasing dismay, Avalon wasn't sure what to ask. She had been angry and wanting answers, but now she wasn't sure where to even start. Then Taggerty, who had been ripping Walthan's shirt and using the pieces to bandage the warrior's legs, looked right into Avalon's eyes, startling her silence into the need for nervous chatter.

"If you weren't working with Brick, then where have you been?"

"Well," Taggerty grit back through clenched teeth, and he now looked as angry at Avalon as she had been with him. "After I saved your life by distracting those charcoal beasts, I foraged in the woods for days and tracked you back to Cormicks." His temper was giving way with each word, and he pulled tighter and tighter as he bandaged Walthan.

"I slept in trees, ate what the paiche birds eat, those berries we had," he pulled his eyebrows up sarcastically, "all the time, and it's not very filling." He pointed at the bush they were next to, and Avalon stole a handful of berries and pushed them into her mouth and swallowed without chewing in hopes of stopping the growling in her stomach.

"I found your Jackie about a week ago and have tamed him to a degree." The jakkow was also eating from the bush Avalon was picking from, and she now noticed that the red lizard did seem to follow Taggerty in every move he made. The lizard had even nudged Taggerty with his nose when he'd heard his name.

"Get off!" Taggerty pushed the wet beak away causing Avalon to laugh. The laughter broke the ice, and Avalon sighed. She was getting erratically emotional and realized that she needed to get a handle on herself before she turned into her sister.

"It looks as though my pet has found a pet."

Taggerty looked at her, and when he saw a smile on her lips, he actually laughed.

"Yes, you might have to keep me in your pocket too."

It was Avalon's turn to laugh now. She knew that Taggerty had always been civil to her because she was a prince, but she couldn't believe that he was actually teasing her.

Now that Avalon had calmed down, Taggerty told her the rest of the story. "I was playing both sides," Taggerty admitted. "I was recruited to help Brick carry out a plan, and I accepted because I knew it was the only way to make sure that you would be safe."

This news shocked Avalon. "Who spoke to you?"

"Brick did. I don't know who he was working for."

"Counselor Glenn," Avalon told him.

"What time is it?" Walthan asked. His eyes were closed, but Avalon was glad that he was still conscious.

"I think dawn will be within the hour, from the look of the moon," Taggerty answered.

"We must go and warn the king."

"I was with the Guide, and he crossed over last night to make sure someone could warn the king if we didn't make it back." Avalon noted that Taggerty had kept this bit of information to himself earlier.

"We are free," Walthan whispered weakly.

"We have to wait, too much blood," Taggerty told Walthan. "I'll hurry things along. You," he pointed at Avalon, "stay here with Walthan."

Avalon watched through the bushes as Taggerty dragged all of the bodies of the dead Runners and Brick together in a pile. He cut down the other two Runners and threw their limp figures on top of the pile, standing back to take a deep breath and admire his work. Then the berries she had swallowed almost found their way up as she watched Taggerty pull his sword over his head and hack several limbs from the dead bodies. She turned her head away as the disgusting, crunching noise made her chest heave once, but she regained herself. She turned back and saw black blood gushing out into a pool, and Taggerty ran out of the clearing. When he saw the look on her face, he apologized.

"Sorry, it was necessary. They'll be here soon and then it will be safe to travel."

"Who will be here?" Avalon asked aloud just as the answer presented itself.

"The everreds," they said simultaneously. Just then the ground rumbled.

"Stay on the rocks," Taggerty yelled over the noise while he looked to make sure that the jakkow was not standing in the dirt.

Avalon remembered that blood drew the ravenous spiders, but she could not prepare herself for what was to come. The ground thundered beneath her feet, and the smaller rocks shook and rolled off the pile they were standing on. As the noise grew, Avalon saw a wave of undulating red ooze over the pile of dismembered bodies. She could make out what looked like a wave of red puss. She held her chest in shock, swept in full awe of their power, unable to even see one of the everreds on its own, but mortified by the mass of energy that destroyed anything in the path of its hunger. A hole opened up underneath the pile of bodies, and the huge swarm of everreds disappeared back underground, leaving a cloud of dust and few body parts behind. Avalon could see a black shadow left on the ground like the one that was on the wall of her cell, and now that she had seen the everreds destructive power, she realized how lucky they had been for the past two weeks underground.

"They respond to the blood," Taggerty told her as the noise dissipated and the ground stopped rumbling. "I think that will buy us the time we need."

Avalon noticed blood dripping down Walthan's legs and she wiped it up with the bottom of her shirt to make sure it didn't touch the ground. They jogged beside Jackie knowing they had one chance to get back home. The cold, night air kept Avalon from sweating, and she breathed it in deeply to heighten her senses any time she felt the exhaustion creeping in. She followed Taggerty's direction, and they moved quickly out of the woods and through a short grass prairie. She could hear Walthan groaning softly at times, and although she didn't want him to feel the pain of his wounds, she was glad to know that he was still alive.

"This is not the quickest way," Walthan said, and Avalon wondered how he could know for sure while riding hunched over on Jackie's back.

"Just wait," Taggerty said. And then Avalon could see the tall, slender trees reaching up to block the moon as they approached the woods. She touched Walthan's leg, remembering their first walk through and how tightly together the trees had grown. She knew he would not be able to make the walk between the trees to the window home.

"He can't walk, Taggerty," Avalon said into the night.

"I know," he said defensively. "Just wait."

They moved along the tree line, each minute wasted closing the door to Fontanasia.

"Here!" Taggerty announced as he turned the red lizard's beak toward the trees. And then Avalon realized that he had found the path bulldozed by Jackie the night that they had crossed over. It was not easy to spot, but once they stepped through the downed branches, Avalon could just make out an area where trees had been knocked apart, some cracked and half fallen, and some almost horizontal before being caught by the trees packed around them.

"Thank you," she said aloud involuntarily. She was grateful that Taggerty did not reply.

They followed a jagged path of trampled branches, Taggerty leading the jakkow, and Avalon following. They had to stop several times to position Walthan so he wouldn't get scraped off Jackie's back by the enclosed trees. She could hear Walthan's stifled grunts as he tried to grit his teeth through the pain. She and Taggerty shared a glance as they tried to move the warrior's heavy limbs closer to the top of Jackie's back so they could squeeze through where the trees had not fallen away.

They moved as quickly as they dared, branches cracking loudly beneath their feet. With her sights set on getting to the window and home, Avalon was not worried about being followed. She found it easy to see the outlines of the others where the moon broke through the tightly packed wood. She was glad to be taking this crooked, more open path, remembering the uncertain darkness and painful cuts on her face of their first night. But those cuts would be easily endured if it meant the difference between getting back to Fontanasia tonight and spending another month in this cold, evil place. Even with stopping and resetting Walthan, they traveled quickly, and Avalon watched the horizon looking for the first glow of the elbagrass. She never saw it in the woods though, and when they finally reached the clearing, the grass glowed dimly in the waning moonlight.

"We missed our window," Walthan groaned. "The full moon is gone." The moon was setting below the horizon as the rising sun canceled its power in the coming light.

"We can hide," Taggerty accepted in defeat as he looked over the grass.

"Not from the everreds," said Avalon. "And not in this cold without making a fire. Walthan needs help."

"We must try to cross over now," Walthan breathed, not concerned with his own fate. "You could survive the elements for a month if you had to, but you have an army after you now." As though their enemy had heard his very words, an unmistakable crack filled the air behind them. Even at this unseen distance, the earsplitting screeching of rock on rock made her flinch, and Avalon knew the sound was the Anthracites unfolding up out of the earth. She could feel a tremble beneath her feet and a panic in her heart.

"He's right," Taggerty told Avalon with a tight smile returning to his face. "Besides, it is summer at home, and I'm freezing." Avalon noticed the sweat on his shirt letting off steam in the cold as Taggerty took a quick look over his shoulder.

"Look at the edge of the grass. Find some green alleya leaf." Walthan tried to point, but he could barely lift his arm.

Taggerty and Avalon left Walthan to search the edge of the grass. It was hard to see the actual colors of the leaves in the dark, but Avalon had already grown used to their feel and she only pulled the softer ones up to her face to see if they were still green. Most of the leaves near the edge of the woods were already brown and dead of their heeling quality. Avalon was losing hope as the full moon waned, and she started to panic as the continuous pounding of the Anthracites far off in the distance shocked her senses.

"They are searching, but blindly." Taggerty touched Avalon's arm and looked into her wide eyes. "We have time, they don't know where we are. We must find the alleya leaf." His touch and his words brought Avalon back to the task at hand. They were able to find six good leaves. They returned to Walthan, Avalon running to his side as he lay on the ground next to the jakkow. She thought he had fallen off, but soon realized his intent.

"Good," he told Taggerty. "Now, give them to Prince Avalon. The grass is fading and we need to be sure that he makes it back."

Without hesitation, Taggerty reached out his hand to give Avalon the full share of alleya leaves. Her astonishment was more than she could suppress.

"No!" she told Walthan. "You are coming with me, both of you!"

Walthan struggled to take off his shirt, and Taggerty helped him, both ignoring her plea.

"Put this on and try to cover any skin that might be showing." Taggerty pulled Walthan's huge, bloodied shirt over his own. He tucked his pants into his boots, and pulled his hands into his own long sleeves until the only skin he had left showing was around his eyes.

"Good," Walthan told him.

Avalon had started to cry silently, not understanding why everything had to fall apart when they were so close to freedom. She tasted the salt in her mouth, helplessly indifferent to the crushing sounds of the Anthracites. But as soon as the hopelessness had swept over her, a soft voice told her that she was in control, and that it was up to her to take action. She wiped her face dry with the backs of her sleeves, determined that Walthan would make this trip with her. She found the will to catch her breath and gave her first command.

"If my father is dead, then that means I am your king, and you will do as I say." Both Walthan and Taggerty regarded her, surprised at her tone. She reached out and took the leaves from Taggerty, shoving three of them in her mouth.

"Walthan, you will get up on the jakkow again," she commanded. He didn't move at first.

"Do you dare defy your king?" Avalon boomed. She swallowed back her tears washing down the alleya leaves.

Satisfied that she was eating, Taggerty helped Walthan back up onto the jakkow, and before either of them could protest, Avalon fed the remaining leaves to her lizard.

"Jackie," Avalon told the lizard, "you have to take us to the pool so we can get home." The jakkow bumped Avalon's cheek with his nose and she climbed on in front of Walthan after pushing his arms into the short sleeves of his undershirt.

"Jackie can do it, Taggerty. Get on, that is an order."

She caught Taggerty's smile before he climbed on behind Walthan who was now sandwiched upright between Avalon and Taggerty. The lizard bent under the weight, but was able to move forward into the tall, blue grass. Taggerty pulled his clothing tight and lifted up his feet, but there was nothing he could do about Walthan's exposed face. The animal moved slowly under their weight, but his strides were long, and they moved through the thick grass quicker than Avalon could have hoped. They were almost to the pool when dawn broke, and what was left of the grass' glow faded fast.

"We can make it, just a little further," Avalon goaded her pet. She was leaning forward to coax Jackie, and she didn't see Walthan pull himself off the lizard's back and drop upright into the grass. Taggerty almost shouted, but Walthan gestured to be quiet as he remained on his feet and tried to limp the short distance to the pool. Taggerty bit his lip as he watched the poisonous grass brush Walthan's cheeks.

The lizard bounced the last few steps without his heavy burden, and they were at the rock-edged pool in seconds. Jackie innocently looked into his reflection in the pool and vanished causing Avalon and Taggerty to fall seven feet to the ground. The thick grass softened her landing, and Taggerty managed to stay upright and not touch any of the grass with his exposed face.

"Prince Avalon, you cross over now," he ordered, needing her to go before their luck ran out. He found three green leaves around the pool and lifted them to his face with his cloth-covered hands, puckering at the bitter taste. Taggerty sighed in relief as the alleya leaf provided him the cure to the deadly grass. He was ready to finish the trip home, but before Prince Avalon looked down at her reflection, she noticed Walthan slowly wading through the grass. His legs were bleeding through the open flaps where Brick's sword had struck, and Walthan's exposed skin grazed the grass. Every step was slower and more deliberate as he felt the effects of the elbagrass' deadly venom.

"Prince Avalon, it is my wish that you cross over now. I am right behind you," he rasped. But she ignored his wish and, protected by the alleya leaf, she ran back out into the grass to help him. She put her shoulder under his arm and tried to take some of the weight from his steps. Taggerty followed her out and helped, trying to move Walthan as fast as he could, his only thought Avalon's return to Fontanasia.

"Prince Avalon, I did as you commanded, and now you must do as I ask. Go." There was little emotion in Walthan's voice, just the deliberate request of a soldier trying to complete his mission. Taggerty patted Walthan's chest in silent response to his wish, letting Walthan know that he would not fail to bring Avalon to safety.

Avalon ignored Walthan's words, making sure he reached the edge of the pool before collapsing. She scoured the area and found three green alleya leaves and brought them back, but Walthan was motionless and did not try to take them out of her hand. His shoulders rested on the brick that edged the pool, and his head hung limp in the air over the dark water. Avalon tried to stuff the leaves in Walthan's mouth, the skin of his face a deathly gray. She cradled the back of his head and tried to make him chew, her hand tugging the bushy curled hair as it tickled her wrist.

"We are there, Walthan! We have made it. Come on," she coaxed. She knew they could make it back to Fontanasia, if only he would eat the leaves and look into the pool. His eyes looked up at Avalon, the life drained out of them, and her tears dropped on his cheeks and rolled into the water behind Walthan's head.

"I am so proud of you," he whispered. She saw a smile on his lips before his head fell to the side and the life breathed out of him. Walthan's eyes met his reflection in the pool, and then he vanished.

Taggerty didn't need to coax her to go next. Avalon looked into the pool barely recognizing the ragged face that looked back, and then she met her own gaze. The air was immediately warmer and silent without the far away pounding of the searching

Anthracites. It was summer in Fontanasia, but she was not relieved for even one second. She was focused on Walthan's lifeless figure, shaking his shoulders and yelling at him.

"Stay with me, Walthan," she yelled, her tears still clogging her eyes.

Taggerty was next to her in an instant, grabbing at her arm, but she shirked him off.

"He needs to eat the leaves, then he will be saved."

"No," Taggerty said sharply but caught himself. "No," he said again, softly, "you have to eat it, to ingest it. Walthan is gone."

Avalon tried to move Walthan's motionless jaw, tried to grind the leaves that were in his mouth. "He will be all right."

"He is gone, Prince Avalon. He died bravely and with honor, in a way he could have never imagined," Taggerty said reverently. "He will be honored for generations. Let him go." Taggerty pulled at her arm, and suddenly her tears became anger and she ripped herself from his grip.

"What makes you an expert on what will work and what won't?" she yelled in his face. "He has the leaf in his mouth, it will cure him!"

Taggerty's shoulders puffed up and he opened his mouth to yell back, but he held his tongue. He didn't need to say anything more. He could see that Avalon had begun to accept his words. Walthan had died well. He had died the hero that he had been all of his days. She knelt beside the warrior and ran her fingers over his eyelids, closing their life from this world. Taggerty removed Walthan's bloody shirt and gently laid it over the warrior's chest and head.

"Your majesty, we must ride to the king, and fast. Walthan wouldn't want us to wait even an instant longer, and if something happens to you, then all is for nothing."

Avalon's eyes looked up at Taggerty, and then her attention moved to his torn sleeve. She recognized the long, black, circular mark on his left forearm as the same one she had seen on the Guides. She unconsciously reached up and touched the black ink on his skin. Her eyes rolled left and right as though she was trying to fit invisible puzzle pieces together.

"Why do you have the mark of the Guides?"

He would have never told the truth to anyone, but he knew Prince Avalon well enough now to know that quick truth was the only way to get them on their way fast. He swallowed hard and tried to find the words he had never been allowed to say. He couldn't believe that tears were making their way from his throat to his eyes, and he grunted.

"Because I am the son of a Guide."

Avalon's mouth opened, but she was holding her breath. She stared at Taggerty stunned, unable to process what he had said. Then she thought of her own secret and realized that this must have been a difficult admission.

"My family wanted someone to serve inside the castle walls, and I was a fair skinned baby, so I was raised by another family who were not Guides, and here I am. Now let's go!"

Avalon was speechless. She knew little of the tribe, but she had never heard of a Guide living away from his own kind. Then she remembered Walthan was dead. She looked down at the great warrior's blood stained and scarred body. She thought of her mother's death and wondered if this is what she had looked like in this lifeless state. But the moment didn't last because aside from pictures, Avalon did not know her mother at all, and Walthan had been larger than life.

"Prince Avalon, Walthan is gone. I am sorry about that. But we need to go," Taggerty pleaded.

Jackie, who had been scrambling around the elbagrass like a fish out of water, now began to shriek. He darted back to the pool as his head and shoulders pulled into themselves, and his giant hips and tail whipped into the grass under his tiny head and shoulders. Then his back end shrank with a pop and he was back in his tiny frame. His transformation broke Avalon's concentration. Jackie clambered frantically along the stones that surrounded the pool of water, and Taggerty grabbed the red lizard and handed it to Avalon.

"Prince Avalon, your father needs you." That brought Avalon back, and she put Jackie in her pocket and followed Taggerty. They ran through the green elbagrass, safe from its poison by the alleya leaf, and out into the day.

Chapter 14
The Other Side of the Moon

The Guide was waiting in the forest, perched on a boulder looking over the tall grass. He called out to Taggerty and, for a man who was typically without emotion, showed his relief when he noticed that the young man was not injured. Avalon recognized the gesture now that she knew Taggerty was a Guide.

"Is that your father?" she whispered as they walked out of the tall grass and into the woods.

"Uncle," he replied in truth. Then he looked to his uncle who was squinting in his direction. Taggerty shrugged. "The prince can be trusted."

"Is there no one else?" the Guide asked gravely. Taggerty shook his head and the Guide gave the young man two short pats on his shoulder before turning into the woods.

"Prince Avalon is starving," Taggerty said. She knew that time was of the essence and could think only of Walthan, but Avalon knew her weak state would slow them down if she didn't eat something soon. They ate quickly, the salty beef jerky and stale bread a feast compared to the mush she had been given in the prison at Cormicks. Avalon stuffed every morsel into her mouth, spilling some of the Guide's water as she tried to drink the entire contents in one gulp. She finally felt a primal relief course through her body. By some miracle, she was alive.

When they were done with the snack, the three trekked back through the forest with the Guide out in the lead. He knew that they were exhausted, it was easy to see, but he pushed them to cover as much ground as possible. When they moved at a slow enough pace to talk, Taggerty told Avalon how he had come to be in the king's guard and chosen for this trip. He'd heard that Brick was looking for a young recruit worthy of the king's guard, and Taggerty had made that his goal at a very young age, so he jumped at the chance. He made himself available to Brick who trained him, and the senior guardsman soon trusted Taggerty.

Brick had hinted to Taggerty that something very important was going to happen, and that he should stay close and not mingle too much with the other guard. Taggerty was happy to comply because Brick was a legend and close guard to the king, but one evening he'd overheard Brick and Counselor Glenn whispering about King Birch, and it was unsettling. Knowing Counselor Glenn had an agenda, Taggerty reported back to the Guides. That is how he came to be on the trip to Cormicks. His uncle, who had been hand picked by King Birch to escort the prince, had asked the king this favor. Walthan would have tried to convince his king otherwise had Brick not also suggested Taggerty for the detail.

"Brick said that Counselor Glenn is king now," Avalon stated.

"We can make this trip in two nights if we hurry," Taggerty told her.

"We won't have time to double back or cover our tracks," the Guide said.

"You can come back later and make sure it is done," Avalon ordered. She was feeling grateful to be warm and back on her side of the window, but the thought of her father brought a panic to her. She felt as though she should run flat out, as though an animal that she had no hope of outrunning was stalking her.

Knowing Taggerty had her back, Avalon followed close to the Guide. She willed herself to hold on to the hope that her father was somehow able to foil Counselor Glenn's plans, and that she would return to Fontanasia and regain her normal life. She wouldn't though. After this trip, she knew that she would never be the same again.

Avalon felt her joints thawing out, and realized she was actually sweating now. She was jealous of Taggerty who had taken off his torn outer shirt and wore short sleeves now. She would never have that luxury. Both layers of her clothing were tattered and torn in spots, and she had lost the ability to smell her own stench a week earlier, but she would not take the chance of even removing her outer jacket.

As they walked, the emptiness of losing Walthan swept over her once more. She had never lost anyone close to her, aside from her mother. Avalon thought of all of the death she had witnessed in the last twenty-four hours and wondered if she would ever be able to push the graphic images from her mind. She didn't carry around memories of her mother because they had only been in each other's presence for the first few minutes of her life. But she knew each death would stay with her like an invisible whisper in the back of her mind, because her mother had been gone her entire life, and not many days passed when Avalon didn't suffer the burden.

Taggerty interrupted her thought. "You are thinking of Walthan?"

"No, I'm not," she snapped back but regretted not taking a softer tone. He had saved her life, and he was a Guide, which made him trustworthy. This made her rethink her position on hating him forever. "Maybe I am in some way thinking of Walthan. I've never been that close to death, not since I can remember. It's making me think of my mother." She stopped herself and looked away into the forest not sure why she had confessed this to him.

"Do you want to talk about it?"

"No, you wouldn't know anything about it."

"I wasn't raised by my mother either," Taggerty offered.

"You wouldn't understand."

"Try me."

Avalon shook her head. "You have two mothers: your mother who birthed you, and your mother who raised you."

"Hurry," the Guide interjected. "It is almost dusk, and I want to make the ravine by then."

Very glad for the interruption, Avalon shrugged at Taggerty and turned back to follow the Guide. They made the ravine when there was still some light left in the sky, and the Guide immediately looked over the side and moved left and right several times. Avalon assumed he was looking for the best place for them to repel down until she remembered they had no rope, and they would each have to climb down untethered. She recalled how easily the wall crumbled, but she stopped worrying about the climb down when she realized that this was the last time tonight she would have the privacy of the woods.

"Excuse me," Avalon said as she walked off.

Taggerty looked around and seemed to get nervous. "We need to stick together," he told her.

Avalon was flustered for a moment and then regained her composure. "I am a Prince of Fontanasia, and I deserve my privacy." She said it the same way that Walthan had on the first night of their outing, and it came out as arrogance, but she didn't mean for it to. She bit her lip and walked away.

Taggerty didn't say anything, but his face turned red. "We don't have time for this," he complained aloud.

"Don't worry, the prince is fine," his uncle told him without looking back, his eyes intent on one part of the overhang.

As she looked for some cover, Avalon patted Jackie who was making the trip in her torn waist pocket. She was angry and pushed aside the thought that the anger might be resentment over pretending to be a boy. Lying to Taggerty was becoming difficult for her, more difficult since she had been able to share her secret with Walthan, and more difficult because Walthan was not here to confide in. She and Taggerty were friends now, and aside from Zaria and Myra, Avalon had no others.

"Shouldn't we stay up here tonight and then go down in the light?" Avalon asked when she returned. She couldn't imagine sleeping amongst the sand eels.

"We're too exposed up here. There is a rock ledge, we will be safe," Taggerty answered as he looked back over his shoulder. Avalon looked for the Guide, and then she realized he had already begun his descent. She crouched next to Taggerty and watched as the Guide expertly lowered himself down the soft side of the ravine to the bottom.

Next it was Avalon's turn. She lay on the ground face down, her hips rolled to one side so she wouldn't squish Jackie. As Avalon pushed her feet over the abyss, Taggerty grabbed the back of her shirt to help her over the ledge. When she had her hands clasped around two large tree roots, she looked up at Taggerty and nodded. He was slow to let go of her shirt, and then she was hanging in the air on her own. She held her weight by her arms and lowered herself slowly, one exposed tree root at a time. Her feet kicked dust and dirt out as the wall crumbled beneath them. Avalon had climbed her own mountain for years, but it was one thing to be hauled up by a rope, and another to try to hold on and hope a dirt avalanche wouldn't spill her to the ground below. Avalon was malnourished and her muscles burned. She panted from the exertion, but she was not injured and was able to make the bottom without a problem. Taggerty was next, and his arms were tired from the fight and the work of supporting Walthan. He took his time and reached the bottom as the sky turned a dull pink.

The moment Taggerty's feet touched the ground, the Guide said, "There is enough time." He turned and started running across the boulders and rocks to the other side of the ravine. Avalon didn't need any encouragement, and she started running behind him with Taggerty in her wake. She closed her hand around the small pouch of keeley dust that was tied inside the bottom of her shirt. It was difficult to balance when she had to duck through the dead fallen trees, but she didn't dare let go of the little pouch. She focused clearly on each rock in front of her, taking one at a time before focusing on the next. They crossed to the other side without incident, the last two hundred feet being the most difficult because the sky was almost completely dark. When Avalon reached the other side, she wondered how this small task had seemed so difficult just two weeks earlier.

Taggerty panted, "I wouldn't mind that bridge you were talking about being put up here."

"No," Avalon said quickly in a high voice, covering it with a cough. She realized that he was making a joke but couldn't leave the thought out in the night. She relaxed herself and said in a deeper tone, "No. Walthan was right, a bridge wouldn't do."

The wall on this side of the ravine was shiny, solid black rock, and was very hard. The Guide showed them onto a wide ledge ten feet off the ground of the ravine. "The sand eels can't reach this ledge," the Guide announced as he lit a fire from the brush and branches he had managed to collect on his run across the ravine. More grateful for this fire than any other in her lifetime, Avalon moved in as close as she dared without singeing her hair.

"And the everreds?" she asked the Guide.

"They are not a problem on this side of the window," he said without looking at her.

They ate the dried jerky meat in silence, and Avalon, who had originally been repulsed by the taste, was growing fond of the salt-leather meal. The Guide was soon snoring, and Avalon was surprised to see him sleep for the first time.

"He knows we are perfectly safe here," Taggerty told her. "And he's been awake for days."

Avalon looked between the two men. "You are very pale for a Guide," she confirmed.

"I was born an albino."

"You don't look albino."

"For a Guide I am."

Avalon looked at the Guide's dark hair and dark skin and could see that Taggerty would be considered very white for their kind.

Taggerty rested his back against the black rock. "I was the son of two Guides, and when they saw how pale I was born, I could have been shunned. But when they read me…"

"They read you?"

Taggerty chuckled. "The chief reads all children to determine their future."

Myra had always been superstitious, and so Avalon understood. "What was your future?" Avalon asked when Taggerty hesitated to offer his reading.

"I was said to be the hope of the king."

Avalon was sure the Guide had been sleeping, but he lifted his head, unsatisfied with Taggerty's answer. "He is the king's future," he said sternly before laying his head back and closing his eyes again.

A small voice inside Avalon couldn't help but ask, *the future of which king*? She immediately put the thought out of her head as Taggerty rolled his eyes. Avalon wondered if he was being humble, or if he didn't really believe in their traditions since he wasn't raised with the Guides.

Taggerty continued, "The Guides took this reading as a great sign, and decided that it was a miracle I was born albino, because I was the perfect person to stay close to the king without raising alarms."

"This all sounds very superstitious," Avalon said.

"The Guides are a superstitious people."

"But you're not?"

"Well, I was born a Guide, but I was not raised a Guide. I hold their traditions to esteem because it is my history and I was taught well, but I was not raised amongst them to accept their beliefs without question."

"So then why are you here now as one of the kings guard?" Avalon asked.

Taggerty paused before he answered, looking up at the growing number of stars in the sky. He sighed heavily. "No matter what your beliefs, when someone tells you that you are destined for a great opportunity, you prepare for it. Whether you do it consciously or not, once you are told, it is in your subconscious waiting to manifest itself."

Avalon should be a princess, and yet here she was, the next king of Fontanasia. She understood him explicitly.

"So, I was raised away from the Guides and accepted as normal society."

"Where you just so happened to become one of the king's guard, and the youngest ever."

"If 'just so happened' means that I trained every day since I was a young boy, then yes, it just so happened."

"But then you should be with my father because he is the king." Avalon was excited now, thinking about her father. She didn't mean to blame Taggerty, but her tone bordered on accusation.

"I needed to see Cormicks. And we weren't sure what Brick was up to, so he needed to be watched. There was no way to know that this trip would go so poorly." Taggerty frowned because he felt responsible for the debacle in not stopping Brick from starting the first fire.

Always aware of his surroundings, and sensing an argument growing between the two youngsters, the Guide interjected. "We still have a lot of ground to cover. Let us rest."

They were soon fast asleep. The exhaustion of the past two weeks seeped deep into Avalon's bones, and she slept in a peaceful blackness most of the night until she became fitful as a story crafted itself in her mind, and she began to dream.

She was in the Hall of Kings confronting Counselor Glenn. She held her sword at the ready, and then lunged forward, but the older man was ready for her and moved to the side, grazing Avalon's side with his blade, causing her to fall to the floor. She put her hand on the cut, and it bled through her shirt.

Counselor Glenn stood over her with a twisted expression bordering on both malice and concern.

"You shut your mouth, you have no idea what is going on here!" he yelled at Avalon whom remained on the floor. "Your father was a great leader, but his time is over. I have a chance now, a chance to work for the people. If King Birch could have only seen…"

Avalon woke up screaming and had to climb through the cobwebs to realize that she was on the rock ledge, in the ravine, with Taggerty and the Guide. She was sweating and noticeably disturbed but tried to compose herself. She noticed that Taggerty had untied his jacket from his waist and placed it on her while she slept. The summer night air was chilly and she could see that he was cold in his short sleeves. She quickly gave the jacket back without a word to save herself the embarrassment.

"I'm fine," she told them, but they continued to watch her.

"You have been dreaming," the Guide told her. Avalon was stunned that the he could know that, but she offered nothing.

"We do know about your dreams," the Guide added. "Tell me what happened."

"What are you talking about?" Taggerty asked.

When Avalon didn't say anything, the Guide continued talking to Taggerty without taking his eyes off of Avalon. "You should know this, nephew. You are old enough now for the story. We all dream in our sleep, but the Hall family does not. They see only a black void, like the darkest night. But many of those born to the Hall family have been able to see a picture of the future in their minds while they are sleeping. These pictures are real. They dream the future."

Avalon was unconsciously holding her side where Counselor Glenn had stabbed her in her dream. She looked at Taggerty, offering the rest. "And dreams always come true," she told him. She had a stricken look on her face.

"What is it?" asked the Guide. "The ravine? Do you fall tomorrow on the climb?"

"No," Avalon told him. "It was Counselor Glenn." Avalon looked to the stars in the sky and thought about Zaria. She hoped her sister was okay because Counselor Glenn was clearly out of control.

"But he is here in the forest?" the Guide asked disbelievingly, looking up the sides of the ravine.

"No." Avalon told him. "He is in the castle. I was confronting him in the Hall of Kings. He was on a rampage."

"But it will take us more that a full day to reach the outer wall," the Guide told Avalon factually but meaning no disrespect.

Avalon half smiled and looked at Taggerty's expression hoping he wasn't thinking that she was abnormal. "I'm a little different. Dreams for me can happen any time in the next week."

The Guide was visibly stunned at her admission because the tale said that the Hall's dreams were to come true in the next day.

He had never heard of anyone seeing farther out than that. "King Birch told me you were special." He lay back down on the rock. "And now I know you make it back to the castle safely, and I can sleep without worry."

The Guide's relaxed demeanor helped little, and Avalon began to lose hope by the minute. She had known that her father's death was a possibility since Brick had told her in the castle at Cormicks, but she had always believed that her father had outsmarted Counselor Glenn. Now, her dream was proof that her father was indeed gone. There would be no other reason for her to be confronting Counselor Glenn. Dreams were selective though, showing the truth but allowing the mind to fold the story in many directions. She shivered as she remembered the dream she'd had as a child of Counselor Glenn pushing her down the stairs. That same expression of malice and concern on his face as he looked down on her all those years ago had shown itself again this night. Avalon felt doomed. She took a deep breath and tried not to assume, but the dread that her father was lost, that he was dead like Walthan, crept into the edges of her every thought.

"Sleep," Taggerty told her. "My uncle is right."

"I don't think I can sleep right now," Avalon admitted, still jilted by the images.

Taggerty dropped some small branches on the fire and offered Avalon a seat against the wall next to him so they could sit up and watch the flames.

"So you can see the future?" Taggerty asked intrigued.

Avalon felt defensive, and the way his eyes sparkled in the flames made her nervous. She wasn't sure what to say. "It's not all the time or anything. Once a year, sometimes more, sometimes less. Usually, when I sleep, I see nothing."

"Wow," Taggerty nodded his head as he poked at the fire. "What do you see in your dreams?"

"I don't know." This was the first time she saw humility in Taggerty as he typically had an answer for everything. "Just stuff, like fantasies."

"Monsters?"

Taggerty laughed. "Sure, when I was a kid like you."

Avalon cringed at that. They were only four years apart in age, but Taggerty made it sound like it was a world of difference.

"Just things that are made up. You could make up a story right now, and that would be a dream. It's hard to explain."

Avalon was intrigued to talk about it since she had been wondering about dreams since she was seven years old, but it was still difficult for her to imagine what a dream would consist of for someone else. She exhaled slowly letting the angst run out of her. The residual emotion from her newest dream lessened, and she tried not to think that it was because she felt safe with Taggerty. Sometime, between talking and watching the fire, Avalon managed to fall asleep. She awoke in the night and Taggerty's coat was on her again. Her arm had fallen off her lap and onto Taggerty's hand. He was sitting up beside her, asleep, and didn't notice, and in her embarrassment, she pulled her hand quickly away.

She watched the sky, a million familiar stars looking down on her, yet this world was all different now that she had seen Cormicks. She wondered how no one in Fontanasia had ever asked why, as a people, they were alone in the world. But the question hadn't even occurred to her until now, now that she had seen the other side. Although life could be complicated at times, time spent in Fontanasia was peaceful and joyous. There had been no reason to look beyond her existence, no reason to question.

The Guide woke them at the first sign of light, and Avalon stretched her weary muscles. She could see that the Guide must have been awake for a while because the fire was gone and there was no trace that it had ever been started. He led, and they climbed the ravine as quickly as their sore bodies would allow. Avalon replayed the conversations she had shared the night before with Taggerty. She had been suspicious of him when the trip set out, but her opinion had changed now that she knew his secret.

The Guide was in perfect health, and he pushed Avalon and Taggerty. It was easier going on the way home, and he didn't need to be as precise with his landmarks. There were no packs to carry, and they jogged through the forest with little rest. In one day, he had led them back to the edge of the woods. When she didn't see the horses, Avalon's hopes sank, but then there was a low whistling, and before Avalon knew what was happening, the Guide had whistled back and a man in a robe crept out of the woods. He was a tall, dark, Guide as well, and the three clasped and shook at the wrists in greeting as Avalon watched.

The tall Guide looked into the woods behind Avalon. "You are fewer than expected."

"Trouble," Taggerty's uncle responded simply.

Another Guide emerged from the woods trailed by seven horses. "Where are the rest?" he asked.

"They are both dead," the Guide said regretfully. They didn't say another word, but Avalon knew that the pained looks on the dark faces were for Walthan.

"We need not rush," the tall Guide added. She wasn't sure what that meant, but the others took his word easily.

They saddled up, and Avalon was struck by the Guides' ability to take the moment for what it was and to move on without asking exactly what had happened. In a world of planning and plotting, she did not think she could have the strength to do that, and she admired them for it, although she had a million questions for them.

"My father?" she asked.

"We have not seen him in almost three weeks," the robed Guide told her without adding more. Avalon had no more questions for him right now as she let her tears flow down her face and into the wind. They didn't ride full out, and Avalon wanted to push the rest so she could get back to the castle in a half a day. She took the lead and then reined back waiting for the others to catch up.

Taggerty galloped his horse next to Avalon's. "It is not wise to rush in when you don't know where you will end up."

"I do know where I will end up. I will confront Counselor Glenn for the death of my father."

"Did you see your father dead in your dream?" Taggerty's uncle asked.

"No".

"Then it is foolish to assume that you know he is dead."

"I don't want him to be," Avalon said defensively.

"And in your dream did you see your own death?" Taggerty asked.

Avalon thought that this was an outrageous question. "Of course not!"

Taggerty replied like a Guide. "So then you don't know where you will end up at all, do you?"

Avalon's face reddened, but she didn't reply.

"And since you know that you will confront Counselor Glenn, we will get there in due time," the Guide added.

They rode on in silence. Avalon had always been so sure of her dreams and had never looked at the whole picture before. She found the reason in their answers, but had a hard time finding patience. They were at the outer wall by evening. Avalon could not find the passage through the wall this time either as the brick construction was designed to deceive the eye on this side in order to keep out intruders. But without even craning their necks, the Guides easily walked the horses down a quarter mile, and they all slipped through the jagged opening. When they approached Fontanasia at dusk, Avalon made to ride straight up through the fingers to the main entrance, but Taggerty stopped her.

"Wait, Prince Avalon," Taggerty placed his horse in front of hers before she could ride.

"Prince Avalon," the robed Guide told her, "you must come with us."

She wanted to storm in. She wanted to draw her sword and order the king's guard to take her to Counselor Glenn immediately. But the Guides were right. She didn't know where she would end up, only that Counselor Glenn would cut her in his final deceit against the Hall family. She didn't need to rush to that moment. She needed to plan.

They led Avalon back to the small outer section of the city where Guides lived between the city's outer wall and forest. They dismounted and led Avalon inside one of the strong stone houses where a lot of people were silently waiting. They gathered around an older man who had presented Avalon with Jackie at her birthday party, and she realized that he was their tribal leader. She looked around the large space and noticed men and women of all ages who crowded in but didn't show any rank aside from their deference to their leader, and deference to her, she noticed.

"It seems that young Taggerty was right," Taggerty's uncle offered.

Avalon noticed a girl approach Taggerty and kiss him on the cheek. The girl hugged his waist and then remained next to him, and Avalon tried to ignore the pang in her stomach.

Taggerty's uncle continued. "The soldier, Brick, tried to get us all killed, and in turn Prince Avalon was captured."

Avalon, who was growing frantic for news, had expended all of her patience. "Never mind that," she told the tribal leader. "What news of my father?"

In the following minutes, she heard many rumors from the collection of Guides, but in the long run, they didn't know what had happened to their king. Three weeks earlier, Counselor Glenn had declared himself Chancellor of Fontanasia and closed the castle to visitors. The people in the town had been left alone, each day business as usual. They asked their questions, but since each day went on without disturbance, there was little uprising. The counselor from each burrow reported that an easy exchange of power was going on between the council and King Birch, and that all was well.

Avalon listened as long as she could, and then she stood. "I don't mean to be disrespectful in any way," she said. "My father has always told me that you are to be trusted, no questions asked. But I can't sit here any longer. I need to get inside the castle to find my father and my sister. I will be allowed to enter the castle or I will break into my home with or without your help!" She thought that she had sounded firm but levelheaded, and wasn't sure what the ravaged expression on her face told them. She could see them all watching her, and she was furious for their ability to remain calm in the moment that her world was imploding. She let out a long sigh in defeat but was saved from her exasperation.

The eldest Guide spoke calmly. "There is way in, but it is a king's secret."

Chapter 15
Long Live the King

When the first king of Fontanasia had the castle built, a secret stone passageway was constructed within the outer walls to give the Guides privileged access to the king. *And to give the king a way out if attacked*, Avalon thought as she squeezed through the tight space. She hadn't known about the passageway until this morning, when, after a solid twelve hours of sleep that helped cure her exhaustion, the Guides had told her of their plan to get her into the castle undetected. Taggerty and Avalon followed a small Guide single file through the tiny maze that had been carved to fit one man. The air was stuffy as the summer sun warmed the bricks, but Avalon could feel a slight breeze move past her skin. They spiraled up on a manageable incline, and Avalon wondered what parts of the castle they were passing, and how many times she might have been in a room when a Guide was creeping past through the walls.

In a few places, they had to crawl a short distance or turn around and pull up onto a new level of rock, and Avalon's hands and knees felt raw from scraping the hard surface. Her legs were burning when the floor leveled out, and she had to turn her shoulders sideways to fit through the space where a concave rock was moved aside by the Guide. She didn't know how Taggerty could have squeezed through the passage, but he surfaced right behind her. It wasn't until they emerged behind a large embroidered rug with the Hall crest that Avalon realized they were in the throne room. A memory sparked from when she was younger of a Guide retreating behind the throne after speaking in confidence with her father. *My father who is dead now.* She tried not to linger on the thought, but it was the reason she was here now, in this moment, a moment that never should have come.

After showing them safely into the castle, the aged Guide left Taggerty and Avalon, pulling the stone snug in its place and retreating down the passageway. The Guides were counselors, not warriors, and it had been decided that Avalon would have her chance to find her family, the Guides' only assistance being a silent entrance into the castle. But Taggerty was a soldier, and he would not leave Prince Avalon to fight alone. He followed Avalon through a series of side hallways, the pair stopping to listen for any movement at every corner. Avalon was determined, but not overly confident, and their reconnaissance took a long time. They finally turned into an abandoned servant's corridor where Avalon led Taggerty to Myra's chambers. Myra had been staying in a room in the king's suite since Avalon was born, but as Attendant to the royal family, she kept this apartment as well.

Avalon's heart leapt with hope as she pushed the door open, but Myra was not there, and Taggerty could find no sign that she had been there recently. Avalon grit her teeth and then gestured Taggerty to a closet. She showed him a loose panel and they both squeezed into the small space. Avalon pulled the hidden panel back in place and whispered for Taggerty to follow her, and soon they were climbing a ladder up through the interior castle walls. This was the same hidden passage that Myra had used to sneak baby Connor to the king's quarters those fourteen years ago. The same passage that Avalon had used as a young child on stormy nights to sneak into Myra's room for comfort, and the same passage Myra would use to escort Avalon back to Zaria's room to ride out the storm. Avalon knew the king's quarters would be the next best place to look. She also didn't know whom she could trust, and if her family wasn't there, maybe Counselor Glenn would be. If he wasn't, she knew where to find him.

Avalon reached the top, subconsciously counting the rungs in the pitch black. She could hear Taggerty well behind her, finding his way slowly in the dark. She remembered the monarch of Cormicks, and shuddering, she realized that this passage must have been meant as an escape route for the king in a time of need.

"Stop," she whispered down to Taggerty as his boots scraped the rungs. He didn't hear her, and she let one foot dangle back in the darkness. Taggerty pulled his head up into her boot and she could hear his muffled grunt. "Sorry," she whispered down. He moved down a rung and waited.

Avalon pulled a corner of a panel aside and looked into Zaria's bedroom. She was flushed with grateful warmth when she saw Zaria and Myra sitting together at the foot of the bed. She almost ran to them, but realized that they might not be alone. She looked around in the dusty space before taking Jackie out of her pocket.

"Jackie, go to Zaria," she whispered to the tiny, red lizard. Jackie immediately scrambled out of her hand and through the paneling. He scurried up Zaria's dress and into her lap, causing Zaria to squeal. Then she realized that it was the jakkow, and Zaria and Myra both jumped out of their seats tossing Jackie under a table set.

"Don't!" Myra commanded in a hiss just as the outer door opened.

"What is it?" a harsh voice asked from out of Avalon's view.

"Nothing," Zaria lied. "I, I…" she stuttered but Myra cut in.

"We saw a mouse!" Myra bellowed. "A mouse in my lady's chambers! This is outrageous! You must let the servants in to clean, and allow us out for some fresh air!" Myra's stern voice could intimidate almost anyone, but there was no reply and the door slammed closed.

"Avalon!" Zaria held her hand to her mouth, gulping her tears back.

Myra was up out of her seat as Avalon burst through the hidden panel. Never so happy to see her family, Avalon wrapped her arms around Zaria and Myra, and the three collapsed to the floor in a hug. Taggerty climbed out of the small hidden space and faced away to the door, not wanting to intrude on this tender moment.

"Where is father?" Avalon asked Zaria who couldn't answer. Myra brushed Avalon's hair back, but it was Zaria who found her voice.

"Father is dead," Zaria said. She'd had some time to come to term with the words, and Avalon, who had known deep down it was true, swallowed back her guilt, her anger, and her tears.

"What happened?" she said gravely.

It was Myra's turn to speak. "He was poisoned at dinner four nights after you left. We were told only after Counselor Glenn had locked down the castle."

"Has he hurt you?"

"No," Zaria answered. "We have been locked in this suite and have been treated well. Counselor Glenn visited once, but Myra spat in his face and he left almost as soon as he'd arrived."

"Where is Uncle Hawker? Is he here with you?" Avalon looked around quizzically. She was firing off questions as fast as she could, knowing that she had to act now and grieve later.

"I heard that Counselor Glenn has him locked in the dungeon," Myra answered.

"Heard from who?" Avalon asked in amazement.

Myra pulled her shoulders back proudly. "From my nephew. He is on the guard."

Taggerty stepped forward. "Will he help us?"

"Who is this?" Myra asked defensively.

"I recognize him," Zaria answered. "This is..." she searched for his name.

"Taggerty," Avalon answered.

"Yes, that's right," Zaria said pleasantly surprised. She opened like a flower under sunlight, Avalon watching as her sister's slumped and defeated figure became postured and pleasant again. Zaria stepped between Avalon and Taggerty looking straight into the soldier's face. "He is no threat, Myra. I saw him escort Avalon home the night of the festival. Apparently, he'd rescued her in a sword fight." Zaria's comment would have bothered Avalon before her trip to Cormicks, but not anymore. Still, there was a small voice that gained volume in the back of her head that noted Zaria's immediate change from captured prisoner into princess and host. Avalon noticed Taggerty rock back on his feet and stare at her for the briefest of seconds before turning his attention back to her sister.

"Princess Zaria." Taggerty managed a slight bow.

Avalon had no time for jealousy, and she moved to the window. There was one person she wanted to discuss these events with, one person she wanted advice from more than anyone else, but her father was dead. "What will I do?" she asked the night. The moon was its familiar black with bright twinkling spots.

"You know what you will do," Zaria said as she took her sister's side. "You will face Counselor Glenn and take back control of Fontanasia as the lawful heir to the throne."

"You will do no such thing!" Myra bit her lower lip. "I won't see you in danger, Avalon. There is a better way," she said sternly and then softly, "There has to be a better way."

The exhaustion began to creep in, and Avalon wanted to be seven years old again, curled up on Myra's lap, and rocked to sleep. She pushed the thought away and focused her eyes. "I saw it in a dream," Avalon told Myra. "I will confront him." Avalon hadn't told anyone the entire vision: that Counselor Glenn would injure and possibly kill her. But she had to go. She had to avenge her father.

Myra met Avalon at the window and resisted the urge to grab her young prince in a bear hug. Instead, she simply put her hand on Avalon's shoulder. "Then you will need the help of my nephew," Myra said. "I will bring him here." Myra moved toward the hidden panel, but Avalon stopped her.

"Wait," Avalon said. "Taggerty, I need you to take Zaria and Myra to safety."

Myra tried to interject, but Avalon put her hand up.

"Have Myra tell you how to find her nephew. We don't know the guard's allegiance, and we will need to have some of the guard on our side to make this work."

"Once they see you, Avalon, the guard is yours," Myra assured her.

"Brick was working for Counselor Glenn," Taggerty told the two ladies. "We don't know who to trust."

Myra looked shaken at that, but she regained her composure quickly. "Well, you can trust my nephew, William," she answered sternly. She pulled Avalon into a long hug, unable to hold back her tears, and then she knelt. She looked up into Avalon's face with the grace and admiration of a mother. "The king is dead, long live the king." Myra drew out her words and then took Avalon's hand, her kiss upon it the final seal of her love and allegiance.

Taggerty knelt and repeated Myra's gesture. "The king is dead, long live the king."

Avalon looked down at Taggerty, all of the features on her face wrestling her command to remain still. She swallowed back tears as she remembered what he had said about preparing for the opportunity before you. All of these years she had prepared for this moment, and it had come too soon.

Zaria approached Avalon and knelt, her actions truly sincere toward her young sister. "The king is dead, long live the king." In all of her grief, and for all of the teasing Zaria managed throughout Avalon's life, Zaria's words were heartfelt as she kissed Avalon's hand.

Avalon pulled Zaria and Myra into a hug and held on tight to what was left of her family. She bit her lip again and stepped away.

"Now go," Avalon ordered Taggerty. "We will meet back here."

"We must not split up, Prince Avalon," Taggerty blurted and then continued with hesitation. "I mean…"

"Never mind," she told Taggerty, not wanting to hear the words yet. "I must look through the suite for weapons and anything that can help us. It's quicker this way."

Taggerty tipped his head forward in a bow, and Myra and Zaria kissed Avalon on the cheek, and then they were gone through the hidden passageway.

Avalon cracked open the side entrance and let Jackie go in ahead of her. When he made one turn of the room and came back, she moved silently through the suite to her father's room half expecting to see his lifeless body laid out on the bed, but it was empty. He'd been poisoned, and her mind raced through painful expressions frozen on his dead face. Her stomach turned, and she had to stop her train of thought before it pulled the bile up her throat. She moved to the immense bed and ran her fingers over the Hall crest that was embroidered on the bedcover. Her heart filled with despair, and she had to choke back her tears again. She was almost there, almost ready to grieve, but it was not time yet. Avalon took in a deep breath and let the rage fill her to her fingertips. Never having intended to wait for Taggerty's return, she moved out of her father's room and snuck back to the secret passageway. She had to make it to the dungeons before finding Counselor Glenn. Her Uncle Hawker was her best hope for help.

The dungeons at Fontanasia had served little purpose since they were built. They were kept clean and had never housed a hardened criminal or enemy of the state. On sparse occasion they housed men who had too much to drink and needed a night in jail to sleep it off. Avalon found her way through the hidden panel and back down the ladder to the servants' corridor. She took her time, making sure to expose herself to no one, and using a seldom-traveled staircase to move slowly down into the basement of the castle.

She crept past the metal workers where no one could hear her footsteps over the constant cracking of hammers on metal. She snaked across the basement to the dungeon area where she encountered her first obstacle. A single guard stood outside the entryway to the cells. She watched him pace, bite his nails, study the ceiling, and stretch, taking time to close his eyes and bare his teeth in a huge yawn. He was obviously bored, and Avalon deduced that the guard could not have found his job here very important. There was one way in, and Avalon had no time to waste. She held her knife in her left hand behind her back and approached the guard.

"Step aside," Avalon bellowed, still twenty paces away. The guard snapped to, but did not move out of the way. "I said step aside!" Her command was the deep roar of her father.

The guard placed one hand on his sword and leaned forward trying to decipher the person approaching in the dim light. He moved forward and was about to challenge Avalon when she stepped close enough, and he finally recognized her.

"I can't, sire. Orders from Counselor Glenn…"

Avalon cut him off. "Do you know who I am?" She was speaking loudly into his face. He was taller than her, but his shoulders slumped forward and he shrank before snapping to attention.

"Y-Yes, Prince Avalon," he stuttered. She was in his face now causing him to look down at the ground, and she knew for certain that he would not pose a threat.

"Counselor Glenn has killed my father," Avalon told the guard whose crinkled forehead and eyes moved up to hers. She'd caught him by complete surprise, and that caught her by surprise. *How could he not have already known?* she wondered. Avalon pulled in a sharp breath and prepared herself for her coming declaration. "I am your king now, and I am ordering you to step aside."

The guard straightened his posture and snapped his heels together, standing at attention before bowing to his king. He then spun around and, in one motion, removed his keys and unlocked the outer door.

"Take me to Prince Hawker," she told the guard who was already three cells ahead of her in a half jog. There was only one person in the dungeon right now, and the guard could not be mistaken as to whom King Avalon Hall was here to collect.

"Right away, your majesty."

His words bounced from the brick walls and faltered Avalon's step. They reached the end of the hall and the guard twisted his key ring, pulling a long key from the bunch. Avalon held her hand out. She couldn't trust that he would not lock her in with her uncle.

"Yes, your majesty," he said as he bowed and handed Avalon the key to the door ahead of her, scrambling out of her way.

"You stay here," she told the guard, hoping he would not sound the alarm. His silent bow was the only answer she needed. When she turned the key in the lock, she was reminded of her cell in Cormicks, and she didn't want to move forward, but she had no choice. However, she was put at some ease when the door did not creak open, and the cell inside was large and lit with torches. She noticed that Hawker didn't even look up when she stepped in. It was only after Avalon called his name that Hawker managed a look of surprise and then a relieved smile.

"Avalon!" He stood, his rail thin frame towering over hers. She rushed in and hugged him noting that his black clothes did not look soiled and actually smelled clean. She felt relieved that at least Counselor Glenn had treated Hawker civilized, even though he was locked up in the dungeon. When he pulled her away, he looked down into her drawn face. "Avalon, you don't look well."

She shook her head, trying not to think about what she looked like or what she felt like, and trying to put the past month behind her so she could face the future. "Uncle Hawker, I have to get you out of here." She pulled on his spaghetti hands as his nose twitched.

"What happened to you, Avalon?"

"I will tell you all about that later, but right now we have to go."

"Wait, Avalon," Hawker said solemnly, pulling back on her shoulder as she turned away to lead him out of the cell. "There is something you should know."

She took his hand and pulled him toward the cell door, knowing what the moment would bring if she surrendered her guard. "Zaria told me, Uncle Hawker. Father is dead." Again, she swallowed her tears down before the river of emotion could wash her away.

"I'm sorry," he told her, this time his long fingers forcing her shoulders around. He pulled her in and hugged her tight, and Avalon realized that her typically studious and unemotional uncle was struggling with the news. He was probably terrified being locked up here as she had been in Cormicks. Avalon squeezed her uncle's back and then pulled away quickly.

"Come with me," she said sternly. "We have to find Counselor Glenn." Hawker pursed his lips and nodded his head. He followed her closely, and they moved quickly up to the dungeon outer door with the guard in tow. Avalon peeked out, and the way was clear.

"Wait," Hawker said in a half whisper. "We shouldn't do this alone, it's too dangerous."

Avalon was impatient, but she listened. Confronting Counselor Glenn in the Hall of Kings was the only true plan she'd made. She hadn't counted on Hawker being locked up, but she was glad to have him with her now. He'd been her counselor her entire life, and he would know what to do. When she paused, he stepped around her in one long stride and grabbed the guard by the lapel, pulling the stunned man up into his own face.

"You," Hawker accosted, "do you swear allegiance to the king, or to Counselor Glenn?"

"The king, of course!" the guard was visibly insulted, and Hawker's grip slackened.

Avalon needed to confront Counselor Glenn alone. If she could contain the situation and stop Counselor Glenn, she could take back control of Fontanasia and squelch any rumors of a rebellion. The people needed unity if they were going to face the Runners. A chill ran up her spine as she imagined the monarch leading his Runners to Fontanasia at this very moment. It was not possible now, but Cormicks would have the full moon back in less than a month's time. Avalon leaned in to the guard who had been released by Hawker and now stood back flattening his jacket. "William George of the king's guard, do you know him?"

"Of course, your majesty."

"Go find him," she ordered.

"Yes, your Majesty," he said to her with a deep bow.

Each time he addressed her in that manner, Avalon thought of her father. "He'll know what to do, find him," Avalon managed.

"Go," Hawker barked at the guard.

The guard left quickly, and Avalon waited a minute, and then she walked out of the dungeon at a casual pace. She wore borrowed clothes and did not look like royalty, so if she was lucky, she would be difficult to identify if someone wasn't looking directly at her. Hawker on the other hand was unmistakable. His beanstalk frame matched no other, and his attire was always the same black clothing covered by black robe adorned with the Hall family crest. He must have sensed Avalon's concern, because he stayed ten paces behind her as she took him up to the main floor. She had to wait at times for servants and guards to move through the many rooms before they were empty and clear to pass, but they arrived in the throne room undetected.

Avalon's eyes moved to the tapestry that hid the Guide's passage, and she wondered if Taggerty had come this way to get Zaria and Myra out. But Avalon doubted it, because Myra's bulk might not make it through the tiny space. Avalon paused hoping Taggerty would be back any moment, wanting to see his face and ask his opinion of everything.

"What is it?" Hawker whispered when Avalon remained still.

"Nothing," she whispered back.

He noticed Avalon's eyes lingering toward the throne and mistook her thoughts. "Try not to think about him right now, Avalon. There will be plenty of time to grieve." She looked back at her uncle and the sorrow on his face immediately reflected in hers. She took a deep breath and the anger filled the empty space within her. "Counselor Glenn is in the Hall of Kings," she told her uncle as she moved away from the throne.

Her uncle remained a few paces behind her as they crept down the final corridor. Avalon pushed the door open a crack and surveyed the room. Counselor Glenn was there, hunched over a marble table with two advisors at his side. Avalon's blood boiled when she recognized one of the men as Counselor Loren of the lower burrow. She wondered just how many had deserted her father in his final hour. She saw a servant enter through a side door and bring them a pitcher with glasses before retreating. The traitors mumbled something, and then, as though the heavens were watching, everyone except Counselor Glenn left the room, allowing Avalon her moment. Avalon pushed on the door, but her uncle held her shoulder.

"Let me," he told her. "I don't want you getting hurt."

"Uncle," Avalon said in a hardened resolve, "you have to let me do this."

He sighed, but ultimately he let his nephew go. She pushed the door open and walked directly toward the marble table, her hand already drawing her sword. Avalon walked past carved statues of former kings. She was very close to Counselor Glenn before he looked up from his work. His expression turned to pure shock and then a flicker of amusement moved to the surface.

"Prince Avalon!" he managed as he stood. Avalon did not slow her pace. "I didn't think you were alive." Counselor Glenn's hands went up in front of him when he saw her weapon.

"Of course you didn't think I was alive. You sent Brick to have me killed, and then you killed my father so you could take the throne for yourself!" Avalon's voice rose to a yell although she was almost upon him. When he realized that she was not going to stop until she had run him through, he sprang for the sword that lay in front of him on the table. Filled with rage and forgetting what had happened in her dream, Avalon raised her sword and thrust at Counselor Glenn. He stepped back, and she lunged forward over the corner of the table, but the older man was ready for her and moved to the side. Her anger prevented her from making a calculated move, and Counselor Glenn grazed Avalon's torso with his blade causing her to fall to the floor, her sword popping out of her hand and spilling out away from her. She put her hand on the cut, and it bled through her shirt, but it was not as bad as it should have been. Here in the room, outside of her dream, Avalon could tell from her mistake that Counselor Glenn could have sliced her in half if he had wanted to. He stood over her with a twisted expression bordering on both malice and concern.

"You shut your mouth, you have no idea what is going on here!" he yelled at Avalon who remained on the floor. "Your father was a great leader, but his time is over. I have a chance now, a chance to work for the people. If King Birch could have only seen…"

Avalon waited for the rest of his words because he had cut off here in her dream, but he didn't finish his thought. He stood over her looking from her face to the bloody wound on her side. Hawker had entered the room, and Avalon tried not to watch his approach. He was very calm as he slinked up behind Counselor Glenn. She looked back at the aged counselor trying to keep his gaze so that her uncle would have the element of surprise. He had never been a fighter, and she didn't know what Hawker would do.

Counselor Glenn must have taken her stare as an act of defiance, because it awoke him from his stupor and he continued. "You see, the time of the king is over. Did you think that you would make a great king? You are a child."

"I am not a child!" Avalon yelled and then grabbed her side tighter from the splitting pain.

"Quiet, boy," Counselor Glenn said with such contempt that Avalon looked to Hawker involuntarily, and Counselor Glenn followed her gaze. Then as if forgetting her, he spun around to face her uncle, his sword at the ready. "I should have known Prince Avalon would find you first," he said to Hawker. Avalon waited for Hawker to make a move as she lay there and bled, but he had never been a warrior, and he hesitated now that he had lost the element of surprise.

"Do you think that your uncle is going to help you?" Glenn spat loudly without looking at Avalon. "He is no longer your advisor, and he is looking to find his place in this kingdom. Is everyone blind of that fact?" Counselor Glenn seemed to ask this question to the stone statues that lined the empty hall. Then he turned looked down at Avalon.

"Do you think he would risk his neck for his nephew after he…"

But he was never allowed to finish the thought. Avalon saw the jerk of his head followed by a spray of red, and she heard blood gurgling out of his windpipe. Counselor Glenn crumpled to the floor. It happened so fast that Avalon lay still in shock, her mouth open, and her mind unable to connect the knife in Counselor Glenn's throat with her Uncle Hawker.

"I wanted to kill that sniveling idiot on the night that my brother died, but he had me locked up," Hawker announced righteously. He tilted his head and shrugged at Avalon, smiling at the lucky throw of the blade.

Avalon let out a stilted sigh and took in a full breath. A tear escaped down her cheek and she laid her head back on the marble floor as weeks of madness came to a pinnacle and dissipated. The trip was over, the journey that had gone so wrong had ended, and she was finally home. Zaria and Myra were safe now, and Avalon could only take up where her father had left off and hope that she could keep Fontanasia safe. She sat up on her elbows and tested her wound holding one hand out to her uncle so he could help her up. He turned on his heel and looked down at her.

"You know, I didn't see that one coming, him locking me up. Smart move on his part." Hawker walked past Avalon and pulled a sword from the nearest coat of arms and turned it over in his hands. He strode to Counselor Glenn's limp body and poked at it, but the old man was dead. "You can't trust anyone." He looked down his long nose with disdain for the elder statesman.

"I was starting to feel hopeless, locked up in the dungeon for weeks, none of the guards willing to free me. But then last night, I knew you were alive. I dreamt this moment, Avalon. Last night I knew you would find me and that I would kill Counselor Glenn."

Avalon was stunned. She had never known that her uncle could dream the future. No one knew, and she wondered why he'd never shared that fact. But it didn't matter now. Looking over at the limp and bloody figure of Counselor Glenn, a man she had been frightened of, and a man whom she had hated since she was seven years-old, she was glad that Hawker had avenged her father. Her anger had brought her here, but Avalon knew deep down that she would not have been able to take his life. She reached out again to her uncle, but instead of coming to her and checking on her wound, he strolled about the immense room, sizing up the statues of each of the former kings.

"Look at these statues, these shells of men!" he yelled. His words echoed in the large marble space. As she was about to call out to him for help, he raised his sword, and to Avalon's astonishment, he smashed the sword down onto one of their forefathers and broke the statue to bits. Avalon was horrified. Her eyes saw her Uncle Hawker, but his face had twisted into a hatred she had never seen. His lanky posture had corrected itself, and she saw the stance of a tall, capable combatant who knew how to wield a sword. She flinched, wondering why her instinct told her to look across the floor to her own sword, which was well out of reach. Hawker strolled to her, and Avalon wanted to reach up for his hand, but she recoiled with fright as Hawker's tall frame tipped over her with an evil grin. She saw in his smooth smile a mask of hatred worse than when his face had been twisted up in smashing the statue, and she felt like a doe about to be swallowed by a lion.

"King...Avalon...Hall?" he laughed. "What do you know at fourteen years old? Nothing!" He yelled at her. "You had to be born a boy, didn't you?"

Avalon was shocked and could only watch as Hawker decided his next move. His slow and studious manner was shed from him like a snake's skin, and he was now strong and confident and moved like lightning. She didn't recognize him at all. She looked at Counselor Glenn's lifeless body and wondered if he had been Hawker's puppet all these years.

"I was so close to taking the throne, and then you had to be born," Hawker ranted in outrage as he sliced through the air with his sword. "I tried to rectify that by replacing your mother's doctor with my own to ensure you would be stillborn, but your precious Myra George had to ruin everything. I never liked that woman," Hawker added as he punctuated his thought by crushing another statue with the sword. Sharp bits sprayed over Avalon and littered the floor, and Hawker crunched across it as he paced.

"Whatever faith in Birch that the council had lost was renewed with the little newborn boy Avalon Hall." Hawker sang this out mockingly, and Avalon's lip quivered. "Makes me sick!" he yelled as he cut a third statue down. "And then Birch got all paranoid and doubled his guard!" Hawker kicked large shards of broken statue at Avalon.

Avalon felt her hands shaking, and her face curled up in anger when she realized that it was Hawker who had been plotting to take the throne all of those years ago. Her throat filled with bile when she imagined herself as a baby, being born only to die at the hands of Hawker's stooge. She dared not think of the years he had pretended to love her, the years he had pretended to love his own brother. She swallowed it all down and steeled herself for what was to come. The electricity that moved through her body numbed the pain of her cut and she barely noticed it anymore. She watched him snake around the room and knew that she would be his next victim. She had to buy time.

"Why would you send Brick to open up the window to Cormicks?" she asked Hawker.

Hawker didn't even think it over as he spewed, "Look at these people, the people in this city!" his arm gestured toward the walls and the people outside them sleeping in their beds. "They are all fools, and the counselors are the biggest fools of all. Look at how many of them were willing to follow Counselor Glenn. A democracy? What a joke! I told your father that it was pointless to try to please the people."

Now, lying on the floor and bleeding, Avalon thought back to many conversations that Hawker had with her father about how to rule the people, but she had never picked up on any hostility he might be harboring. She remembered overhearing his conversation with Counselor Glenn near the armory in the basement and heard its meaning now clearly for the first time. She wished her dream had shown her this moment.

"The people of Fontanasia need to be shaken up. They don't know what despair is, and the best way to introduce them to true discontent and to make them appreciate their lives is to introduce them to Cormicks and the Runners, and the true beautiful chaos that they create. Only then will the people appreciate what they have."

"When it is lost," Avalon said.

Hawker looked up suddenly, awaking from his reverie, and looked at Avalon with his eyes wide. "My smart nephew. Of course, when it is lost."

Hawker stepped toward Avalon, and she immediately tensed.

"You know, Avalon, this is actually better than I could have planned. Now, I am the hero because Counselor Glenn killed you, and I had to kill him in defense of my own life. Now Fontanasia is mine, free and clear." Hawker took a candle from the table and looked down at Avalon who still held her bleeding torso. "I could distract you from the pain of your wound." He smiled, his rabbit's nose twitching in anticipation.

Avalon remembered the burning mouse in the basement and the rumors she'd heard from Myra, and she knew that he intended to burn her alive. Avalon panicked and tried to think of anything, but her mind was blank of all but a crippling fear. "So," she swallowed hard, "you know about Cormicks?"

Hawker cackled. "Know about it? I have fantasized about it. A place where I could be among people like me. Where I could test fire on anything or anyone without disapproval or judgment from anyone. Where I could take my senses for a spin and not have to be *good* or *nice*," he whined those words like a child. "I have spent years reading every document that I could find about Cormicks." His eyebrows lifted in consideration. "It was named Hawkerness, you know. I was named for it." He looked down at Avalon and noticed the flame dancing at his fingertips. "Cormicks is the place where I won't have to live up to anyone's expectations but my own."

Avalon's spine tingled. She was betrayed to the core, unable to recognize any of her uncle in this man. It was appalling to her that this relationship was over, destroyed, and what's more was never true. She had loved her Uncle Hawker, hugged him, spent hours with him, listened to his stories, and sought his advice. She'd loved him. Just ten minutes earlier everything had been fine between them, and now that love was gone, and all of her memories came into question and crumbled down so fast that it took her breath away.

"Are you crying?" Hawker sniveled.

She wasn't though. Taggerty, who had come to her aid four times before, had let himself in the same door she'd come through from the throne room, and Avalon had been washed with relief. No matter what happened to her now, Hawker would not get his hands on Zaria or Myra, nor would he be able to destroy the whole of Fontanasia.

Still, Avalon was stunned, and as Hawker spoke, she realized that she was still lying on the floor holding her side. She had been reliving her dream for two days, and the whole time she had thought about her moment with Counselor Glenn, she had been lying on the floor. The pain of her wound had dissipated, and it hadn't occurred to her before now that she should stand up. Avalon got to her knees and tried to reach her sword, but the bleeding had made her light headed. Hawker was standing over her now, and Avalon looked straight into his wicked face. Without another word he jolted forward, and Avalon flinched, expecting the point of his sword and the hot flame of the candle to plunge into her at the same time, but nothing happened.

She opened her eyes to see Hawker's arms had dropped, the sword and the candle clanging to the ground in front of her. Taggerty had run Hawker through from behind, and a crimson red blade protruded from the front of Hawker's chest. Two guards Avalon recognized as her sword trainer, Gamon, and a man deeply resembling Myra, rushed to her side and pulled her safely out of Hawker's reach. Hawker's tall frame waved to the left and the right before he toppled over. Avalon looked down at Hawker's bleeding body, and ignoring the stab of pain in her side, she pulled Gamon's sword from his hip and took a step forward.

"King Avalon," Taggerty warned as he stepped toward her.

"Roll him over," she told Taggerty. He watched her for a minute and then did as his king ordered. He pulled his sword from Hawker's back and used his foot to roll Hawker over, but he didn't move away. Avalon stared down at her uncle, his hands clutched at his stomach, his eyes full of disbelief. She stepped forward and elbowed Taggerty out of the way. Then she stepped one foot on Hawker's chest and held the sword to his neck. She squinted, the hurt and anger pushing tears to her eyes, but in the end, she could not avenge her father. She watched Hawker bleeding, and then handed the sword to Taggerty. He looked at Avalon who simply shook her head.

Chapter 16
The Oath

Avalon spent many days in seclusion. She rested and allowed the cut on her torso to begin healing, but she had unseen wounds that might never heal. Her father was dead, she was king, and everything that she thought was real was not. She had spent years of energy blindly hating Counselor Glenn, and her true enemy for all of her life had been Hawker. She spent hours wondering if it was Hawker who had pushed her down the stairs all of those years ago. Hawker had been right there on site, running down the stairs immediately to assist Avalon on the landing below. And she could remember the sneer on Counselor Glenn's face, but now saw it as the same expression of mixed anger and concern that he had shown in the Hall of Kings when she attacked him. And when Avalon had overheard Counselor Glenn threaten Hawker in the basement, she could now see that it was Hawker threatening Counselor Glenn. Everything was open for question now. The plans and plots, the deaths, it was all so confusing.

"Good afternoon, King Hall," Myra announced when she entered Avalon's room. The slit of light pouring in the door made Avalon squint, and when Myra pulled open the blinds, Avalon had to pull her blankets over her head to shield her eyes from the glare.

"Pish posh," Myra said to the pile of blankets. Avalon was glad to hear Myra's familiar voice, but she wasn't ready to face anyone.

"I said I didn't want to be disturbed," Avalon's deep, muffled voice bellowed from under the blankets.

"Yes, Zaria told me," Myra responded, unperturbed. She crossed to Avalon's closet and pulled out clothes, placing them on the trunk at the foot of the bed. Avalon could hear Myra's steps as she left the room, and she peeked out from under the blankets, taking time to allow her eyes to adjust. Just then, Myra returned with a washbasin and placed it on the side table.

"Up now," Myra said as she bolted the door to the suite.

Avalon lazily complied, pushing the covers off and standing up for the first time in a day. Myra cleaned Avalon's wound and put fresh bandages on it. Then Avalon washed with the warm water and a soft towel, but in the end, she didn't feel clean. Darkness hung on her like a cloak, and Avalon stared at herself in the mirror wondering if anyone else would notice the lump that remained lodged in her throat. She had so many questions but asking any of them would only tie knots in her mind that she would never be able to unravel. She pulled on a clean undershirt and returned to her bed, throwing back the blankets that Myra had just fixed.

"Avalon," Myra chided. Then she said more softly, "Avalon, you can't stay in this room forever."

Avalon's lips pursed and turned down, and her eyes filled with tears, but none spilled out onto her cheeks. "I don't know where to start." Myra sat on the edge of the bed as Avalon dropped her head back into the pillows and covered her eyes with the crook of her arm.

"Start at the beginning, Avalon."

"I can't."

Avalon sounded as though she was begging, and Myra sighed heavily, her concern for Avalon's well being swelling over. "You have to start somewhere, Avalon."

She had intended to keep the secret, but when their eyes met, Avalon decided that she would tell Myra the entire story of Cormicks. She had no one to trust now but Myra and Zaria, and Myra always had answers.

"Why would Brick tell the monarch that it was Counselor Glenn who killed my father?" Avalon asked Myra after she had told her about the entire journey to Cormicks.

The truth of the story was overwhelming, and for the first time in her life, Myra hesitated to answer. Avalon waited patiently, and Myra nodded her head and slowly answered. "I think it is because Hawker needed anyone who survived with Brick to think it was Counselor Glenn, in case you made it back. Then Counselor Glenn would still take the fall. Brick might have never even known the truth." Myra took Avalon's hand. "Hawker is just that smart, Avalon. You will come to see it clearly, when this is all far behind you and the emotion of it is mollified by time." Avalon was glad to be back with Myra and her indecipherable reasoning. It was the only part of home that she could recognize anymore.

Myra's words cleared some of Avalon's vision, and she began to put the pieces in place, but it would take more than mere days to reconstruct this puzzle. "Counselor Glenn didn't announce that my father was dead, because if I didn't return, that would make Hawker the rightful heir, and Counselor Glenn didn't want to chance the people rising up against him on behalf of Hawker," Avalon surmised.

Myra's eyes widened and she nodded slowly as she pulled the blankets up to Avalon's chest and tucked her into bed. "You can't stay here forever, but a little more rest wouldn't hurt."

"You don't have to nanny me anymore, Myra."

"I will take care of you until the day I die," she told Avalon forthright. Myra stood up and brushed her apron off, looking down at Avalon.

"What is it, Myra?"

"This might not be the right time, but I was just wondering: what will you do with Hawker?"

"I don't know," Avalon squinted hard as if trying to see the future in her mind. She was sure Hawker was dead when

Taggerty had run him through, but her uncle had been treated and somehow survived. Avalon wasn't sure how to feel about that either. "We've never had a prisoner in Fontanasia, and I won't be the first king to keep one."

"Oh," Myra breathed, clearing her throat.

"I'm not going to have him killed either, Myra." They remained silent for a few moments. "I just don't want anything to change," Avalon whispered.

"I know, honey," Myra said longingly as she leaned down and brushed Avalon's short bangs to the side, "but you can't stop time. Change is always in motion." Myra gave a parting smile and took the washbasin, closing the door to the suite behind her, and leaving the young king to her own thoughts. Avalon threw back the covers and dressed.

A small contingency of the king's guard escorted Avalon to a row of magnificent houses just outside the castle. She was made to wait at the end of the walk as the lead guard knocked on the front door which was promptly answered by a servant who stepped aside and knelt, allowing the guard to secure the house before the entourage entered. The moment she arrived, Avalon recognized Counselor Glenn's wife from many social gatherings, although she hadn't realized that was who this woman was at the time. She was rail thin and pleasant, and paler than the moon. When Mrs. Glenn knelt, Avalon wanted to tell her not to go through the trouble, but all of the residents of the home were kneeling at once before taking their seats.

They sat in silence for a moment before Avalon realized that no one would speak before her. She cleared her throat. "Mrs. Glenn, I am very sorry for your loss."

When the woman was sure that was all her king had to say, she responded. "Thank you, King Hall, and I am sorry for your loss. I knew your father from when we were young, and he was a great man." She dabbed her nose with a handkerchief, and it was then that Avalon realized this woman was grieving for both men. It was very difficult for Avalon, who was so deeply torn, to comfort anyone else. She wasn't sure exactly what she would say. After years of thinking Counselor Glenn was working against her father, Avalon had been ashamed to realize that in the end, he was a pawn to Hawker, and he died protecting Fontanasia.

"I am sorry to disturb you in a time of such grief, but I wanted to tell you, all of you," Avalon gestured to the family and her lips smacked together so she could keep at bay the growing lump in her throat, "that your husband, your father, was an honorable man. And in a time of quiet uprising, he protected his king as well as he could."

Mrs. Glenn sobbed aloud now and three of the children moved to her side. There was a shroud of silence over what had really taken place in the castle, and the truth would never come to light, but this was confirmation that Counselor Glenn had acted honorably, and Mrs. Glenn had her absolution. Avalon felt uncomfortable. She had always practiced a reserve at showing any outward emotion, and she was finding it difficult to keep her composure. It was then, as she adjusted her eyes away from the counselor's crying wife and to his surviving children, that Avalon realized that Counselor Glenn had only daughters.

The man had no sons, Avalon thought. As foolish as Glenn had been, he wasn't going to kill her. He was ambitious, but he could not have been trying to take the throne for the future of his own family. He was simply using this opportunity to fulfill his own dreams of a democracy. He had been leading his own agenda, but in the end was simply a pawn for Hawker to use. Counselor Glenn didn't hate her. He hated what she had come to represent which was the perpetuation of having a king instead of a ruling council. Still, Avalon knew what was far out in the field of glowing elbagrass, on the other side of the window, and she would never step down.

"He always respected King Birch," Counselor Glenn's wife managed between sobs. "I know they had their differences, but he was your father's servant."

Avalon stood and everyone in the room simultaneously bowed their heads in respect. Turning fourteen hadn't made her an adult, but the events of the past month had aged her in irreparable ways. She wanted to ease the burden for everyone in that room, and for everyone in Fontanasia. She wanted to believe that life would go on as it had been for hundreds of years, but she could not swallow those words for herself, so she left the house without another word.

When King Avalon told Gamon, who had taken the temporary roll as head of the king's guard, that she would be seeing Hawker in the dungeon alone, he insisted that Hawker be chained down. And so wrist and ankle cuffs that had never been used before in Fontanasia were employed, and Hawker's recovering body was bolted to the brick cot and the cell floor. He'd been placed in the deepest dungeon, and Avalon walked slowly down the stairs in his cell, her childlike features matured heavily in one month's time. She stepped in front of him trying to look strong, but it was difficult. She tried to brush aside the need for his approval, even though he was not her uncle nor her advisor, nor her friend anymore. He was nothing to her now.

She looked at Hawker and saw a slight smile on his face, his rabbit's nose twitching steadily in the torchlight. He did not look like a man searching for redemption. He was bandaged but looked fit, for a destroyed man. Avalon could see clearly the events that led to her father's death. First, her birth and her being announced a boy, and then her becoming of age to be king. Her father was dead because she'd dreamed of a trip to a bright blue sea and convinced him to let her take the journey to Cormicks. Her father was dead because his own brother had waited fourteen years to make his move, and could wait no longer.

With chains on his wrists, Hawker couldn't physically touch her, so she was safe, but Avalon could feel the widening hole in her chest as though he had punched the wind from her lungs. She had to face him, to resolve with him his crimes, yet in all of her mental preparation to remain calm at this moment, looking at him, she had to grit her teeth to keep from being overcome. He was her uncle, and he was not. It was as though Avalon had another person to mourn, and between her father and Walthan, she had no tears to spare in her drowning.

She had thought about this moment for weeks, ever since the doctor who had been treating Hawker told her that he would recover from his wounds. And looking at him now, it was though he had died, and she had to come to terms with that in spite of the duplicate figure of the man who sat in front of her now. It looked like Uncle Hawker, but it wasn't. Avalon wanted to scream at him, to cry, to hug him and to kill him. She was heart broken, but she held herself upright with lips pursed.

"So, Avalon, you are to be king, I hear."

The formal ceremony was to take place in hours, but Avalon needed to see Hawker first. She wanted to clean up the old garbage before starting her official reign.

"I am king; the ceremony is but a formality."

"You are anxious, boy," Hawker snapped, but then recovered his typical composure. "You wanted the throne more than I thought."

"I want my father." Avalon looked away from Hawker for a moment to keep her temper. He was manipulating her now, and she knew it. Myra had warned her, and Avalon regained herself, pondering inconsequential details like what she would have for lunch tomorrow to keep herself from exploding.

Hawker went in for the kill. "We can rule together, Avalon. It was inevitable, really. Your father said when he made me your advisor that I was to help guide you. I can still be of assistance," Hawker slurped.

"You are neither my advisor nor my uncle. You are nothing to me."

"I am something, or you would have run me through when you could have."

Avalon knew that this was all too true. "I'm not a killer."

"And I am?" Hawker opened his hands as far as he could against the shackles. "You're standing here." His tone was light, as though they were out on the lawn sipping tea together. Avalon didn't respond. She was sure that he would have finished the job started by Counselor Glenn if Taggerty hadn't intervened.

Hawker clucked his tongue and shook his head. "You've been listening to Myra George again, haven't you? I swear that woman never liked me."

"Leave Myra out of this."

"You would defend her. You think the way she thinks." Hawker's nose twitched. "Of course, she is the only mother figure you have had."

He meant for this to sting Avalon, and it did, but she didn't respond. It made her sad that someone she had loved so much could hate her equally. She looked right at him though, because she didn't want him to sense the pain he was causing. She said slowly, "Against the pleas of the entire council, who would prefer to have you hanged, I have decided to banish you from Fontanasia."

Hawker's eyebrows dipped in anger and then crumpled into his forehead in mock despair. "But how will I live? Where will I go?" His plea sounded convincing, as though Avalon should really care as to where he ended up. She hated him, and yet she did feel a nagging concern for him. She could not throw away fourteen years of love so easily as he could.

"You will go out of Fontanasia, and never come back."

Avalon noticed Hawker's twitch of a smile, and it reminded her of Myra's warning to heed her instincts around Hawker. Here, in a dungeon, clasped in chains, he was playing a game.

"Thank you for your mercy, nephew." But she saw the smile that he'd barely tried to hide.

"So, you will go look for Cormicks?"

Hawker's brow pulled together, and he looked at Avalon as though this was the first time he was really seeing her. "You are so much smarter than I ever gave you credit for."

Avalon turned her back. "You will never find it." She walked through the shadow of her uncle cast by the torchlight to the top of the stairs and Gamon opened the cell door.

Hawker called after her. "My brother knew where it was, and now you do as well. What makes you think my father never sent me out to see it?"

Avalon should have walked away, but she felt compelled to explain herself. She needed the last word, so she called down the stairs. "I have come to realize that Brick was sent to Cormicks on your behest. He knew a lot about the journey because he had been there once before, but only Walthan and the Guides really know how to get to Cormicks.

"You expected all of us to be killed and Brick to come back and show you the way. But Brick never made it back, and you have no idea how to get there." Her voice was deep and sound, and she played the role of king perfectly, every bit the strong male king her father had hoped for. She wondered, if she had actually been a man right now, if she would have the compassion not to kill her uncle.

"Brick was a coward," he managed, and Avalon could hear his teeth mash together with a grunt of rage.

"Brick said that Counselor Glenn had probably already aligned himself with you. At the time, I didn't realize what he was saying. You poisoned your brother and killed him, only you didn't count on Counselor Glenn not being able to live with you as king so much as he couldn't live with any king. So he had you locked up and decided to rule on his own."

Hawker answered her with silence, and Avalon held her breath, taking one last look back into the darkness. She swept past Gamon who quickly locked the cell behind her. It was more difficult to confront her uncle than she'd thought it would be, and the hole in her chest had grown more painful. The following day, Hawker was to be blindfolded and escorted by a small detail far north, past the mountains and through the forest as far away from Fontanasia as they could get him, and farther from the door to Cormicks. She had instructed them to leave him there alone to wander for the rest of his life, which might have meant his quick death in the wild as he'd never been an outdoorsman. That was still more mercy than he had planned for her.

She made her way up to the king's suite, avoiding the throne room, and struggling each step with Hawker's deception. How could he have taught her so many things and been such a large part of shaping her into the person she was now, and not really be true at all in the end? It was bewildering to Avalon. She couldn't find truth in anything. She caught herself in the mirror in clothes fit for a king, and knew that even she was a lie.

"Are you ready to take the crown, brother?" Zaria asked with reverence instead of the sarcasm her little sister was so accustomed to. She'd found Avalon at the tomb of her father. It was a stone crypt that was being crafted by hammer and chisel into a beautiful monument. Avalon had missed her father's casket being closed as Counselor Glenn had done so in secrecy, just as she'd missed her mother's being closed. She wondered if she would ever be able to lay either of her parents to rest.

"I never wanted this," Avalon told Zaria.

"Of course you didn't," Zaria said. "Neither did I, but there is no way back, Avalon. There is only what lies ahead."

"You don't understand," Avalon snapped back. "Since the day I was born, I have been raised to become king, and I knew that. But I never really thought it would happen. I never thought that our father would die. I thought we could go on pretending forever." Avalon stared off into the distance seeing nothing in front of her.

"If you are having second thoughts, father would understand." Zaria gently took Avalon's hand.

Avalon shook her head. "No, he wouldn't."

"Yes, he would." Zaria spoke softly. Her badgering sister had aged just as quickly as Avalon had in the past month, turning from a young lady into a graceful woman. "You are living Father's lie, Avalon, not your own. You don't have to continue if you don't want to. The day has come when you choose the life you will lead."

But in Avalon's mind there was no choice to be made. It wasn't her family's honor she was defending, and there was no concern in perpetuating her family's kingdom in her name. There was a side of the world no one in Fontanasia could comprehend, and it was Avalon's job, just as it had been the job of the kings before her, to protect this land that she loved. She would take the throne in order to make sure Fontanasia was properly prepared for a war that she hoped would never come. She would take the throne because she was destined to be king, and unlike any other in Fontanasia, she had prepared for this her entire life.

Avalon offered Zaria her arm, and the sisters returned to the king's suite where Myra was waiting.

"Pish posh," she said in a manner of scolding them for being late. Myra wordlessly helped Avalon dress for the ceremony, reverently cloaking Avalon in a cape fit for a king.

"I guess I have outgrown Zaria's dresses," Avalon quipped. Myra bit her lip but could not help the tears that streamed from her eyes. She gave Avalon a tight squeeze and then pulled her apron over her own face to wipe her tears.

"I am so proud of you, Avalon." They shared a hug before Myra kissed Avalon's forehead. Then she grabbed Avalon's shoulders and took a step back to take one last look. Myra bit her lip and then released Avalon, forced to let her young charge go. "You'll be late already," was all she could say.

Zaria pulled Avalon's hand and led her out of the suite, escorting Avalon down through the Hall of Kings. The staff had cleaned up, and the statues that Hawker had destroyed were removed, artists already somewhere in the Fingers working on reconstructing replicas along with a new statue of King Birch. When they stepped through the arch to the throne room, Zaria left Avalon to walk forward alone. Avalon passed the council members and the King's guard and stepped to the throne where she turned to face her inner circle. Councilman Nelson shared a decree with the onlookers, but Avalon had not heard a word. The counselor stepped forward with two others to complete the ceremony. Standing strong and upright throughout the ceremony, Avalon held still, trying not to let the power of the moment effect her. She held the torrents of emotion at bay until the crown was placed on her head.

"The King is dead," the room thundered. Avalon had to choke herself to keep the tears from flowing. Then they chimed in unison, "Long live the King." When Walthan had uttered these words, she was not focused on the real possibility. When Myra, Zaria, and Taggerty had said this back in the king's suite weeks earlier, all Avalon could hear was 'the king is dead'. Now that she understood the words she would never hear again, she tried to breathe as they gripped her with devastating excitement.

She stepped down from the throne and walked through the hall as all of the councilmen and King's guard knelt and kissed her ring. It was a very strange experience for Avalon. She was used to being watched, but not touched. She had not been on the receiving end of this kind of attention as Zaria and the other ladies of the court had been, and she tried not to let her face flush red. They were showing their allegiance to the new king, but Avalon couldn't help but be very aware that men were holding and kissing her hand no matter the reason.

Then Taggerty was there, and he bowed his head and knelt. He took her hand and Avalon's breath stopped in her throat when his salty green eyes peered up into hers. He smiled his cocky smile, and she squinted at him realizing in that moment that the feelings rising inside her could not be dislike nor residual hate. Avalon became aware of a deep liking she held for Taggerty, beyond the bond of the ordeal that they had experienced together. She knew then that she had been mistaken about the anger she'd felt toward him from their beginning at the tournament. It was not dislike, but her internal defense against a feeling of the complete opposite. She considered this for a heartbeat, discarding the thought just as quickly because it led to an impossibility.

"Long live the king," Taggerty said, and she had to turn her head so that no one could see that she was blushing. When Taggerty kissed the ring on her hand, her heart fluttered. She looked down once more into the sunshine of his expression before stepping out onto the parapet.

Zaria was there waiting, and she held her hand out to escort Avalon to meet the people of Fontanasia. This was the same platform her father had stepped onto fourteen years earlier when he had shown Fontanasia their new prince. But it was Avalon on the balcony today, not a stand in. When she stepped forward, a large cheer erupted. Born a girl and raised a boy, she waved her hand to salute her people, now king of Fontanasia.